THE CURSE OF BLOOD AND SILENCE

M GUIDA

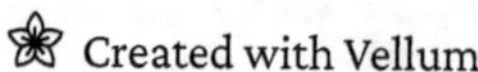 Created with Vellum

CHAPTER

ONE

A*ngelo*

THE LEATHER SEAT creaked as I slumped back. "The last thing I wanted to do was disappoint Serenity," I grumbled to Enzo. Jazz seeped in through the limousine's windows as the heady scent of blood mingled with the lingering aroma of bourbon in the air—the unmistakable essence of New Orleans at night.

Dimitri Dragan—my driver and brand-new brother-in-law—caught my eye in the rearview mirror, a sardonic smirk on his lips. "Trouble in paradise, Your Majesty?" he quipped. "Or just another night failing to find a certain human girl in a city full of them?"

1

I scowled at him. "Just drive, Dimitri. Your 'wit' is as unwelcome as it is unimpressive."

He chuckled, but I caught the brief flicker of genuine concern in his eyes. As my sister's husband...and a royal pain in my ass...Dimitri never missed an opportunity to push my buttons. Yet despite being a born vampire—typically a weakness in my eyes—he'd proven himself time and again, even taking on a powerful wolf who threatened my sister, dispatching the beast with a mix of charm and brutality that was uniquely him.

In other words, his dedication had earned him my grudging respect, if not my full trust.

"Joking aside, Angelo," Dimitri said, his tone turning somber, "we need to find Joy. For Serenity's sake...for everyone's."

Serenity. My Nephilim. The prize I'd won at auction and now refused to let go. Her celestial blood sang to me, a siren's call I couldn't resist. But she was more than just a captivating creature—she was our salvation. Her powers had healed the Aeternum Stone, which had been fading. If it had gone completely dark, Dracula would have found us and wiped out not only me, but my entire family for not following his rules. The stone was the only thing that kept him at bay, a shield against our enemy.

My mind filled with images of Serenity anxiously pacing the halls of Crescent Manor, our mansion overlooking Bourbon Street, waiting for news about her best friend Joy DuPont who'd vanished into the labyrinthine streets of the French Quarter without a trace. Serenity's anguish clawed at my gut, fueling a primal urge to hunt down Joy and prove my unwavering devotion to my mate.

Enzo Di Salvo, my most trusted enforcer, ran his piercing gaze over me. His handsome face held a flicker of guilt. "You mustn't blame yourself for her disappearance, Angelo. I was the one who was supposed to be watching her." He looked out the window at the raucous crowds on Bourbon Street, his jaw clenched. "If it hadn't been for that damn explosion at Crimson Stakes…"

Enzo had been following Joy as she passed out flyers about Serenity near my casino Crimson Stakes when an explosion had occurred. He had raced into the casino to find out what happened, and while his back was turned, Joy had disappeared without a trace.

I ran my tongue over my fangs, feeling the pulse of the city outside. Serenity might not have chosen this life with me, but she was now integral to our survival. The delicate balance of power, life, and death rested on her slender shoulders.

"We'll find Joy," I said, my voice low. My hand instinctively moved to the hilt of my sword concealed beneath my coat. "And whoever turns out to be responsible will learn why crossing the Santi family is a death sentence— one delivered as inevitably as the tide of the Mississippi."

Frustration rolled through me. As king of New Orleans' vampire underworld I commanded legions of immortal warriors and controlled a vast criminal empire that stretched from the Mississippi to the bayous. Yet I couldn't find one missing girl? My failure choked me like the suffocating humidity of a Louisiana summer night.

Dimitri stopped the limousine at the back of Crescent Manor and opened the door for Enzo and me. He always let us out at the rear entrance of the antebellum mansion, away from curious eyes on Bourbon Street. I didn't like my movements being tracked.

I approached the door, my heart heavy. Serenity had been frantic for days, pleading with me to find Joy. I'd pursued every lead, even following a false trail to Simon Cartier's auction house at Ravenwood Estates. Now, returning empty-handed, I braced myself for Serenity's disappointment.

I reached for the doorknob, expecting her to burst out, eyes wide, bombarding me with questions about her best friend's whereabouts—the best friend she feared had been sold into slavery.

Instead, the door creaked open and silence whisked over me like a cold wind.

No running footsteps.

No anxious face peering around the corner.

No excited voice calling out for news.

The quiet was oppressive, the kind of silence that made your skin prickle and your shoulders tighten. Something was wrong—terribly wrong. Serenity's absence screamed louder than any words could. As I stepped inside, the silence seemed to thicken, filling the air with almost tangible dread.

Enzo glanced over at me, his lips pressed to a worried line. His eyes asked the question we were both thinking: Where was Petar? He was supposed to be guarding Serenity. His absence set off alarm bells in my head.

As I stood there my nostrils flared, instinctively seeking out information. The familiar scents of vampire and Nephilim lingered, but something was off. I strained my ears, but the only sound was the thunderous pounding of my own heart.

Step by cautious step, I entered the house. My heightened vampire senses worked overtime. No wolf. No human. No Fae. The side hallway loomed before me, a tunnel of growing dread. My movements were measured, silent. I was a hunter now, stalking an unknown threat in my own home.

Then it hit me. Metallic. Unmistakable.

Blood.

I signaled to Enzo to cover the rear as we moved silently through the mansion. Years of survival had taught me never to announce my presence to my enemies.

Enzo nodded, drawing his blade with a whisper of steel. His eyes scanned every corner, every shadow. "I don't like this, boss," he muttered under his breath.

I didn't either, but I kept it to myself.

I worked to keep my face impassive, but beneath my stony mask panic was rushing through me like wildfire.

My fingers twitched, longing to tear through the mansion, to call out her name, to find her safe and unharmed. But I knew better. Any display of emotion, any hint of weakness, could be fatal—not just for me, but for Serenity and everyone under my protection.

The scent of blood grew stronger as I moved deeper into the house. Where was Serenity? Was Petar protecting her? If anything had happened to her, he would pay with his life.

Soft footsteps approached from behind, and Dimitri joined us. His usual smirk was gone, replaced with an uneasy look that matched our own. A glint of fear flashed in his eyes, no doubt at the idea of losing my sister. She was his life, just like Serenity was mine.

A soft whispered moan reached us, like thunder in the oppressive silence.

"Dimitri..."

Gianna!

Dimitri raced past us, drawing on his vampire speed. He could be heading into a trap, but no one could tell him anything—not when it concerned Gianna.

"Dimitri, wait!" I hissed. Too late. He had already disappeared into the depths of the mansion.

I exchanged a quick glance with Enzo, seeing my own tension mirrored in his eyes. We had to move fast. This might indeed be a trap, but we couldn't let Dimitri walk into it alone.

As I cautiously followed Dimitri's path, my thoughts

were a chaotic mix of concern for Gianna, fear for Serenity, and a growing dread of what we might find. The scent of blood grew more pronounced with every step.

Enzo and I entered the living room. The air was thick with the metallic scent of blood, mixed with the lingering aroma of bacon and Elena's famous beignets—a bizarre contrast of homely comfort and violent intrusion that made my stomach churn.

A vase lay shattered on the floor, jagged shards glinting in the dim light filtering through the heavy curtains. Water from the vase had pooled on the floor, seeping into the hardwood and leaving a dark stain that spread like a sinister omen. But I was sure that wasn't what hurt my sister. Hitting her over the head with a vase wouldn't take her out.

No, something else did this. The air felt heavy, oppressive, carrying an undercurrent of...dark magic? The hairs on the back of my neck stood up when I tasted the acrid remnants of powerful, malevolent energy on my tongue.

Dimitri was sitting on the antique leather couch, cradling Gianna in his arms. The crimson of her blood stood out starkly against the rich, dark leather as it slipped down the side of her temple. The cocky grin on his face that I'd grown so accustomed to had vanished entirely, leaving only an uneasiness that matched our own.

He gently pushed back her hair, his fingers trembling slightly—whether from fear or fury, I couldn't have said. "Who did this to you?" His voice was low, dangerous, so different from his usual sarcastic tone. The fury vibrating through his words almost charged the very air around us.

His eyes burned with a cold fire as they flicked up to meet mine. "Whoever did this is dead," he remarked to me in a lower tone, his voice deceptively calm. "They just don't know it yet."

"I... I'm not sure," Gianna murmured, her usually melodious voice now weak and uncertain. "Elena was making breakfast, then she cried out. I came to investigate and... Someone hit me." She rubbed her head, wincing.

I scanned the living room, my eyes darting from the overturned side table to the paintings hanging askew on the wall. The grandfather clock in the corner had stopped, its pendulum frozen mid-swing. It was as if time itself had paused in this moment of crisis. "Where is Serenity?" I asked, unable to keep the note of desperation from my voice.

Gianna gave me a dazed look, her usually sharp eyes unfocused. "I don't know," she whispered, each word seeming to cost her effort.

Dimitri's head snapped up, his piercing blue eyes locking onto mine. "Let me guess. Daddy Dearest is MIA. How positively shocking." He arched an eyebrow, his tone biting. "I thought guarding damsels in distress was his specialty. But I guess I was wrong."

Cold anger gripped me. My fangs lengthened, aching to rip someone's throat out. "If you're right and Petar has betrayed me, he'll learn a new definition of pain."

I turned to Enzo, keeping my face a mask of cold determination despite the fear clawing at my insides. "Search the house," I ordered, my voice quiet. "They could still be here."

A floorboard creaked upstairs.

In that instant, my predatory instincts took over. I didn't hesitate, didn't waste time with caution or stealth. Whoever was up there had made a fatal mistake.

"Secure the perimeter," I snarled to Enzo lethally.

Then I moved.

My vampire speed transformed the world into a blur. One moment I was at the foot of the stairs, the next I was on the landing, my preternatural senses scanning for threats. The scent of blood was stronger here, stoking a dangerous mix of fury and hunger within me.

I refused to skulk around my own home like prey. I was the predator here. The vampire king. And someone had dared to intrude on my territory and threaten what was mine.

My fangs yearned for blood as I stalked down the hallway, every muscle coiled, prepared to unleash devastating violence. Whoever was responsible for this would learn the true meaning of fear. They would beg for death long before I granted it.

But first, to find Serenity. And God help anyone who might have dared harm her.

CHAPTER
TWO

S *erenity*

THE DREAM of Angelo melted away from me...

My eyes fluttered open, and panic immediately gripped my chest when I found myself on a strange bed in an unfamiliar room. "Not again," I whispered, my voice trembling with both pain and fear. Memories of waking up at Crescent Manor after Angelo bought me at the auction flooded back, intensifying my anxiety. At least this time I still had my red sundress on, I realized. It was something.

A horrible headache pounded between my temples. I pressed my palms against my eyes, trying to will away the pain and the rising tide of dread threatening to engulf me.

As if from a distant dream, the melody of "Wishing You Were Somehow Here Again" from *Phantom of the Opera* drifted through my mind. I couldn't shake the feeling that this was important, that it was tied to Angelo somehow. The song's wistful notes mirrored my own longing for him, making my heart ache for his presence. Why did this music make me think of him so strongly?

Where was I? I let out a shaky breath, fighting back tears. That question was important enough, but it paled in comparison to the one that truly mattered: How do I get back to Angelo?

My chest tightened with each passing moment. I wanted to return to him. No, not wanted—needed. He was my home, my safety, my world. And I would crawl through Hell itself to get back to his arms.

"I'm coming, Angelo," I whispered, my voice filled with determination. "I don't know how, but I'll find my way back to you, I swear."

I forced myself to stand, ignoring the way the room spun around me. Every instinct screamed at me to curl up and wait for rescue, but I refused. Angelo was out there, and nothing—not fear, not pain, not even whoever had taken me—would keep me from him.

On shaky legs, I began to explore my surroundings. Each step was an agonizing battle against my own body. But I pressed on, driven by a desperate, all-consuming need to return to Angelo. I had to get back to him. The alternative was unthinkable.

Where was Petar? Why had he betrayed us? Did he have a death wish? Angelo would kill him! My stomach churned as I recalled how Petar had lured me into that delivery truck with a lie about Joy being wounded inside. He'd claimed Angelo was in there too. How could I have been so stupid to believe him? Guilt and self-recrimination joined the cocktail of emotions swirling inside me.

I had to escape and get back to Angelo, but how? I thought back to when I had believed Joy was dead, and I had thrown objects around telekinetically. Perhaps I could use those powers to could break out of this place?

Heart racing, I eased myself off the bed, wincing at every squeak of the springs.

Please don't hear me Please don't hear me.

I focused, reaching for my Nephilim powers, the ones Angelo believed in. They had manifested before—they had to manifest again now.

Tiptoeing across the room carefully, my bare feet silent on the cold floor, I fought the urge to run. I couldn't afford a single mistake.

Reaching the window, I threw open the plantation shutters with trembling hands, desperate for some indication of where I was, some chance of escape. My heart sank when I was greeted by thick iron bars, their presence a mocking reminder of my captivity. Beyond them, no comforting, familiar sight of the French

Quarter met my eyes. Instead, an endless sea of trees stretched out before me, draped in eerie Spanish moss. Tall thistles and plants covered with flowers dotted the landscape.

My eyes were drawn to the colorful blooms. They were a deep, majestic purple, like something you'd see adorning a king's robe. Their beauty seemed out of place in this nightmare.

As the full reality of my situation sank in, a sob caught in my throat. I was alone, trapped, and clearly miles from anything familiar. From Angelo. Each thought of him sent a fresh tumult of emotions through me—fear for myself, worry for him, and above all a desperate hope that somehow he would find me, since escaping myself was clearly out of the question.

I sank to the floor beneath the window, hugging my knees to my chest. "Please, Angelo," I whispered to the empty room. "Please come for me." Even as I pleaded, a darker fear took root. What if he couldn't? What if this time I was truly on my own?

The sudden, scraping sound of a key turning in the lock sent my heart racing. I scrambled to my feet, pressing my back against the wall, as if I could somehow disappear into it. The door creaked open agonizingly slowly, each inch revealing more of the figure behind it.

A tall, muscular man with shaggy brown hair stepped into the room. His gray eyes, cold and calculating, locked onto me immediately. I felt naked under his gaze in a way that made my skin crawl. He moved with a predator's grace, each step deliberate and menacing.

"Ah, Serenity, you're awake. Good." His voice was smooth, almost pleasant. Why did that make it all the more terrifying? He bowed slightly. "Allow me to introduce myself. I'm Gage Bray. You are now my...prisoner."

The way he said "prisoner" sent a shiver down my spine. It wasn't just a word; it was a sinister promise of things to come, none of them good.

I squared my shoulders, summoning every ounce of courage I could muster. Tears pricked at the corners of my eyes, but I held them back. I wouldn't give him the satisfaction of seeing me cry.

"What do you want from me?" I asked, pleased that my voice didn't give away the fear coursing through my veins.

Gage's lips curled into a cold smile. He looked at me as if he wanted to devour me, his gaze continuing to roam over my body in a way that made me feel dirty.

"Oh, Serenity..." he purred, taking a step closer. I pressed myself harder against the cold wall, wishing I could melt through it.

"It's not about what I want from you. It's about what you represent." His eyes gleamed with anticipation. "You're the key to bringing down the mighty Angelo Santi and the arrogant Trystan Hunter."

The name sent a jolt through me and my breath caught in my throat. "Trystan? The wolf mafia king?" He had tried to buy me at the auction but Angelo had outbid him.

My captor's eyes shone bright, a gleam in them that made my skin crawl. "Not for long." His voice dripped with a dark promise.

That's when I noticed he held a mirror in his hand, and he followed my gaze to it. "This is the Moirai Mirror. Ever heard of it?"

I shook my head. "No."

"Angelo is clearly keeping secrets from you. This mirror has the power to show you both present and future."

He reached out, brushing a strand of hair from my face. I flinched away from his touch.

"Don't touch me," I spat, surprised by my own vehemence.

Gage chuckled, but it was a sound devoid of real humor. "Hmm. Fiery. I can see why Angelo is so...invested in you." He stepped back, giving me a little more room, but his presence still dominated the space. "Get comfortable, Serenity. You're going to be here for a while. And you'll do as I say, or two friends of yours will die. Look."

He thrust the mirror at me. I gasped, my heart plummeting at what I saw in it.

Joy's brother Steve and her father Louis—my protector, and a good friend—sat motionless in a sparse bedroom. Their haunted, vacant stares chilled me to the bone.

"Is this real?" My voice quavered.

Gage's eyes flashed with cruel delight. "Very real, I promise you."

"You're lying," I spat. Even so, doubt gnawed at me.

Without a word, Gage dropped a silver Celtic cross into my trembling hands. I'd have known it anywhere. It was the one Steve's dying grandfather had given him. The one he never took off.

My fingers clenched around it, nausea rising. Gage turned to leave, triumph radiating from him in waves.

"Angelo will come for me," I called out, my voice stronger than I felt. "He'll save the DuPonts, too. And when he does, you'll beg for mercy. But you won't receive it."

"I don't think so. Look again." The mirror rippled. Angelo and Enzo were in the back of a limousine, talking softly. Angelo didn't look at all upset.

"He doesn't seem overly concerned to me, Serenity."

Something wasn't right. This guy was messing with my head. "Angelo must not realize I'm missing yet. When he does, he'll tear New Orleans apart to find me."

Gage paused at the door, looking back with an amused expression. "Oh, I'm counting on that. In fact, I'm looking forward to it." With that, he was gone, the lock clicking shut ominously behind him.

I slid down the wall to the floor, my legs no longer able to support me. My brave facade crumbled, and all the tears I'd been holding back finally streamed down my face. Angelo would come for me, I knew he would. But as I sat there, alone and afraid, I now wondered: at what cost?

What twisted game was Gage playing? Challenging two mafia kings was madness...unless he had a secret weapon. What power could possibly overshadow Angelo's?

The answer whispered through my thoughts, freezing my breath: Dracula.

Angelo's words echoed in my mind: "Dracula wants me dead." I trembled, terror and rage warring within me. If Dracula himself was involved, we were all in danger beyond imagination, and I was trapped here while Angelo faced this nightmare alone.

Desperation clawed at my insides. I needed out now, so I could get to Angelo and warn him. I wasn't going to be a damsel in distress.

Angelo's words echoed in my mind: "Your power is limitless, Serenity."

I closed my eyes, reaching deep within myself. Remembering the Aeternum Stone, and Angelo's unwavering belief in me.

At first, nothing. Then—a spark.

Tingling sensations skittered across my skin, raced down my arms, danced along my spine. My breath caught.

"Come on," I hissed, fingers curling into fists. "Come on!"

The spark ignited. Power surged through me like wildfire in my veins. Every nerve ending crackled with energy. My body felt too small to contain this force.

I gasped, my eyes flying open. The world looked sharper, brighter. I could feel every molecule of air around me.

It was both exhilarating and terrifying.

I turned to the barred window, heart pounding. This was my chance. Possibly my only chance.

"Angelo," I whispered. "Watch me fly."

The energy surged. Nothing happened to the bars, but suddenly, heat licked at my back. I spun around, my heart in my throat.

Shitshitshitshit

The quilt on my bed was engulfed in flames, hungry tendrils of fire reaching for the ceiling. Smoke billowed, thick and choking.

"No, no, no!" I coughed, my eyes stinging.

As panic flooded my system, my concentration was broken and my powers slipped away. The warmth drained from my limbs, leaving me cold and shaking. That incredible strength, that sense of invincibility—gone in an instant.

My knees buckled as the last whispers of power faded. I was empty, hollow, utterly drained—and now, helpless in the face of the inferno I'd unleashed.

Noxious smoke filled my lungs. The unbearable heat was closing in from all sides. My eyes darted frantically around the room, searching for an exit that wasn't there.

What had I done? I'd wanted freedom. Instead, I'd created my own fiery tomb.

The door swung open with a bang. Gage stood there, his eyes widening at the inferno before him.

"What the hell?" he growled. "Fire. FIRE!"

He seized my hand and pulled me out of the smoke-filled room. I twisted, trying to get away, but he was too strong and easily slammed me up against the wall, his hands at my throat. His long fingers squeezed tighter and tighter, cutting off my air.

Tears sprang to my eyes as I batted at his hands, but he didn't loosen his grip. His gray eyes turned gold, and he released a growl that stopped my heart.

"Were you trying to burn down my home, Nephilim?" he snarled.

I didn't answer, just kicked and scratched, but it was useless. He shook me violently. "Do not disobey me. Do not resist. I am your master, and you will stay here. If not, the DuPonts die. Remember that."

As suddenly as he'd grabbed me, he dropped me to the hardwood floor. I fell in a heap, sputtering and gasping for air.

I looked down the empty corridor, wishing I could speed away and escape. But something told me the DuPonts were here, too, and I couldn't leave them to die. Aside from Angelo, they were my only family.

As I lay there, my throat still burning and my body still aching, despair seized me. It appeared I was only able to control my abilities when Angelo was present. His presence and belief in me gave me confidence, almost like a shot of adrenaline. My feelings bubbled up inside me like a volcano, exploding into frustration. I wanted him so badly.

Tears streamed down my face as I curled myself into a ball on the cold, hard floor. The intensity of my longing for Angelo overwhelmed me. It was more than a desire to feel safe or protected; it was as if a part of me was missing. The void left by his absence left an almost physical ache deep in my bones.

Angelo, where are you?

THREE

I WAS STALKING down the hallway toward the bedroom I shared with Serenity, every sense on high alert, when sharp, sudden pain lanced through my skull like a white-hot blade. My vision blurred, the familiar walls almost twisting and warping around me. The familiar scents of the manor—old wood, leather, and a lingering trace of Serenity's perfume—were suddenly obliterated by the acrid smell of smoke and fear.

I staggered, my usual vampire grace deserting me. I shot out a hand, bracing myself against the wall as my knees threatened to give out, but it did little to steady me.

"Boss?" Enzo's concerned voice floated up from downstairs, sounding distant and muffled, as if I was underwater.

I shook my head, trying to clear the fog that had descended over my senses. It was incomprehensible. In all my centuries, I'd never experienced anything like this.

I staggered to our bedroom as the smell of smoke grew stronger, suddenly mixed with Serenity's scent. She was here. Here, and in danger.

I forced another step, fighting the pain that threatened to bring me to my knees. "Enzo!" I snarled. "Up here. Now!"

He appeared in seconds, eyes scanning for threats. "Boss?"

"Smoke," I growled.

His frown deepened. "I don't smell anyth—"

"Serenity's here," I cut him off, my voice raw with desperation. "Serenity. I can smell her perfume. It has to be her."

Another wave of pain hit. I swayed but caught myself. Now was no time for weakness.

"Find her," I ordered, already moving down the hall. "Now. Search every room. Go!"

My heart, long silent, felt like it might burst. Serenity was close. In danger. And nothing—not this bizarre pain, not any force on Earth—would stop me from saving her.

My hands trembled as I flung open the door and burst into our bedroom, desperately praying to find Serenity waiting for me. But as my eyes darted around the room, my heart sank.

Nothing was out of place.

No smoke.

No Serenity.

Our crimson canopy bed, where we'd shared so many tender moments, was perfectly made. The bookshelves stood like silent sentinels, neatly dusted and every book in place, taunting me with their orderliness. Not a lamp was out of place, not a stick of furniture overturned.

A wave of frustration washed over me. I clenched my fists, fighting the urge to tear the room apart in my desperation to find any trace of her. "Serenity," I whispered, my voice cracking with emotion. "Where are you?" The thought of her in danger, possibly hurt, made my centuries-old blood run cold.

I took a deep breath, fighting to stay in control, but I could feel my composure slipping. My mind spun with terrifying possibilities, each worse than the last. If the wolves hurt her like they had my sister... A red haze of fury threatened to overtake me as the memory of my sister's broken body in the alley flashed before my eyes.

My fangs lengthened involuntarily, pricking my lower lip as I allowed the rage bubbling inside me to boil over. The taste of my own blood fueled my rage. I'd skin Trystan alive, hang his hide as a warning to every wolf. And yet the savage thought brought little relief against the fear chewing on my insides.

"Angelo, come quick." Enzo's urgent cry shattered my dark fantasies.

I burst from my bedroom, the world blurring as I moved at vampire speed. My beating heart nearly stopped when I saw the woman on the ground at Enzo's feet.

I skidded to halt. It wasn't Serenity.

I didn't know if I should feel relief or frustration. The figure Enzo was bent over in my sister's room was Elena Moreau, my housekeeper who was almost like a mother to me. I gritted my teeth and my heart clenched as he slowly rolled her onto her back. Her face was pale, a bloody wound on her temple matching Gianna's. Unconscious. But alive, thank God.

"Take her to her room. Stay with her," I ordered, moving toward my sister's and Dimitri's room, nerves crackling.

Enzo's voice was tight with tension. "Do you smell that? Something foul."

"Yeah, I do." As soon as I crossed the threshold, an oppressive energy swirled around me like smoke, making every hair on my body stand up. The air felt thick, making it difficult to breathe, as if the very atmosphere itself was tainted by something unnatural.

The stench was unmistakable—a mixture of decay and ozone, the telltale scent of dark magic. I'd been around dark forces enough to recognize the reek of evil. As I made my way deeper into the room, the pull became stronger, an invisible current tugging at my senses.

My eyes were drawn to a drawer left open in Gianna's dresser, as if magnetized. I held out a hand and a wave of cold energy washed over me as I drew closer, raising goosebumps along my arm. My stomach churned with a mixture of dread and anticipation, and a cold sweat broke out over my brow.

My eyes fell upon a wicked-looking dagger nestled in some delicate scarves in the drawer. Its wavy, iridescent blade appeared to writhe in the dim light, alive and hungry for flesh. The hilt was adorned with black diamonds, their facets greedily absorbing what little light there was in the room. The gems, often associated with darkness and mystery, pulsed with an inner malevolence that made my skin crawl.

The dagger wasn't the only magical object in my sister's dresser drawer. My breath caught when I spotted my missing ring—the Solarite ring—lying next to it. It glittered with gold, a beacon of hope in the darkness, its bronze stone shaped like the sun. It had the power to negate magic or break a spell at sunrise. I had been anguished when it had been stolen, and my heart sank as a sickening realization washed over me and the pieces fell into place.

Dimitri. I should have known.

White-hot anger surged through me, threatening to consume everything in its path. I had never wanted my sister to be with him. He'd proven himself a traitor too many times, but this... This was beyond the pale. He was now my own family, and yet still he conspired against me. Against Serenity. The sharp points of my fangs pressed against my tongue.

Was this the tool used to subdue Serenity? The thought of the dagger touching her and draining her essence made me want to tear the room apart. Worse—had my sister played a part in this nightmare? Bile rose in my throat as images of Serenity, weakened and afraid, flashed through my mind. The mix of fury and anguish they brought threatened to bring me to my knees.

"Enzo," I called, my voice ragged with the effort of maintaining control. My hands shook as I clenched them into fists. "You need to see this."

Enzo came up alongside me, cradling Elena to his chest. Surprise flashed in his eyes. "The Nightshade's Thorn Dagger?" He glanced up at me, surprise hardening to cold fury. "Where the hell did Dimitri get this?"

"I don't know," I said, a maelstrom of emotions—rage, fear, and a deep, aching betrayal—threatening to overwhelm me. "But I intend to make Gianna a widow."

Enzo pursed his lips and growled. "Never trusted that bastard."

I glanced down at Elena in his arms, my heart squeezing at the sight of her unconscious, pale face.

He followed my gaze, his expression softening slightly. "She's okay. I gave her some blood. She'll be fine. But I'll take her to her room to rest."

"Good. Don't let Gianna near her," I growled, my low

voice rumbling. The beast inside me was surfacing together with my anger, deadly fangs ready for blood. I snatched up the dagger, its weight ominous in my hand, then slipped the ring onto my finger. The cool metal pulsed against my skin, a comforting reminder of the power I now wielded.

I whisked down the stairs, my vampire speed blurring my movements. The scent of fear and blood hit me as I entered the living room, my eyes narrowing on the scene before me.

Gianna sat next to Dimitri on the couch, her face flushed with unnatural vitality. The coppery scent of vampire blood lingered in the air. It confirmed my worst fears: Dimitri had given her his blood—tainted blood. Well, I'd drain every last drop of it out of his throat. My jaw clenched as I considered this might be the last time she'd ever see her husband alive.

I rolled my shoulders and cracked my neck. Gianna's eyes flicked to me, fear flashing in them. "Angelo? What's wrong?" Her voice trembled.

In a blur, I crossed the room and shot out my hand, fingers wrapping around Dimitri's throat with crushing force as I slammed him hard against the wall.

"You stole my ring," I snarled, my face inches from his. "And where did you get the Nightshade's Thorn Dagger? Did you use it on Serenity?" Her name tore from my throat. "Answer me, you fucking bastard!"

The Solarite ring glowed on my finger, its power

thrumming against Dimitri's skin. I saw a flicker of fear in his eyes.

Dimitri gripped my wrist, his eyes watering. "Your ring... Yes, I took it," he sputtered. "I won't...deny that." He paused, trying to swallow, but my fingers tightened around his throat. His eyes darted to the dagger. "But that's not...mine. I swear. I've... I've never seen it before in my life."

Spittle dripped down his chin.

Gianna frantically beat her fists on my back. "Angelo— let him go. You're going to kill him." Her voice was laced with a desperation that I might have once cared about.

I threw her a withering look. "That's the idea," I growled, narrowing my eyes, my vision tinged red with bloodlust. I pressed the blade against his jugular until blood began to trickle down his neck. The coppery scent filled the air, mixing with Gianna's perfume.

"Enzo!" Gianna screamed, her composure shattering. "Please help."

The soft sound of hurried footsteps announced Enzo's arrival. I glanced over my shoulder and saw him enter the room.

Tears swam in Gianna's eyes as she made one last, desperate appeal. "Enzo, please," she cried, turning to him for mercy or intervention. "He's my husband."

Enzo's face remained impassive, unmoved by her distress. He shrugged, and his voice was devoid of emotion. "He shouldn't have betrayed us. You know what happens when someone does that."

Her eyes widened. "Angelo—no!" she screamed.

Her plea fell on deaf ears. I poured on my vampire speed, taking Dimitri to my secret room. I would get my answers, even if it meant extracting them from his dead corpse.

FOUR

S *erenity*

I HUDDLED on the floor in a ball, wishing I could disappear. My throat throbbed, each breath bringing a painful reminder of Gage's brutality. I pressed my head into my knees, trying to block out the world, desperately wanting Angelo to come. In my mind's eye, I pictured him bursting through the door, his face contorted with rage at what had been done to me. He'd tear my captor limb from limb for choking me, I was sure of it. The thought was both comforting and terrifying.

The silence in the hallway was suddenly broken by soft, firm footsteps approaching. The slow, measured pace sent chills down my spine. This wasn't the angry, impulsive stomping of Gage, but someone potentially more dangerous in their restraint.

"Tsk, tsk, Gage," a smooth voice cut through the air, laden with false disappointment. "Must you always be such a brute?" The words were chiding, but there was an undercurrent of amusement there too that made my stomach churn.

I didn't look up, but I could feel the newcomer's presence, hear the rustle of expensive fabric as they came closer. The air itself seemed to shift, filling with a new kind of tension.

Gage's furious voice suddenly came from across the room, sending my heart into a panicked frenzy. "But look what the bitch did to her room!"

The newcomer hummed thoughtfully. "Indeed," they finally said, closer now. "It seems our new guest takes quite the creative approach to redecorating."

I tensed when I felt a gentle touch on my shoulder. "Come now, my dear," the voice coaxed, a dangerous edge beneath the silky tones. "Let me see the face of our aspiring escape artist."

Trembling, I slowly raised my head, dreading what—or who—I might see looming over me in the aftermath of my failed rebellion. The last thing I expected was for the second kidnapper to be dressed as a rock star—long black hair, skintight black leather pants that hugged well-muscled thighs, and a sculpted chest, shirtless.

He knelt down and offered me his hand. "Please stand. I won't let him hurt you."

I bit my lip, not sure if I should do as he said.

He glanced up at Gage. "I mean, I *could* leave you with the big bad wolf..."

My choice was made. I reluctantly placed my shaking hand in his. An electric zap ran through me, as if I had touched a live wire. My stomach roiled and I fought down a wave of nausea. I'd never experienced such a touch before, not even with a vampire. What was he? I doubted he was a wolf.

He scrutinized me closely as he pulled me to my feet, then flashed me a seductive smile. "Let me introduce myself—I'm Balthazar. I've been watching you for some time, Serenity."

That was creepy. I pulled on my hand, but he didn't release it, not before kissing the back of it. Another jolt rocked through me. What was happening?

"What are you?" I asked nervously. "I don't think you're a wolf..."

He tilted his head back and laughed. "No, little one. I'm not. And I'm not a vampire, either."

Gage gestured with his thumb. "He's a demon."

I looked up at Balthazar, his eyes gleaming with ancient malevolence. I suddenly wondered again if my dad was a demon. Would he be drop-dead gorgeous like Balthazar?

I could feel the blood rush from my head, and Gage's

and Balthazar's faces spun around me. I felt a strange connection to the demon.

Don't pass out Don't pass out Don't pass out

I put my hand on the wall to steady myself, refusing to turn into a fainting violet. Where was Angelo? Just thinking of him gave me a little strength. I had to remain strong for him.

Balthazar's dark eyes burned red. "Do not steal my moment, cur. Or our deal is broken."

I looked between them. "Deal? What deal?"

Gage narrowed his eyes. "Not one that concerns you."

For some reason I didn't believe him. I had the feeling that any deal he made with Balthazar had everything to do with me, but the question was—what?

Balthazar shrugged casually. "Gage here wants to be king."

King? How could I make this guy king? But I kept the question to myself. I watched them warily, getting the uneasy feeling I was a pawn in a game I didn't want to play.

"Balthazar," Gage gritted his teeth, a warning clear in his tone.

"Tit for tat," Balthazar smirked in an amused voice. He walked around me, his gaze raking over my body, sizing me up. I felt exposed, craving Angelo's strong arms around me for protection, but having to settle for the cold comfort of my own embrace.

He moved his palm inches away from me, close

enough that I could feel unnatural heat radiating from his skin. "Such a little thing," he purred, his eyes shining with malevolent curiosity. "And yet containing all that power."

My heart hammered against my ribs, threatening to burst from my chest, and I swallowed hard, tasting bitter fear on my tongue.

"What do you want?" I spat venomously. I might be terrified, but I'd be damned if I'd let this demon see it.

Balthazar lifted my chin with his long fingers, his touch sending another jolt of that strange, painful energy thrilling through me. "He wants you to heal the *Luparion Crystal*. It keeps the little curs at the top of the wolf food chain."

I pulled away from him, surprised when he released me. This sounded almost exactly like Angelo wanting me to heal the vampires' Aeternum Stone. Angelo had said that the other supernaturals wanted me too but had never said why. Now I knew. I crossed my arms. "Are there other stones besides the *Luparion Crystal* and the *Aeternum Stone* that need healing?"

"Yes." Balthazar's eyes glinted with approval. "The Unseelie's Anchoring Obsidian. If it fades, the whole lot of them can be sent packing back to the Elder Dimension. Something that good King Keir doesn't want to happen."

My mind reeled, the world around me suddenly becoming unstable and unreal. The very air felt different, as if the laws of physics themselves were breaking. "Elder Dimension? You mean...a dimension other than this one?"

The words exploded from me, half-shouted, half-gasped, my voice cracking, and a hysterical laugh bubbled up and out my throat, startling even me.

I pressed my palms against my temples, trying to physically hold my thoughts together as they threatened to spiral. The room spun as if I was body surfing, the waves crashing over me, smashing me onto the sand.

"How is this possible?" I demanded, my voice rising with awe and terror. "How have we not known about another dimension all these centuries?"

"Because you humans have such tiny minds." He ran his hand down my arm, making me shiver. "What do you think Heaven and Hell are if not that, my dear?"

I had never thought of them as different dimensions before, but a cold feeling of uncertainty slowly crept through me as I realized how little I truly knew. Still, I hadn't read anything about dimensions in Angelo's library. Was Balthazar telling the truth? He was a demon, and demons weren't exactly known for their honesty. My stomach churned with anxiety and doubt.

Gage's eyes bored into me, his expression a toxic blend of condescension and impatience that made my skin crawl. His next words sliced through the air, sharp as a blade. "You must realize that's the only reason your precious vampire king wanted you. He needed you to heal his stone. Did you do it?"

A flicker of doubt threatened to ignite in my chest, but I extinguished it firmly before it could take hold. Gage clearly expected his accusation to shatter me, to make me crumble, but he had severely underestimated both me and Angelo.

I met his gaze unflinchingly, my resolve hardening like steel. "You don't know anything about Angelo or me," I said, my voice low but steady, holding an edge of defiance. "Angelo would tear through New Orleans and rip apart the bayou to find me."

The statement wasn't just fueled by hope—it was a certainty that warmed me from within, a beacon cutting through the darkness of my nightmare. Love, loyalty, and determination swelled in my heart.

I allowed a small smile to spread across my lips. "You have no idea what you've gotten yourself into," I added for good measure.

Gage seized my hair in a vicious grip, fingers twisting the strands until my scalp screamed in protest, and his nails raked across my skin, leaving fire in their wake. "Don't underestimate me, Nephilim," he snarled, his breath hot in my ear. "You're my slave, and at my mercy." He yanked harder, tears springing to my eyes. "Do you understand, bitch?"

"Yes," I whispered, all the fight suddenly draining out of me. The taste of fear flooded my mouth, bitter and metallic. Taunting this wolf had been a grave mistake, one I wouldn't soon forget or repeat.

"Release her." Balthazar's voice cut through the air like the crack of a whip.

Gage's eyes widened, wild fear replacing his earlier bravado. "As you wish, demon," he muttered, the words hushed. His grip on my hair loosened immediately and he let go of me so abruptly I stumbled into the wall.

Gage stalked toward me, his eyes glittering with malice. He stopped mere inches from my face, his hot breath washing over me. "I'm going to ask you again, bitch, and this time, I want an answer." His hand shot out, fingers digging into my cheeks with bruising force. "Did you heal the Aeternum Stone?"

I braced myself for what was coming, but to my utter shock, Balthazar moved with inhuman speed, clamping his hand around Gage's wrist, yanking it away from my face. "You don't get it, cur," Balthazar snarled, his voice dripping with contempt. "She's not your property. She's mine." The muscles in his arm tensed, and Gage's eyes widened in what I could only assume was pain. "She wouldn't even be here if it wasn't for me."

My heart lurched at Balthazar's words. "His"? The idea of belonging to this demon terrified me even more than Gage's brutish threats. And what did he mean when he said I wouldn't be here if not for him?

Angelo's face flashed in my mind, his eyes filled with all the love and protectiveness I'd come to rely on. I belonged with him, not this creature of darkness. The memory of Angelo's touch and his unwavering support gave me a flicker of reassurance amid the fear. He would come for me, I was certain. I just had to stay strong until then.

Gage hastily stepped back from me and a whimper escaped his throat as Balthazar sent him flying across the room with a casual flick of his wrist as if he weighed no more than a rag doll. The wolf crashed into the far wall with a sickening thud.

I flinched, but couldn't tear my eyes away from Balthazar. His casual display of power only underscored the danger I was in, caught between two monsters—one loutishly brutal, the other terrifyingly sophisticated.

Balthazar's eyes, glowing with an otherworldly light, fixed on Gage's crumpled form. "Of course she healed the Aeternum Stone, you fool. She's a Nephilim." His lips curved into a cruel smile. "And yes, she can heal the Luparion Crystal, too."

Panting, Gage shook his head and then slowly stood, his eyes never leaving Balthazar. "You want her, demon? Fine, you can have her." He jabbed a finger in my direction, his voice venomous. "But she heals the Crystal tonight, or she's dead."

Balthazar's eyes gleamed with amusement as if Gage's threat was nothing more than a child's temper tantrum. The casual, dismissive way he treated Gage's demand sent a fresh wave of fear through me. Balthazar was clearly far more powerful than the wolf.

If he could toss Gage so easily, what could he do to Angelo? The image of Balthazar hurling Angelo across a room, breaking him, maybe even killing him, flashed unbidden in my mind. My heart clenched painfully at the thought. The mere possibility of it played havoc with my lungs, turning my breath into short, panicked gasps. I had to find a way out of this, but surrounded by these monsters, one brutal and the other terrifyingly powerful, I felt more helpless than ever.

I need you, Angelo. Find me. Please.

I KICKED open the door to my secret room, the heavy wood splintering under my boot. With a snarl, I hurled Dimitri inside. He careened across the room, crashing into an array of gleaming instruments of torture hanging on the far wall. Metal clattered to the floor around him as he slumped, gasping.

Dimitri raised his head, blood streaming from his nose and a fresh gash on his forehead. Newly formed bruises on his neck had already darkened to an ugly purple. He spat out a mouthful of blood, then looked around the room with exaggerated interest. "Private party, eh?" he wheezed, attempting a smirk that came out more as a grimace. "Your events are getting rather exclusive, Angelo."

His flippant tone made my blood boil. I flew across the room, pinning him to the wall, my hands at his throat. "Joke while you can, Dimitri. This might be the last time you use that smart mouth of yours."

Dimitri's eyes glinted with amusement and dangerous defiance. "Promises, promises. You know, your hospitality leaves something to be desired. No wine? Not even an imported cheese platter? Tsk tsk."

"I'm a centuries-old made vampire with Dracula's blood coursing through my veins, you insignificant ingrate," I growled, my face inches from his. "You're nothing but a born vampire playing little power games." I tightened my grip, feeling his pulse flutter weakly under my palm. "Your pathetic quips won't save you here. Keep them up, and the only thing you'll be tasting is your own blood."

"Hmm, well, they do say a liquid diet is good for the figure," Dimitri smirked, though I did notice a flicker of genuine fear pass through his eyes as they darted over the bloodstained implements around us.

I grabbed a wicked-looking blade from the wall, pressing it against his cheek. "Last chance, Dimitri. Tell me everything about Serenity's disappearance, that dagger, and my ring. Or I'll show you just how creative I can get with my toys."

Dimitri's smirk faltered for a moment before he regained his composure. "Well, since you put it that way... How about we start with truth or dare? Though I have a feeling you're not much for dare right now."

I leaned closer, my voice a deadly whisper. "I have countless ways to make you talk, Dimitri. Your screams won't leave this room, and neither will you if I don't get what I want."

Dimitri's breath turned ragged and gasping, each inhalation painful against his bruised throat. Blood trickled from the corner of his mouth as he spoke, and his words were slurred and broken.

"L-look," he wheezed, wincing, "I... I'll admit I took the ring." He paused, coughing violently, specks of blood spraying from his lips. "N-needed it to melt the Malefic Puppets—a curse the high priestess put on...my brother and Gianna." His eyes, glassy with pain, sought mine. "Only...only thing...that would negate her power."

My jaw clenched, fury and skepticism warring within me. Part of me wanted to believe him—to think that this betrayal had a purpose beyond greed. But a larger part, the part consumed by fear for Serenity's safety and rage at her disappearance, wouldn't let me accept his words so easily.

"A likely story," I snarled, my voice trembling with barely contained anger. I leaned in closer, my face inches from his. "If that was true, why not just ask me for it?" The question came out as a roar, bouncing off the walls of the torture chamber.

Dimitri flinched, fear flashing across his battered face. His eyes darted away for a moment, a flicker of shame or possibly regret in them. It was gone before I could be sure.

"It's...complicated."

His hesitation ignited something savage within me. With a roar that tore from the depths of my soul, I unleashed a barrage of punches. Each impact sent a sickening crunch through the room, blood and spittle flying with every blow. My knuckles split, but I barely felt it. Betrayal, fear for Serenity, helpless rage—it all poured out in a tsunami of violence.

"What else?" I snarled between strikes. "What. Aren't. You. Telling. Me?" Each word was punctuated by another devastating blow.

Dimitri's head snapped back and forth like a broken doll's. Blood streamed from his nose, his lips split and swollen. He gurgled, choking on his own blood, struggling to form words. His face was so beaten as to be unrecognizable.

I paused to let him speak, my chest heaving. My hands trembled, knuckles coated in his blood and mine.

"P-Petar," Dimitri rasped, the name barely understandable on his ruined lips. "He...made...me..."

I froze, my fist raised for another blow, the name hitting me like a physical blow. "What did you say?" I hissed, grabbing his hair and yanking his head back.

His eyes, almost swollen shut, held pain and desperation. "Petar..." he choked out, each word a struggle. "Would have killed Valentin if I didn't...get the mirror."

The mention of a mirror sent a fresh wave of rage through me. My grip on his hair tightened, a growl building in my chest. "The mirror? You took the Moirai Mirror as well? Why, you bastard, why?"

"He... He wouldn't tell me," Dimitri gasped, his words slurred. "Just said he had to give the mirror to someone. I don't...don't know who."

"Wrong answer." The words left my mouth in a feral growl as I plunged a blade deep into his shoulder—not just any blade, but one imbued with the essence of sunlight, a weapon that inflicted unimaginable pain on our kind.

His anguished scream echoed off the walls of the chamber. Blood, darker than human blood, poured from the wound, and the scent of burning flesh filled the air. The blade worked its cruel magic, simulating the agony of sunlight coursing through his veins.

Dimitri struggled against me, his body in torment, but he was no match for my strength. His eyes, wide with shock and pain, locked onto mine, silently pleading for mercy.

I leaned in close, my face inches from his. The acrid smell of his burning flesh mixed with the metallic scent of blood in my nostrils, but I didn't flinch. My voice was a deadly whisper, each word dripping with lethal intent.

"Tell me everything, Dimitri. Every word Petar said." I

twisted the blade slightly, eliciting another agonized howl. "Your life depends on it. And trust me, this pain is nothing compared to what I'll do if you hold anything back."

Dimitri's labored breathing filled the silence as he struggled to form words through the haze of pain. Finally, panting and trembling, he managed to rasp out, "Petar... he didn't tell me much. Just that it was... the only way... to save Valentin and Gianna."

I arched an eyebrow. "So you decided to play hero, steal from me and endanger my mate? How wonderfully noble of you." I slow-clapped, the sound echoing ominously in the chamber. "I'm touched. Truly. Maybe we should alert the Nobel Peace Prize committee."

I leaned in again, my smirk fading into a dangerous glare. "Did it never occur to your brilliant mind that perhaps coming to me might have been a better option? Instead of, you know, stealing my things?"

Dimitri leaned his head against the wall, a mirthless chuckle escaping his bloodied lips. "For some reason, I didn't think you would take it well if I asked," he rasped. "And I thought you'd believe Petar over me."

"Poor choices, Dimitri. Now, you're the guest in my special room." I narrowed my eyes. "Perhaps next time you'll remember that stealing from me has... consequences."

He clicked his tongue. "Well, well. Look who's got trust issues. I'm hurt, Angelo. Truly." Dimitri pressed a hand dramatically over his heart. "And here I thought we were besties. Sharing blood bags, braiding each other's hair..."

Dimitri let out a choked laugh, wincing as the movement jarred his injuries, a ghost of his usual smirk flitting across his battered face.

The copper scent of blood hung thick in the air between us, mixing with the cloying humidity that seeped through the old mansion's walls. Outside, a thunderstorm rolled in from the Gulf, each rumble vibrating through the shuttered windows of the converted attic. The ancient floorboards had witnessed a century of secrets, and now they'd keep ours too.

I circled him slowly, my shoes creaking against worn wood. "You know what I find interesting?" I ran my finger along the edge of the metal table beside him, centuries of practiced control in every movement. "You're still trying to joke your way out of this. Old habits die hard, don't they?"

"What can I say?" Dimitri's eyes tracked my movement, tension betraying his casual tone. "Comedy's my coping mechanism. Though I have to admit—" he gestured to the array of implements on the table, their steel surfaces gleaming dully in the gas lamp's light "—your decorating choices aren't exactly inspiring my best material."

"Then perhaps—" I selected a slender blade, watching his reflection fragment in its surface "—we should focus on inspiring your honesty instead. Tell me where my mirror is."

A muscle twitched in Dimitri's jaw, the first crack in his facade. "Angelo..." His voice dropped its playful edge. "I don't have it anymore."

"No?" The blade caught the lamplight as I turned it. "Then who does?"

Dimitri's eyes dropped to the floor, something like shame crossing his features. "My father. He said... he said someone wanted it. Wouldn't tell me who." A bitter laugh escaped him. "Guess betrayal runs in the family, huh?"

"Your father." My voice went flat. "Petar has my mirror." The blade stilled in my hand. "And you gave it to him without asking who wanted it?"

"I didn't think—"

"No," I cut him off, cold fury seeping into my voice. "You didn't think. I gave your father a chance. That was my mistake. Yours was handing over something that doesn't belong to you, to a man who's spent years perfecting the art of betrayal. Like father, like son."

Dimitri's eyes flashed with fear and desperation. "You don't understand," he rasped. "I've never trusted my father. I thought... I thought he was setting me up, and now I know I was right." He swallowed hard, wincing at the effort. "That dagger you found? He must have planted it in my drawer. He's always three steps ahead. I'm just another pawn in his games."

I paused, studying Dimitri's face, trying to figure out if

he was telling the truth. He was so bloodied and in so much of pain, I didn't think he would lie to me, but then again... He was Dimitri Dragan.

And he always had tricks up his sleeve.

After a moment, I twirled the blade between my fingers, the threat still clear. "Interesting theory. But even if your Daddy Dearest is playing chess while we're playing checkers, it doesn't change the fact that you're in a mess. Here's a wild idea. How about you start trusting me? Because believe me, the alternative..." I gestured around the torture chamber. "Well, let's just say I'm just getting warmed up."

Dimitri's lips twitched into a pained smirk. "Funny you should say that," he breathed, each word an effort. "I'm starting to think Petar's idea of a family reunion might be less painful than your idea of a party."

I couldn't help but let out a dark chuckle. "Oh, Dimitri. Always with the jokes. Let's be real—you've seen what Petar's capable of. You really want to test that theory?"

Grabbing his chin, I forced him to meet my gaze. "We're going to try this again. Start talking. Every detail about Petar's plan. What he said, what he didn't. Hell, you're going to tell me what color underwear he was wearing. And if you don't..." I let the blade hover near his other shoulder. "Let's just say I have a lot more creative ideas that make this sunlight blade look like a moonlit stroll on the beach. *Comprende*?"

As I hovered the blade near Dimitri's shoulder, a

sudden jolt of energy surged through me, the world around me blurred, and the torture chamber faded away.

I need you, Angelo. Find me.

Serenity's voice, clear and desperate, penetrated my mind. It was followed by a series of images: dark rippling water, moonlight, the smell of swamp and decay. Serenity's face came into focus, pale and drawn. It was bad enough that her eyes were wide with fear. But what really made my blood run cold were the dark, ugly bruises marring her delicate neck, standing out against her pale skin.

There was something else too that made my ancient blood run cold—a presence, dark and malevolent, hovering just out of sight. The unmistakable taint of powerful evil permeated the vision.

Demon.

The word flashed in my mind, certain and terrifying.

The vision fizzled out, leaving me gasping and shaking. I stumbled back from Dimitri, the blade clattering to the floor. A feral growl rumbled in my chest as my predatory nature took over.

Dimitri just looked at me, fresh fear etched on his battered face.

I whirled on him, my vision tinted red with fury. "Someone's hurting Serenity," I snarled, snatching up the blade. "She's alive, but she's injured and... There's something else there. An evil presence. Demonic."

Dimitri's one eye that wasn't swollen shut widened in

genuine shock. "Demonic?! Angelo, I swear, I don't know anything about—"

A pounding on the door cut him off. Enzo's deep voice came through the thick wood. "Boss, it's important. You're going to want to hear this." At the same time, I heard Gianna's voice, frantic and muffled. "Angelo! Angelo, stop! You need to hear what I have to say! Don't listen to Enzo. He's lying!"

She sounded so desperate. It must be something truly horrible for her to be turning on Enzo.

I stood frozen, torn between my burning desire to continue extracting information from Dimitri and my need to hear what Gianna and Enzo were arguing about. Serenity's plea rang in my ears, her bruised neck and the evil presence flashing in my mind. Every second wasted was a second she remained in unimaginable danger.

"Tick tock, Angelo," Dimitri whispered, his voice still wheezing but with a hint of his old smugness. "Sounds like the cavalry's here. What's it going to be?"

CHAPTER

SIX

S*erenity*

As the sun began its descent over the bayou, I turned my attention back to the untouched plate before me. The aroma of spicy shrimp jambalaya wafting up, normally so enticing, now served only to turn my stomach. I pushed the plate away, the fork clattering harshly against the ceramic in the quiet room.

My appetite had been replaced by a gnawing anxiety that tightened my throat. The thought of Gage with his hands around my neck made even the idea of swallowing difficult. I stood, leaving the cooling jambalaya, and moved closer to the barred window.

Outside, the bayou was transforming in the fading light. The setting sun painted the sky with vibrant oranges and purples, its reflection shimmering in the murky water below. Cypress trees cast long shadows across the swamp, their silhouettes stretching like dark fingers over the water's surface.

As twilight deepened, a chorus of frogs began their nightly serenade, their croaks echoing across the water. The humid air carried the rich, earthy scent of decaying vegetation mixed with the sweet fragrance of blooming magnolias, overpowering the aroma of the abandoned meal behind me.

In the growing darkness, fireflies emerged, their tiny lights blinking on and off, and an owl hooted in the distance. Its mournful call sent a shiver down my spine— or perhaps that was from the memory of Gage's threat, and the impending visit to the wolf mafia king's estate to heal the Luparion Crystal.

As the last light faded, the sounds of nocturnal creatures grew louder, a symphony of chirps, croaks, and rustles that spoke of a world blissfully oblivious to my predicament. I pressed a hand against the cool glass, my reflection ghostly in the window, and listened to them, hoping they might soothe my fear.

The creak of the opening door sent a jolt through my body, causing my heart to race. "Time to go, beautiful." Balthazar's words felt like a death knell.

I stiffened, my muscles tensing as if preparing me for a

fight or flight response. Turning around, confusion gripped me. Dread swelled within me when I saw Balthazar. Yet the sight of his bare, muscled chest glistening in the dim light stirred an instant attraction in me. I immediately felt ashamed. How could I feel anything but revulsion for my captor?

"What if I can't heal the Crystal?" My voice quavered as I asked. The question hung heavy in the air, and cold dread settled in the pit of my stomach as I contemplated the possibility of failure and its consequences. Would death be preferable to whatever they had planned for me?

Balthazar's outstretched hand seemed both an offer and a threat. "You will be able to heal the stone if you choose to—if you do so willingly. Come," he commanded. The way he pointedly ignored my question amplified my fear, allowing my imagination to run wild with horrific possibilities.

Reluctantly, I placed my hand in his, feeling as if I was sealing my own doom. The eerie sensation that washed over me once more at his touch sent shivers down my spine. It was a feeling of wrongness, of the unnatural, that penetrated to my very core. Confusion mingled with my fear; why did touching him feel so terrible and yet so pleasurable? Was this a normal reaction to all demons, or was it something unique to Balthazar?

I hated lacking this crucial knowledge and feeling so woefully unprepared, ignorant and helpless in the face of evil. If Angelo was to find me, he needed something to track, some way to reach me before it was too late. Meanwhile, my powers were uncontrollable, as I was constantly finding out. If I didn't heal this wolf stone, I was a dead Nephilim.

As Balthazar led me out of the room, a cocktail of emotions swirled within me: fear of the unknown, shame at my body's reaction to Balthazar and confusion over the strange sensations his touch evoked, and a deep, pervasive sense of vulnerability and powerlessness. Yet beneath it all, a small spark of defiance remained, urging me to stay alert and watch for any opportunity that might arise to change my fate.

That's what Angelo would do. To survive, I was going to have to be ruthless, like him.

Balthazar led me down the hallway, my heart rate quickening with each step. At the far end, standing next to an exterior door, I could make out three figures waiting for us. Gage's imposing silhouette was unmistakable, even at a distance, causing my breath to catch. The memory of his hands around my neck flashed through my mind, making me instinctively want to retreat.

As we drew closer, the figures came into sharper focus. Gage stood in the middle, his muscular frame tense and alert, ready to pounce. His eyes, cold and calculating, locked onto mine, making goosebumps erupt up all over my skin.

To Gage's left stood a man I didn't recognize. He was shorter than Gage but no less intimidating, with broad shoulders and a deep scar running down the side of his face. His presence radiated danger, and I found myself unconsciously leaning away from him. But it was the man on Gage's right that truly made my heart stutter, and my blood run cold.

Petar Dragan.

I stumbled, my legs suddenly weak. Bitterness swelled inside me as memories of his betrayal and the terror of my kidnapping crashed over me.

Petar's gelled-backed hair gleamed under the hallway lights, reminding me of an oil slick on water. His eyes darted around nervously, never settling on one spot for long, until finally they locked on mine. In that moment, I saw dark cruelty flash behind his nervous facade, and my stomach lurched.

"You," I whispered through gritted teeth.

It was all I could muster. I couldn't even bring myself to say his name. Rage boiled inside me as I remembered how he'd manipulated me, lying about Joy being hurt to lure me away. The memory of my panic, my desperate rush to help my friend only to fall into his trap, made me want to lash out at him right there.

He would pay for that deception, for turning my love for Joy against me. Angelo would see to it.

Petar's thin lips curled into what I suppose he thought was a charming smile, but it only served to heighten my unease. Something about him had always set my teeth on edge, but now, knowing what he'd done, the feeling had erupted like a burst boil, oozing with foul-smelling pus. He reminded me of every sleazy used car salesman and unscrupulous politician I'd ever encountered, rolled into one unsavory, festering wound.

As we approached, I could smell Petar's overpowering cologne, a cloying scent that stuck in my throat and mingled unpleasantly with the aroma of the bayou still clinging to my clothes. The combination was nauseating.

I tried to steel myself, to project an air of confidence I didn't feel. Inside, my mind was racing. What was Petar even doing here? His presence suggested that whatever was about to happen involved not just supernatural politics, but the human criminal element as well. The situation, already dire, suddenly felt even more complex and dangerous.

Despite my fear, I forced myself to stand tall, meeting each man's gaze in turn. I might be their captive, but I refused to let them see me cower. Angelo never showed fear. I was his mate and had to show that I was worthy of being so. I had survived Freaky Freddie and I would survive this. Angelo always said, "I believe in you." Right now, those words were my lifeline, the only thing keeping me from crumbling under the weight of their collective stares.

"Hello, Serenity," Petar said, his face splitting into a big, oily smile. "Enjoying your stay?"

His smug tone ignited my fury. Without thinking, I lunged forward, my hand raised to slap his face. But before

I could make contact, Balthazar caught my arm in his iron grip, yanking me back. As I struggled in his hold, a sleek limousine pulled up outside, is arrival momentarily distracting me.

Petar's eyes flashed with anger. "You'll pay for that little outburst," he snarled. Then his tone shifted and became sickeningly sweet. "I have a gift for you."

It was only then that I noticed the burlap sack in his hand, the words 'Idaho Potatoes' stamped across it in faded letters.

"What—" I started to say, but Petar was too quick.

Before I could react, he lunged forward and pulled the sack over my head. Darkness engulfed me, the rough fabric scratching against my skin.

I was hustled outside and into the vehicle, then the car door slammed shut and the vehicle lurched into motion. The world outside the burlap sack was a cacophony of muddled sounds—the purr of the engine, the crunch of gravel under the tires, the low murmur of voices I couldn't quite make out.

My neck still hurt where Gage had gripped me yester-day, and I didn't want another round of him trying to squeeze the life out of me. The stale smell of potatoes from the sack mingled with the leathery scent of the car inte-rior, creating a nauseating cocktail that made my stomach churn. Each inhalation was a struggle.

As we drove my mind raced, trying to piece together the fragments of information I had. Petar's betrayal...the

Luparion Crystal...Gage's threats... They all swirled in my head like a chaotic storm. What did they really want from me? And more importantly, how was I going to get out of this alive?

I tried to focus on my other senses, attempting to glean any information about where we might be heading. The car felt like it was moving fast, with few stops or turns. Were we on a highway heading away from the city? The thought of being taken even further from potential help sent a fresh wave of panic through me.

Despite the fear coursing through my veins, I forced myself to take slow, deep breaths. *Stay calm*, I told myself. *Look for opportunities. Be patient. It's what Angelo would do.*

That was how I had escaped Freddie for years, too. Until—no. I didn't want to think about that.

My fingers twitched, itching to summon my Nephilim powers. But I knew better than to try that now. I was blindfolded, surrounded by enemies in a moving vehicle. One wrong move and I could kill all of us. This wasn't the time. I'd just have to wait for another opportunity.

I focused instead on filing away every detail I could—the duration of the ride, the turns we took, any distinctive sounds or smells outside.

As the car continued its journey to the wolf mafia king's home, a grim determination settled over me. I might be their captive, but I refused to be their victim.

The car hit a bump, jostling me against whoever sat beside me. A familiar wave of revulsion, automatic and completely unbidden, told me it was Balthazar. His presence, though threatening, was oddly reassuring. He had shown some mercy earlier when he called off Gage. Perhaps, if things went south, I could use the apparent tension between them to my advantage.

Hope crystallized in my mind. I would survive this, whatever it took. I'd survived living with a single mom, survived her death, even survived Angelo buying me. I could do it again. I would get back to Angelo.

I settled back in the seat and recited a silent prayer, wedged between my two of my captors.

Angelo, be safe. I'll find you. Just know I love you.

SEVEN

ENZO KEPT POUNDING on the door. "Boss, it's important. Open the door."

My jaw clenched, my hand tightening on the blade I held. The vision of Serenity, bruised and surrounded by evil, still burned in my mind.

If Petar hurt her, he would never know a minute without pain. I would keep him alive and in misery for the rest of his life.

"Don't want to keep him waiting, do you?" Dimitri murmured. "I'm not going anywhere."

I threw open the door, still clutching the blade.

Gianna ran her gaze over me and clapped a hand over her mouth. "How could you?" I glanced down at my shirt and trousers, stained with Dimitri's blood.

Pain flickered in her eyes. "Don't listen to a word Enzo's about to say. What he found is a forgery."

Now that grabbed my attention. I focused on Enzo. "What did you find?"

Enzo's eyes darted to Dimitri and Gianna, then back to me. He handed me a folded paper, his expression grave. "This. Hidden in a pocket of one of Dimitri's leather jackets."

"Someone planted that there. Someone's trying to frame him," Gianna insisted.

My curiosity piqued, I unfolded the paper and scanned the letter. The elegant handwriting was instantly recognizable. Each word felt like a blow as I read it:

Dimitri,

Your loyalty to the pack will not go unnoticed. The information you provided about the Nephilim's location was invaluable. Our plans will proceed as discussed.

Ensure the path to Crescent Manor remains unguarded. Your role in weakening the vampire coven's defenses will prove crucial, and you will be handsomely rewarded when the Luparion Crystal shines again and the Nephilim is mine.

Betray us, and the hunt begins with you as our prey.

Trystan Hunter

When I finished reading, a tidal wave of fury washed over me. My hands shook with rage, nearly tearing the letter. Trystan had tried to take Serenity once before, at one of Simon Cartier's private auctions. I had had to fight him to secure her. And now, with Dimitri's help, he was trying to reclaim her? This betrayal meant death.

Wordlessly, I handed the letter back to Enzo, who took it with a grim nod. Gianna looked up from where she cradled Dimitri's head in her lap, his blood smeared on her dress and hands. Her eyes were wide with fear and pleading. "Please, Angelo. Don't kill him," she begged, her voice breaking. "There must be some explanation. Dimitri isn't allied with Trystan and the wolves, I swear."

I stared down at Dimitri, determined to drain the bastard.

I could smell the fear radiating off him beneath his bravado. The one eye he could see out of darted between Gianna and me. I saw the silent plea there, his desperation to spare her from witnessing what was about to happen.

"Come on, Angelo," Dimitri rasped, managing a weak smirk despite his battered state. "You wouldn't deprive a wife of her husband's charming company, would you?"

I nodded with my chin, unmoved. "Take her out of here, Enzo."

Gianna shook her head violently, her dark hair flying around her. "No. No! Stay away from him. You're going to kill him."

I gave her a level look, rolling my shoulders. "Yes, I am."

"No!" Gianna shrieked, her voice raw and desperate.

She lunged forward, throwing herself over Dimitri's body, her hands slick with his blood as she shielded him. "Angelo, don't do this! I'm your sister. As you love me, don't kill him!"

Enzo moved to pull her away, but she fought him like a wild animal, kicking and clawing. "Get your hands off me!" she screamed, her eyes flashing with fury and terror. "Dimitri, I won't let them hurt you!"

It took both Enzo and me to pry Gianna off Dimitri. She thrashed in our grip, her nails leaving bloody scratches down Enzo's arms. "You're a monster, Angelo!" she spat, tears streaming down her face. "If you do this, I'll never forgive you!"

I tightened my grip on Gianna, feeling her fury and fear. For a moment, our eyes locked, and I saw the desperation there, a plea for mercy I couldn't grant.

"Enzo," I said, my voice grim. "Take. Her. Out."

With a sharp nod, Enzo reached for Gianna. I released my hold, allowing him to take full control of her, pulling both of Gianna's arms behind her back, restraining her very effectively.

"No!" Gianna screamed, renewing her struggles against Enzo's grip. "Angelo, please! Don't do this!"

I ignored her entreaties. In our world, betrayal was the ultimate sin, and Dimitri had crossed a line that couldn't be uncrossed. Family or not, I couldn't let this go unpunished. The safety of our entire organization—not to mention of Serenity—depended on it.

I cracked my knuckles, the sound sharp in the sudden silence of the room. The smell of Dimitri's fear intensified with the coppery scent of his blood. Time for him to die.

"Angelo, non. *S'il vous plaît.*"

I stopped in my tracks and turned to the frail voice. Elena stood there, leaning heavily against the door jamb. Her silver hair, usually piled up into a bun, now hung loosely over her shoulders. Her vibrant blue eyes, typically so full of warmth and wisdom, were tired and sad as she looked between me and what was left of Dimitri. Her arrival here was so unexpected that, for a moment, I forgot to breathe.

There was a fierce determination in the set of her jaw. Whatever she had to say, she considered it important enough to drag herself down here, barely recovered from her attack as she was.

I glared at Enzo. "What is she doing here?"

I didn't want her to see what I was going to do any more than I wanted Gianna to witness it.

Enzo shrugged, looking as bewildered as I felt. "I don't know. She was unconscious when I left her."

I turned back to Elena, my voice softening. "Elena, what is it?"

As Elena opened her mouth to speak, the tension in the room was like a rattling lid on a boiling pot. "Angelo, I...saw who put the dagger...in Gianna's drawer."

I remained perfectly still, except for my thundering heart.

She took a deep breath. "It was Petar. I came in to put away some laundry and he was in there." Fear flashed in her eyes. "He was angry and told me that I shouldn't be there. And that he...had to...shut me up."

I clenched my fists. "He attacked you?" Another nail in Petar's coffin.

She nodded. "Yes. The look in his eyes... I believe he is mad, Angelo."

Gianna gasped, and from behind me, Dimitri let out a weak, humorless chuckle that ended in a wet cough. "Well...well," he croaked, his voice rough. "Looks like... Someone's been a naughty boy." Each word seemed to cost him effort, but his sarcasm still cut through. "And here I thought... I was your favorite punching bag, Angelo." He wheezed, a pained smirk twisting his bloodied lips. "I'm hurt...truly."

I shot him a warning glare, but he merely attempted another smirk, wincing as the expression pulled on his split lip. His words came out slurred and breathless, punctuated by pained gasps.

"Don't...tell me you're...surprised." He paused, struggling to pull in breath. "In our line of...work...betrayal's practically...expected."

Dimitri's labored words had barely left his bloodied lips when sudden, searing pain lanced through my skull. I staggered as I tried to keep from falling.

I caught my breath. The room spun around me, colors whirling around as if I had turned into a spinning top.

Serenity's sweet voice echoed in my mind.

Angelo, be safe. I'll find you. Just know I love you.

Enzo gripped my arm. "Boss, what's wrong?"

I braced my legs, fighting to stay upright as the world around me tilted and faded. Darkness enveloped me, and then... The smells hit.

Rich leather, new. The unmistakable scent of a luxury vehicle.

Champagne. Sharp and bubbly, perhaps spilled on upholstery. Potatoes... Why potatoes?

A man's cologne—expensive, but applied too heavily to be anything but oppressive.

And beneath it all, the faintest trace of her perfume. Serenity.

"Angelo," her voice whispered in my mind, fragile yet determined. "Be safe. I'll find you. Just know I love you."

I gasped, the connection breaking and the room snapping back into focus, Dimitri's heavy breathing distracting me from my racing thoughts.

Gripping the edge of a nearby table laden with instruments of torture, I tried to make sense of what I'd experienced. A limousine. She was definitely in a limousine. But going where? The smells offered no clue as to her location, just the agonizing certainty that she was out there, afraid.

With a roar of frustration, I hurled the instrument table against the wall, sending metal tools clattering to the floor. The crash echoed through the room, doing nothing to quiet the rage inside me. Every vampire instinct screamed to hunt, to tear apart whoever dared touch what was mine.

"What's happening, boss?" Through my haze of fury, I saw Enzo appearing in my peripheral vision, his stance wary as he blocked the doorway.

"It's Serenity..." I snarled through clenched fangs. "She's on the move, in a limousine. But I don't know where. I can't fucking find her!"

I broke away from him, then grabbed Dimitri by the throat and hauled him off Gianna's lap. I shook him hard, making his head flop around like a chicken's. "Who has her? Tell me your dad's plan."

Blood trickled from his split lip as he choked out a laugh. "If I... knew Daddy Dearest's plans," he coughed wetly, "...don't you think...I'd have better things to do...than get tortured by you?" His eyes rolled briefly before focusing again. "Although...this is...rather cozy."

Despite his battered state, a weak smirk returned. "But hey...if we're taking bets...my money's on...Dear Old Dad making a deal with...our doggy friends." Another painful wheeze. "He always did...want to be king."

I dropped him on the floor and he crumpled into a ball, his eyes fluttering shut. Gianna pushed herself up from where I'd left her, stumbling as she rushed to close the distance between her and her husband.

"Stop, Angelo, please. You're going to kill him." Her voice cracked with desperation, but I barely heard her over the roaring of my blood in my ears.

I stared at Dimitri, trying to decide if he was telling the truth. Either way, the scent of his blood called to the monster inside me, making my fangs ache.

Enzo came up next to me. "Petar wouldn't be able to take you down without an army, and then Trystan would get his Nephilim prize."

"Serenity." Her name tore from my throat like a curse. Fury like I'd never experienced in all my centuries rushed through me, a red miasma clouding my vision. My fingers curled into claws, itching to tear into flesh. My body trembled with barely contained violence, the need for bloodshed thrumming in my veins. The beast inside me howled for retribution, demanding blood for blood.

"This note is Trystan's declaration of war." I crushed the paper in my fist, my voice dropping to a guttural snarl barely recognizable as human speech.

The predator inside me was rising, hungry for vengeance.

CHAPTER
EIGHT

ngelo

A SILENCE as heavy as a burial shroud descended over the room at my assessment of Trystan's note as a declaration of war. Rage flowed through my veins like molten steel, burning away every shred of reason.

"We need to go now." I lunged toward the door, but Enzo's grip found my arm, his fingers digging into muscle.

"Boss—wait."

Something snapped inside me. I whirled around, my vision blurring red at the edges, and slammed him against the wall, my hand crushing his throat. "Don't. Ever. Argue. With. Me. Enzo." Each word was filled with venom.

69

Enzo didn't flinch. His dark eyes bored into mine, steady despite my grip on his windpipe. In them, I saw not fear, but my own savage desperation reflected back at me. "If you go after him without a plan," he croaked, "he'll rip you to pieces." His face softened with concern. "I can see the grief eating you alive, boss. But charging in blind—that's exactly what he wants. You know that."

I narrowed my eyes as I squeezed tighter, feeling his pulse hammering against my palm. "What do you suggest I do instead?" The words came out as a guttural snarl, my teeth clenched so hard my jaw ached.

Enzo's eyes watered. "Set...up...a...meeting." Each word was a desperate wheeze.

I stared at him, rage and reason warring within me. Every cell in my body screamed for blood, for immediate vengeance. Serenity's face flashed through my mind; her smile, now stolen from me. My grip tightened as fury surged anew. I wanted—needed—to rip someone, anyone, apart for daring to take her from me, for thinking they could challenge my crown.

The throne I'd fought to build. The family I'd fought to protect.

"*S'il vous plaît.*" Elena's trembling hand pressed against my back, her touch warm, melting my ice-cold fury. "I don't want to lose you too, Angelo." Her soft voice cracked, reaching through the red haze of bloodlust and pulling me back from the pit of hell, a lifeline.

For now.

The darkness still churned beneath my skin, patient. Waiting.

I released Enzo abruptly, and he gasped, coughing and sputtering, looking shocked. I'd never attacked him before.

Never.

This obsession with Serenity could bring me down. I knew it with the same certainty that I knew my own name. The realization hit like acid in my veins. If I didn't wrestle this beast back into its cage, I'd not only burn New Orleans to ash, I'd tear apart the only family I had left. The family she'd helped me build.

I stumbled away from Elena, fighting for air. The rage was a living thing inside me now, clawing at my ribcage, demanding blood. Each breath felt like swallowing glass as I tried to force it back.

My gaze found Enzo over my shoulder. He stood there, fingers gingerly touching the angry red marks blooming across his throat; marks I'd put there. Guilt twisted in my gut to see them.

"Set up a meeting at Bourbon Street Burgers." My voice was sandpaper rough. The Santi family's burger joint—our territory, our rules.

Enzo shook his head, still massaging his throat. "Trystan won't go for that, boss. It needs to be somewhere neutral, where you'll be on equal footing." His eyes held mine steadily. Still looking out for my best interests, even after I'd nearly killed him.

I gritted my teeth tight. This wasn't what I wanted. I wanted the advantage, wanted to corner that bastard like the rabid dog he was on Santi territory. But Enzo's logic cut through my bloodlust like a knife through fog. I dragged trembling fingers through my hair, pulling some strands loose. "Fine. Call Keir."

Keir Rankin, the Unseelie king, was the only one of us with ice in his veins instead of fire. While Trystan and I were creatures of impulse and violence, always one heartbeat away from carnage, Keir remained a glacier of calm in even the bloodiest storms.

I bolted for the door, my control fraying with each passing second. The people I loved were too close to danger, and the monster inside me was too hungry for violence to tell friend from foe.

"I won't be able to set it up until tomorrow or tomorrow night," Enzo murmured quietly, cautiously, like he was talking to a wild animal. Maybe he was.

"Just set it up." Using my vampire speed, I shot down the hallway, the world blurring around me. My hand found a bottle of wine at the bar—not nearly strong enough to dull the pain and quiet the screaming in my head, but it would have to do. Anything to soften the razor edges of grief that threatened to slice me to ribbons from the inside out.

CHAPTER

NINE

Serenity

THE LIMOUSINE finally pulled to a stop. Balthazar's hand wound around my waist as the doors opened, drawing me close like I was already his prize. The leather scent of the limo gave way to crisp night air. All I could think of was Angelo. Balthazar could force my body to his side, but he'd never own my heart the way Angelo did.

Gage came up next to me. "One word and you're dead, bitch." His voice stole my breath.

I concentrated on the smells around me, desperate for any clue as to my location:

Bubbling water with a faint sulfuric odor—perhaps a hot spring or a swamp?

Damp earth and decaying leaves, hinting at a forested area.

A whiff of smoke, from a distant campfire or chimney.

The unmistakable scent of moss and algae, strong and earthy.

A trace of something floral—magnolias? Their sweet perfume was barely noticeable under the stronger scents.

Musky animal odor—wild, not domesticated. Wolves?

Balthazar's expensive cologne, mixed with sweat now.

And Gage's aftershave; cheaper, sharper, with an undertone of gun oil.

All the scents seeping through the burlap sack told a story. I focused on each one, trying to build a picture in my mind of where I was, where we might be going. If only I could see, touch, or hear more clearly. But with my other senses diminished, these fragments of smell were my only connection to the world—my only hope of escape.

Suddenly, someone lifted me into their strong arms. The moment skin touched skin, a jolt of energy surged through me and an unmistakable aura enveloped me, setting every nerve on fire. My blood recoiled yet at the same time was oddly drawn to the conflicting energy.

I struggled against the bare chest, fingers brushing against smooth, unnaturally warm skin. "Put me down."

"If I do," Balthazar said, his voice a low rumble against my side, "you'll sink into a marsh. Do you really want to tramp through mud and water that would go up to your thighs?"

The heat radiating from his body was suffocating, intensifying the humidity in the air around us. I could smell his unique scent—a mixture of brimstone, exotic spices, and something indefinable and otherworldly. It made my head spin.

"N-no," I said miserably. Why on earth were we walking through the swamp?

The sounds of water sloshing and reeds rustling filled the air. Frogs croaked in an endless chorus, punctuated by the splash of something large sliding into the water. Insects buzzed around us, a constant, irritating whine, while cicadas screamed in the trees. With the bag over my head, every sound seemed amplified, making it impossible to tell direction or distance. The pungent odor of decay and stagnant water assaulting my nostrils was made worse by my proximity to Balthazar's overwhelming presence.

With each step Balthazar took, I felt his muscles shift. My body alternated between wanting to melt closer to him to escape the swamp's perils and recoiling from the strange energy that simultaneously repulsed and attracted me.

A cool breeze ghosted over my exposed skin, a brief respite from the swamp's oppressive heat, carrying the scent of night-blooming flowers, a jarringly beautiful note in this treacherous environment.

"Watch your head," Balthazar warned, ducking slightly. I felt something brush against the sack over my head—low-hanging moss or branches.

As we moved deeper into the swamp, I clung to every detail my senses could grasp—the squelch of footsteps through mud, the tang of cypress and stagnant water, the way our path curved left and then right. Remembering each sound and smell might be the difference between escape and captivity.

Heavy footsteps squished through the marsh. "Gage," an unfamiliar voice said, gruff and low. "The king is gone, off visiting his favorite whore. He won't be back until tomorrow night."

"Good, that makes it easier." Gage's voice was like a sleazy pimp's. "She'll keep him busy."

I stiffened in Balthazar's arms. A whore? That was their grand plan to overthrow the wolf king—thinking he'd be distracted by a woman? Everything I'd ever heard about Trystan painted a picture of cunning and power. Gage's certainty made my stomach turn. He was either a fool or knew something I didn't.

"The Luparion Crystal is locked in his office, but I have a key." The unfamiliar voice paused, and I felt the weight of unseen eyes on me. "Is that the Nephilim?"

"Yes," Gage replied, his tone clipped and cold.

"Do you think she can really heal the Crystal?"

"She'd better hope so," Gage said, malice dripping from every word. "If she doesn't, she's dead."

The marshy scent around me intensified, mirroring my rising panic. I tasted acrid fear in my mouth. Balthazar's arms tightened almost imperceptibly around me, whether in reassurance or warning, I couldn't tell.

Balthazar finally set me down, and my legs wobbled under me like a newborn colt's. The ground felt solid enough—a pebbled path, judging by the crunch under my feet—but after being carried blindfolded, my sense of balance was way off. And without my sight, every sound, every sensation felt amplified and yet impossible to place.

"I've got Trystan's key and sent the other guards to the east side of the compound so they won't see you enter Trystan's office," said the unknown voice. "Just make it quick. If she fails and we're caught, we're going to become a bonfire."

"Getting cold feet, Ivan?" Gage taunted.

"Just make sure she does it," the other voice growled.

A chill ran down my spine. Bonfire? God, I hoped they didn't roast their enemies alive. The casual way he mentioned such a gruesome fate made my stomach churn.

I tried to look down, but all I could see through the small gap in the tie around the neck of the bag were my sandaled feet trying not to stumble on the pebbled path. The stones crunched beneath us, each step a reminder of my helplessness. I wanted to run, but Balthazar's grip on my arm was relentless. Escape was impossible.

Someone opened a door, its hinges squeaking ominously. I was led up some stairs, the wood creaking under our weight. The scent of wolves grew stronger, musky and wild. I had to be in the compound now. But there were other scents too, creating an unsettling tapestry.

Roasting meat, making my mouth water despite my fear.

The clean, sharp smell of waxed hardwood floors.

And a sweet floral scent—jasmine or maybe bougainvillea—floating on the air. Mom used to have those planted in her garden and I would know them anywhere.

The mix of scents was jarring—the homey smells of cooking and flowers so at odds with the underlying threat of violence. It was as if someone had built a pleasant home over a slaughterhouse.

As we moved further into the building, the temperature dropped slightly. Air conditioning, I realized. Such a strange comfort in this den of wolves and conspirators. The sack over my head rustled with each breath, a constant reminder of my vulnerability.

Another door creaked open. Finally, the sack was ripped off my head. I blinked, my eyes adjusting to the dim light after the suffocating darkness. We were in a turret study, apparently Trystan's. It seemed to float in shadows, illuminated only by the moonlight filtering through tall, arched windows and the ethereal blue glow from a modern gas fireplace set into one of the walls.

My attention was immediately drawn to the massive

oil painting above his desk—a white wolf with piercing blue eyes. Something about those eyes tugged at my memory, familiar yet just out of reach.

The eight walls of the room rose high above me, dark wooden panels climbing halfway up them before giving way to deep burgundy wallpaper that disappeared into shadows near the ceiling. A mahogany desk dominated the center, its polished surface bare except for a sleek computer monitor casting a faint glow. No papers, no pens —just a deliberate, calculated emptiness.

Against one wall stood an ornate floor-to-ceiling bookcase, its shelves filled with leather-bound volumes whose gilded spines winked in the firelight. A small octagonal table, also mahogany, sat in one corner, surrounded by four high-backed chairs upholstered in deep red velvet. Every detail spoke of power and control—exactly what one would expect of Trystan's private domain.

Balthazar leaned closer to me, his demonic presence making the air feel thicker, heavier. "Welcome to the wolf king's private office, Nephilim." He pointed toward the painting, a knowing smile playing over his perfect lips. "Just in case you're wondering, the painting is of Trystan."

I stared at the magnificent white wolf, really seeing it now. The massive paws that could crush bone. The powerful shoulders built for tearing prey apart. A memory flashed: Angelo's face when I first met him, angry red scratches marring his beautiful features. He'd said they were from a "scrape with a cur"—over me. Even Angelo, with all his vampire strength and power, hadn't walked away unscathed from that fight.

My heart clenched painfully in my chest. If the wolf king could claw someone as powerful as Angelo... What else could he do to him? The thought made my blood run cold.

Gage pulled on a book and the bookcase swung open like something out of a Gothic horror novel. Behind it sat a safe, its metallic surface gleaming dully in the firelight. He twisted the combination lock back and forth, each click echoing in the tense silence.

He opened the safe door and took out a small black velvet case. "Showtime, Nephilim. Heal the Luparion Crystal." His eyes turned gold. "Or you're dead."

Balthazar put his hand on my lower back. I didn't know what the gesture meant. Was it for reassurance, or was he simply urging me forward?

Gage opened the case to reveal the Luparion Crystal. What might have once been a magnificent stone now lay practically lifeless, its gold and black stripes dulled like a tiger's pelt left too long in the sun. The crystal's surface looked almost cloudy, as if a film of ash had settled over it, muting its natural luster. Even in the dim light, I could sense its weakened state—like a dying heartbeat, barely pulsing.

I knew what healing a mystical stone felt like—the Aeternum Stone had nearly drained my life away with its sharp, angular need clawing at me, like a thousand knives scraping the power out of my veins. This was different. Where the vampire stone had been all jagged edges and violent hunger, the Luparion Crystal's rounded curves were somehow softer as it lay dormant before me.

Balthazar and Gage stalked forward, shepherding me back until the sharp edge of the bookcase dug into my spine. I tried to wriggle away, but Balthazar's arm shot out, his palm slamming against the shelves next to my head. Gage did the same on the other side, their bodies forming a cage of muscle and menace. The twin scents of wolf and demon surrounded me, closing off any hope of escape.

Gage cocked his eyebrow, one claw extending to trace a burning line down my arm. "I'm waiting. Or do you need some friendly persuasion?"

My skin crawled where he had scratched me, but I refused to give him the satisfaction of flinching. The sharp sting was nothing compared to what he could do—would do—if I failed.

I held my head high and scanned the bayou, wishing desperately that Angelo in bat form would burst into view and through one of the windows. But there were only clouds.

Balthazar met my worried gaze. "That's it, Serenity. Show him what you can do."

Were they both delusional? The Aeternum Stone had admittedly been larger than the Luparion Crystal, but both were crafted by witches. Healing the first stone had nearly killed me—my body still remembered the way it had drained my life force. And now Gage expected me to heal another one just so he could overthrow Trystan?

I reluctantly took the black velvet case.

Gage glared at me. "Put your hand over the stone and heal it, just like you did for Angelo. Do it, or the DuPonts die."

I put a shaking hand over the stone, my fingertips barely grazing its surface, and waited for that rush of power I'd felt with the Aeternum Stone—that surge of energy that had coursed through my veins like liquid lightning, the overwhelming flood of sensations and feelings that had nearly brought me to my knees.

Nothing. No warmth, no pulse, no whisper of magic. Just a cold, lifeless crystal beneath my trembling fingers that felt as dead as any ordinary rock you'd find on the street. My stomach twisted with anxiety. What if I couldn't do this? What if whatever power that had worked before had abandoned me?

Gage's claws dug into my shoulder as he shoved me forward. "Are you even trying? You don't want to find out how creative I can be with pain. I can make death feel like mercy."

I stumbled back and smacked into the bookcase, the wooden edges digging into my spine. Something heavy tumbled off and hit the floor with a dull thud. A quick glance showed what looked like an old tome—thankfully still intact. Just what I needed, to damage something in this room.

"Yes, I'm trying." My voice came out smaller than I intended, fear and frustration making it quiver. I squeezed my eyes shut, pressing my hands against the crystal until my fingers ached.

Nothing. Not a single tremor of power, not the faintest whisper of magic. The crystal remained cold and lifeless under my touch. Why was this happening? The Aeternum Stone had practically sung to me, its power flowing through me like a river.

Was it because this was a crystal and not a stone? Or was there something else missing, some key to unlocking my power that remained frustratingly out of reach?

My heart slammed into my ribs as I felt Gage's impatient presence looming over me. Time was running out, and I had no idea how to make this work.

"She can't do it," Balthazar said softly, his words falling like a death knell in the quiet study.

"Bitch," Gage hissed. There was a blur of movement, then white-hot pain exploded across the back of my skull. The study spun around me, the moonlight fragmenting into stars behind my eyes. My arms went limp, useless. As consciousness slipped away, I thought I heard Balthazar sigh. Then I fell into darkness, and knew nothing more.

CHAPTER

TEN

S*erenity*

WHEN I WOKE UP, my skull felt like it had been bouncing around a pinball machine. Sunlight streamed through the barred window, sending fresh spikes of pain through my temples, and I winced.

"I'm sorry Gage hit you," Balthazar said softly. It sounded like he was right next to me.

I scrambled to the other side of the bed, my heart pounding. The sudden movement made the room spin. Balthazar sat beside the bed, staring at me with those unsettling eyes. His long black hair flared over his muscular shoulders and once again, he was shirtless. His legs were crossed and he had on a pair of jeans. High black boots hugged his calves. The casual pose didn't fool me—there was nothing casual about being locked in a room with him.

"I didn't mean to frighten you, beautiful." He sighed, and regret crossed his face. "Gage hit you before I could stop him. It was my fault."

The acrid smell of smoke still hung in the sparse room, a reminder of my failed escape attempt. Through the barred window, Cypress trees draped with Spanish moss swayed in the breeze. Somewhere in the distance, a bird called out across the bayou. I was miles from civilization, miles from help.

Miles from Angelo.

I clutched the blanket tightly, trying to hide the way my hands shook. "What are you doing here, Balthazar?"

He shrugged, the movement making his muscular shoulders ripple. "Protecting you. What else?"

"From...?"

"You didn't think Gage would be content with just hitting you once, did you?" Something dark flashed in his eyes.

I thought of Gage's threat, and fear jumped into my heart. "He won't kill me, will he?"

Balthazar walked over to the window and peered out, his reflection ghostly in the morning light. "No. At least... Not yet." A bird's cry echoed across the bayou, as if in warning.

His broad back blocked my view. "What's going on out there? What's happening?" I asked fearfully.

He turned back to me, and for a moment, the way the sunlight caught his face made him look almost angelic. But I knew his beauty was a mask for something ancient and deadly. "Nothing that concerns you."

Another lie. But instead of confronting him, I changed the subject, trying to ignore how my head pounded with each heartbeat. "What did you mean when you said I had to be willing to heal the crystal?"

"Tell me..." His voice dropped lower, more intimate as he moved closer. The air seemed to thicken at his nearness. "When you healed the Aeternum Stone, did Angelo force you?"

The memory rose up sharp and clear—Angelo revealing how the stone was all that stood between him and Dracula's vengeance. He hadn't begged, hadn't threatened. Just spoke a truth I couldn't bear: his death if the stone failed. Angelo was a killer, a monster by any human standard. But the thought of him being destroyed had left my heart aching with a fear deeper than any moral judgment.

I shook my head. "No, I wanted to."

"Because you love him?" His lips curved into a wicked smile. "Sweet, but your love won't save him if he tries to interfere. I could end him with a thought."

His words made me uneasy and I didn't respond. The way he watched me—like he could see right through my silence—made my skin crawl. He moved with the fluid grace of a creature that had had centuries to perfect its predatory movements.

"Why didn't Gage kill me?"

"Because I told him I could teach you how to use your powers to heal the Crystal." He grinned, and there was nothing human in that expression. "That is, if you wanted to."

"That's why you want to teach me? So I can heal the Crystal?"

He chuckled, the sound turning my insides to ice. "Not exactly. I couldn't care less who is wolf king. Trystan, Gage, it means nothing to me." He traced a finger idly along the window bars.

"Then why?"

Balthazar turned to me and ran a finger along my jawline, his touch electric against my skin. "Because you're a Nephilim and possess power that I want. Your father... He's quite something, isn't he? All that celestial blood running through your veins. So much power, just waiting to be unleashed." He leaned closer, his breath ghosting across my cheek. "Don't you want to know who your father was? What you really are? I could show you things Angelo never dreamed of."

My heart slammed against my ribs. After years of questions, someone finally had the answer. "You know my father?" The words came out raw, desperate. "Is he a demon?"

His laugh filled the space between us, head tipped back in genuine amusement. "To some, yes. I've encountered him once or twice over the centuries." His gaze raked over my features. "You look just like him. That golden hair, those green eyes—the minute I saw you, I knew exactly whose daughter you were."

My fingers trembled as they nervously went to a strand of my hair. All my life, I'd wondered about that. My mother had been a brunette with brown eyes. Every time I looked in a mirror, I'd been seeing pieces of him without even knowing it. "Is he demonic?"

Balthazar's smile curved slow and dangerous. "Like I said, to some he is. But trust me, sweetheart, there are others that are worse. Far, far worse." He prowled closer. "Present company included. Now, if you want to save your favorite vampire, I have a proposition for you."

My mind spun as it raced through impossible choices. Balthazar was offering me everything—knowledge of my father, power, maybe even a way back to Angelo. But at what cost? The way his power reached for me, tried to wrap around whatever celestial essence flowed in my veins, made my skin crawl. Angelo might have bought me for my Nephilim blood, but he'd never tried to twist me into something dark.

A small voice whispered that perhaps I should play along, let Balthazar think he had won me over until I found a way back to Angelo. But there was something so seductive about Balthazar's darkness that called to parts of me I didn't understand. If I gave in—even just pretended to—would I be able to pull back? Or would I become something even Angelo couldn't control?

Yet Balthazar's words about my father were like a siren song that sang to my blood, even as my instincts screamed to run. Angelo had never offered me these answers, this knowledge of who—and what—I really was.

"You will become powerful." He ticked off each point on his fingers as if he was offering me a particularly good deal. "You will be in control. And—" His smile turned wicked. "You will be mine."

"What?" The word came out as a strangled yelp.

"Don't look so scandalized, my dear." He leaned against the window frame, completely at ease. "I don't do anything by force. That's too easy, too boring. I prefer...persuasion."

I frowned. "What's that supposed to mean?"

"Come, come, didn't your precious Angelo teach you anything about supernatural creatures?" His voice dropped to a velvet purr. "We're hunters by nature. And you, my forbidden little Nephilim, are the most tempting prey I've seen in centuries." His eyes glittered. "Your power calls to mine. It's only a matter of time before you will want to know more—about who you are, what you can do. What you could become."

I shrank back against the headboard. The last thing I wanted was to turn into a demon. "I don't want to become evil."

He shrugged, that devastating smile still playing on his lips. "Never said you would. It all depends on you." His words dripped with dark promise, each one designed to make me forget about Angelo, about myself, about everything except the answers he dangled before me like delicious bait.

Still... There had to be another way. One that didn't entail me losing myself.

The door banged open, and I jumped. Gage stormed in with murder in his eyes, making the room feel suddenly smaller. My fear skyrocketed. Balthazar's dangerous charm was infinitely preferable to Gage's raw aggression.

"Did Balthazar tell you yet what you're going to do?" Gage's voice was a growl.

I glanced nervously at Balthazar, seeking the lesser evil. "You mean him training me?"

Gage slowly approached me. "You will do everything he asks."

"Don't touch her," Balthazar warned, his demonic energy crackling in the air like static electricity before a storm.

Surprisingly, Gage obeyed, but his eyes flared like hot brass, pupils contracting to predatory slits. His lips curled, revealing fangs sharp enough to tear through flesh. "You will heal the Luparion Crystal." His voice dropped to a guttural growl. He gestured toward Balthazar, power rolling off him in waves that made the air thick and heavy.

"If you don't, he'll kill your precious vampire king...right after I tear out Angelo's heart."

My own heart thundered against my ribs, but I lifted my chin, channeling every ounce of defiance I could muster. "You're not strong enough to take down Angelo. He'll drain you dry." Even saying his name made my voice waver—not from fear, but from the ache of wanting him here, needing him to burst through the doors and end this nightmare.

"Oh, but I am." Gage stalked closer, his boots silent against the floor. The scent of pine and wilderness clung to him, with something metallic under it. Blood. "There's more than one way to rip out a vampire's heart."

A deadly silence filled the room like a poisonous fog. My magic flickered weakly beneath my skin, exhausted from fighting. I tried to think of all the ways to kill a vampire, but none of them seemed lethal enough to kill Angelo. He was ancient, powerful—untouchable. Wasn't he?

I clenched my fists until my nails bit crescents into my palms, using the pain to ground myself. "You'll regret taking me. Angelo will find me—"

"You still don't get it." Gage's cruel laugh echoed off the walls as he leaned in close enough for me to see the madness dancing in his golden eyes. It punched me in the gut, knocking the breath out of me. "I want him to find us." His voice dropped to a whisper that chilled me more than any shout could have. "I want him to watch you die, just like he made me watch when he killed my mate. That's the precise moment when I'll rip out his cold, dead heart."

The pure anguish in his words made me take a step back. This wasn't just about power or territory; it was about vengeance born from love twisted into hatred. And I was caught in the middle.

God, what had Angelo done? He'd created a monster. The realization settled in my stomach like lead. Every terrible possibility of how Angelo might have killed Gage's mate flashed through my mind.

"In other news, Nephilim…" Gage's lips twisted as he prowled closer, satisfaction rolling off him in waves. "I'm meeting with your precious vampire mafia king." A dark chuckle rumbled from his chest. "My plan is beginning to come together. He thinks Trystan kidnapped you, and I'm going to lay breadcrumbs leading your dumb bat right to you."

The casual way he spoke about manipulating Angelo made my blood run cold. Gage wasn't just acting on blind rage—this was cool, calculated revenge, planned and perfected over who knew how long. And he was using me as bait in his twisted trap.

He laughed, the sound almost a howl as he left the room, echoing off the walls like a wolf's victory cry.

I stood there, as numb as if I'd fallen through ice, my bones heavy with dread. Even breathing felt like an effort. Balthazar looked at me steadily, his dark eyes holding ancient secrets and unspoken promises. "You have a choice, Nephilim." Each word was honeyed venom. "The only way to save your vampire is to develop your powers. I can teach you"...he paused, letting the words sink in..."but you'll have to pledge yourself to me."

"I thought you said you wouldn't force me." Each word fell soft as a shadow.

"Oh, I won't have to, beautiful." A knowing smile curved his lips, demonic energy crackling around him like a dark halo. "You'll come to me willingly."

ELEVEN

WITH DIMITRI still recovering from my questioning, Pascal Broussard had temporarily taken over as my driver. He was one of Enzo's guys—short and stocky, but quick as a snake and loyal to the bone. I still wanted to keep my eye on Dimitri, though, so I brought him along, even if every breath seemed to pain his cracked ribs. His face was a patchwork of healing bruises, his jaw still swollen where I'd broken it, his fingers bent at angles that hadn't quite straightened. He shuffled forward like a battered marionette. As a born vampire, he took longer to heal compared to a made vampire like me.

In the limo, I sat across from him, contemplating my handiwork, studying the purple-black bruises that still covered his skin. My knuckles tingled with the memory of each blow, and satisfaction curled within me when I saw him try to hide his winces every time we hit a bump in the road. He'd clearly learned his lesson about crossing me.

Dimitri gave me a signature smirk, though it pulled at his split lip. The casual way he swirled his bourbon couldn't quite hide how he favored his right side.

"You know," he drawled, voice rougher than usual, "you and I really need to work on our relationship since we're brothers now."

I cocked an eyebrow, fighting the urge to add more bruises to his collection.

"By marriage, I mean." His smirk widened despite the obvious pain I saw in his eyes. "Here I am, being a perfect brother-in-law, and you treat me like your very own personal punching bag." Despite the dark bruises mottling his face, his eyes still held that dangerous glint of amusement. "Using me to make Trystan squirm? Now that's the kind of petty I can appreciate." He took a deliberate sip of bourbon. "I'm afraid you're going to be disappointed, though: Trystan isn't my bestie."

The way he said 'bestie' made my fingers itch for another round of questioning.

Enzo shook his head. "You're poking the bear, Dimitri. I'd shut up if I were you."

"Please," Dimitri drawled, inspecting his bourbon like

it was suddenly the most fascinating thing in the room. "I've been poking bears since before you were born, Enzo. I just love the way their fur feels."

Enzo gave him a scowl.

"Okay, I know: you're older than me. Like, Old Man Winkle old. Anyway—" His eyes flicked to me with that infuriating mix of amusement and challenge, though I noticed that he shifted carefully to avoid putting pressure on his ribs. "What's my dear brother-in-law going to do? Beat me again? Kill me? Pretty sure his sister would have something to say about that. Though I have to admit"—he gestured to his face with his whiskey glass—"this new look is growing on me. Very *Fight Club* chic, don't you think?"

My fingers twitched. If the bastard wasn't married to my sister, I would've torn his sarcastic tongue out by now. And something in his eyes told me he knew exactly how untouchable that bond made him. Gianna's tear-stained face from this morning over what I had done to her mate flashed through my mind. But Dimitri had stolen from me, and I'd do it again if I had to.

Enzo sighed, but I caught him fighting a smile. Dimitri had that effect on people, making them either want to laugh or kill him...or both, simultaneously.

The limo curved along the river road, the Mississippi's dark water gleaming under the moonlight. Keir's yacht loomed ahead, a floating fortress of steel and luxury. It was a smart choice for our meeting—neutral ground that limited how many soldiers either side could bring. I could already sense Trystan's powerful presence on board.

"Well," Dimitri drawled, draining his glass with a wince, "this should be fun. Nothing like a friendly chat between mortal enemies aboard a boat. Very *Godfather* meets *Titanic*." He paused, that dangerous glint returning to his eyes. "Though let's face it, Trystan wasn't exactly sending me holiday cards even before I killed his man. Now he has another reason to want my head on a spike." His smirk turned predatory. "At least I had a good reason. His guy went after Gianna. You, dear brother-in-law"—he gestured toward me with his glass—"killed just to make a point."

I didn't bother responding. We both knew exactly why I'd torn that warrior apart. Nobody touched my sister and lived.

"Yes, yes, we're all very badass," Dimitri continued, though his smirk looked more like a grimace through the bruises mottling his face. "A regular family of assassins. Speaking of family reunions..." He gestured at the approaching yacht. "Shall we?"

I pinched the bridge of my nose, fighting back a surge of homicidal irritation. Why did my sister have as her mate the most infuriating vampire in New Orleans? "Just keep your mouth shut unless I tell you to speak."

"Yes, sir, boss, sir, three bags full, sir." Dimitri mock saluted, and immediately grimaced at the movement. "Though you might want to work on your negotiation skills. The whole strong-silent-murderous thing? Super last century."

Pascal opened the door for us and Enzo got out first. After learning of Petar's plan to possibly take me out, he had insisted on assessing whether it was safe for me. Not that I needed protection. I was the strongest and deadliest vampire in New Orleans—stronger than King Nico and the Headmaster Tarus of Red Rose Academy combined. But I let Enzo play watchdog; it made him feel useful, and truthfully, having an enforcer who truly cared enough to check for threats was...kind of nice.

I watched Enzo scan the dock, his eyes tracking from shadow to shadow before checking the sky. His fingers brushed the Void Chain at his hip—a gesture that told me he sensed trouble. The magical restraints had the ability to bind any supernatural creature and neutralize their powers. He had fought Keir's enforcer Lorcan Blackthorn for it in a battle that had left them both half-dead. The Unseelie enforcer had never forgiven Enzo for claiming the prize, and the two had been bitter enemies ever since.

Dimitri climbed out next. He stumbled and had to grab the roof of the limo to keep from falling down.

I got out last, buttoning my jacket. Two of Keir's goons approached, including Lorcan. He was tall, and unlike the other Unseelie he wore his hair cut short—practical, like the warrior he was. He wore a gray suit that matched his cruel eyes. His gaze twitched when he saw his former prize in Enzo's hand, and for a moment, the temperature around us dropped several degrees. Classic Unseelie tell.

"Santi." He completely ignored Enzo and Dimitri. "This way."

As I approached the yacht, Trystan Hunter caught my eye. He leaned over the port side, raising a glass of champagne with unhurried confidence of a predator who knew his prey was trapped. His long blondish-brown hair was pulled up in a man bun, and instead of his usual suit, he wore black denim jeans and boots, and a blue shirt that matched his eyes. The casual attire made my jaw clench. Every detail—from his leisurely pose to his deliberate underdressing—was designed to remind me that he held Serenity's fate in his hands, and I could do nothing but play by his rules.

Not bothering to put on a suit was another slap in the face, and he knew it. My rope of patience, already worn thin from the past twenty-four hours, began to fray and snap. I pulled back my upper lip, revealing razor sharp fangs that would like nothing better than to sink into his flesh and drain him dry. A savage sound tore from my throat as my inner monster stirred.

Beside me Enzo tensed, his hand drifting to the Void Chain. On my other side, Dimitri's smirk had vanished entirely, and for once, he kept his mouth shut. Even he could feel how close I was to snapping.

Lorcan turned around as if he sensed my anger. "Keir

had a concern you'd have a problem keeping your cool, Santi." He snapped his fingers.

Three harpies burst from the port side of the yacht, their human faces twisted into cruel smiles above their eagle bodies—some of Keir's Elder Dimension pets. My fangs dropped as one swooped close enough for me to see the poison gleaming on its talons, but I forced myself to hold my ground even as every predatory instinct screamed to strike. Leave it to the Unseelie king to bring creatures whose smallest scratch could reduce even me to ash. One wrong move, and all my power would mean nothing.

"That's...not something you see every day," Dimitri murmured, the amusement in his voice forced.

Lorcan grinned, and there was nothing human in it. "Just a little insurance. There will be no war on this ship." He inclined his head. "Come. My king awaits you."

Three harpies. Three of us. My eyes narrowed as I did the math. Was this a coincidence, or were we walking into a trap? Enzo had the Void Chain, but was it strong enough to take down a harpy? Three harpies? My gaze drifted to Trystan, still watching us with that infuriating smirk, then back to the deadly creatures circling above. One wrong move and this peaceful meeting could turn into a bloodbath. Still...

Serenity was worth the risk.

LORCAN LED us up onto the deck of Keir's yacht, but I barely registered the luxurious polished teak beneath my feet. Every shadow, every cabin could be hiding Serenity. The vessel's vast expanse of glass and steel spread across two decks meant countless places to conceal a captive.

My eyes swept past the ostentatious outdoor bar and plush loungers, focusing instead on the multiple staircases leading below deck. How many rooms were down there? Which one might hold her? So close, and yet so unreachable.

The upper deck offered clear views through several

cabin windows, but heavy curtains blocked my view into others. Each covered window felt like another taunt. Even Keir's renowned stateroom, with its mahogany panels and floor-to-ceiling windows, drew my interest only for the hidden spaces it might have. Somewhere in this floating palace, Serenity could be trapped, waiting. Every locked door I passed felt like another barrier between us.

Lorcan opened the door. Trystan and his top two enforcers, Stark Winters and Gage Bray, were already seated at the table. Trystan stared at me with an open challenge in his gaze, his blue eyes turning amber, holding all the menace of a wolf about to strike. If he wanted a fight right here, I was ready to paint this yacht with his blood.

Keir sat at the head of the table, appearing every inch the neutral mediator in his custom-tailored suit, but I knew better. No one survived as long as Keir had by being truly neutral. He stood and gestured to three seats oppo-site of Trystan and his men, his smile cool. "Good evening, Angelo. Enzo, Dimitri—please have a seat."

His gaze lingered on Dimitri, taking in the mottled bruises that purpled his face and disappeared into his collar with the calculated interest of a hunter noting its prey's weakness. The silent question of where he had received the wounds stretched between us like a thread about to snap.

"I see you brought some birdies from the Elder Dimen-sion." My fingers traced the crystal glass in front of me, refusing to give Keir the satisfaction of seeing my unease about the creatures circling outside.

Keir leaned back in his chair, the picture of casual power. "Merely an added precaution. The harpies will patrol the outside to ensure that no one breaks the deal by calling in more men. My yacht will move into the middle of the river as another precaution."

I took my seat with deliberate casualness, though every muscle was tense and ready for action. Enzo flanked me, placing his fists on the polished table with the Void Chain wrapped around one hand—a not-so-subtle reminder of what we were capable of.

Trystan cocked an eyebrow and leaned back in his chair with feigned relaxation, a smirk playing over his lips. He turned to Keir, who offered only a slight shrug in return. The gesture spoke volumes.

Keir's gaze slid between Trystan and me, cold calculation behind his diplomatic facade. "It's come to my attention that there is a possible war brewing between the vampires and the wolves. This would jeopardize our way of life and draw unwanted attention from the humans." His tone held false gentleness.

"I'm not the one who wants a war," Trystan blurted, a growl in his words like distant thunder.

"Really?" Dimitri drawled from his seat, touching his split lip with exaggerated care. "Because framing me for kidnapping... That's a bit desperate, even for you."

I glared at the wolf king, my fingers digging into the

chair's upholstery until the fabric threatened to tear. The scent of his lies made my fangs ache. "If you didn't want war, you shouldn't have stolen Serenity."

There was a flash of genuine confusion in his expression that made my dead heart stutter. "Are you serious? I didn't steal her." His lips curled into a surprised smile. "Oh, my... Are you saying you lost her?"

"I didn't *lose* her," I snarled, my voice dropping to a register that made the crystal decanters vibrate. "She was kidnapped." I snapped my fingers, the sound sharp as a gunshot. "Enzo."

Enzo reached into his jacket and pulled out the letter. He handed it to Keir, who scanned the words with eyes that had seen centuries of deception. His gaze flicked to me. This wasn't going to go well for Trystan. Stealing mates crossed the line in our world—it was an offense that had started wars and toppled kingdoms.

The letter passed from Keir's hands to Gage, who delivered it in turn to Trystan. Trystan's brows furrowed as he read, his face darkening like storm clouds gathering. With deliberate care, he placed the letter on the polished table. "I didn't write this."

"It's your handwriting," Keir said simply, his voice quiet but carrying the weight of judgment. "There's no mistaking it."

My fangs dropped, darkness bleeding from my skin as my control slipped. The wolf king had taken her, lied about it, and now sat here playing innocent while Serenity was fuck-knows-where. Only Enzo's warning hand on my arm kept me from lunging across the table and ripping out Trystan's lying throat.

Trystan bristled, his wolf rising to the surface as it stared down my vampire darkness. "Where did you get this letter?"

"In my sister's dresser drawer." I held up a hand, cutting off his inevitable protest. "Gianna is not part of this war. Target her, and you'll truly wish for death." My voice turned to ice. "The culprit was trying to pin it on Dimitri. Care to explain that, Trystan?"

"I do not." Trystan's voice carried a razor's edge. "I haven't set eyes on your precious Nephilim since the auction. Whoever stole her, it was not the wolves."

"That's your handwriting," Keir said quietly, each word falling into the silence like stones. "I suggest you take another tactic."

Trystan pulled his upper lip back in a snarl, power rolling off him as his blue eyes dissolved to molten gold. "Handwriting can be forged. I didn't write it, Keir."

Dimitri went very still, the kind of stillness that preceded a massacre. "Are you seriously trying to involve my mate?" His smile was all teeth, eyes darkening with deadly intent. "Bold choice. Stupid as fuck, but bold. Shall I show you what I do when someone threatens what's mine?"

Gage's lips curled into a cruel smile as he studied Dimitri's bruised face. "You don't look like you could do much damage right now. Word is your own family doesn't even trust you." The taunt hung in the air like cigarette smoke over a late-night poker table.

"He claims his father's behind it." I leaned forward, each word heavy with meaning. "Says Petar's making a move for my crown. But he needs muscle." I let my gaze slide to Trystan. "Your muscle."

Trystan looked at Keir, then back at me, the surprise on his face turning to darkness. "You actually think I'm fucking stupid enough to get into bed with Petar Dragan?" He leaned forward, voice dropping to a dangerous whisper. "That bastard's got a body count longer than Bourbon Street, Angelo. You brought that rabid dog into your family —not me."

He'd hit a nerve, but I kept my face smooth as marble. Years of running New Orleans' supernatural underworld had taught me to wear my masks well. Yes, I had made a mistake with Petar. It was a mistake I would bury him for.

"Let me be crystal clear." My voice turned to arctic ice. "If Serenity isn't returned safely to me, I will declare war on the wolves. I will systematically hunt down and slaughter every last cur in your pack until there's nothing left but memories and blood-soaked earth."

"Tell me." Trystan traced a finger along the edge of his glass, the movement precise as a surgeon with a scalpel. "What's the latest on those murdered girls?"

I growled, rage simmering beneath my skin. Someone had been draining young women dry, staging their bodies like macabre artwork to implicate my family. The last victim was Emily Bastion, one of my favorite girls at Simon's Ravenwood Estates. The same damn auction house where I'd bought Serenity was now a hunting ground.

For days, I'd had my best men working every connection we had in the French Quarter to trace Emily's movements, her history, anything that might give us a lead. The careful staging of her body, the deliberate way all traces of her past had been erased—someone wanted me to find these bodies, wanted me to see the way they'd arranged every detail. But why Emily? What made her special enough to become a message to me?

"For example, have you been dining on them?" Trystan's eyes glittered with accusation as his words slithered through the room like poisonous snakes. "All the intel points to you and your bloodsuckers."

I jabbed a finger at him, power crackling between us like static electricity. "I suspect you framed me, Trystan. With Detective Louis DuPont and his son and daughter missing, the police will be circling us like vultures." The weight of his accusation pressed on us all—humans going missing meant attention on us that could unravel everything we'd built in New Orleans.

Enzo's growl thundered through the room at the mention of DuPont's daughter. The sound was pure possessiveness. His connection to Joy DuPont was becoming a liability I'd need to address, dammit.

"That's something we cannot afford," Keir cut in, shoulders tensing as he pressed his palms against the table. His words cleaved the room like an executioner's axe. "I refuse to have my family threatened over a trifle like a missing Nephilim." The word trifle cut like a blade, a reminder that he could become an enemy as easily as an ally.

"You wanted her too, Keir," Trystan snapped, his words dripping with venom. "Or tell me, has your precious Anchoring Obsidian healed itself?" The challenge in his voice brought a sudden chill to the room.

The Anchoring Obsidian was the Unseelie jewel that kept their enemies from dragging them back to the Elder Dimension like rats onto a sinking ship. I'd seen it once—a crystalline heart that pulsed with ancient magic, its surface etched with symbols that made even my vampire blood curdle. I'd always suspected it had been carved from some ancient being in the Elder Dimension, maybe even while it was still alive, but Keir guarded its origins like a dragon guarding his hoard.

Keir's expression turned glacial, generations of iron discipline splintering beneath the surface for just a moment. "I'm not the one who kicked this particular hornet's nest, Trystan." He traced an ancient sigil in the air between them, the gesture heavy with unspoken threats and magic that made the air grow thick and cold. "The missing piece here is Petar Dragan." He leaned forward, power radiating off him in waves. "I suggest you produce him."

"He's not a member of my pack," Trystan growled, fangs flashing. "He's on Angelo's payroll, not mine."

A phone's shrill ring cut through the tension.

Keir's expression turned to carved ice. "I specifically said all cell phones were to be put to silent during this meeting." His tone of voice could have frozen hell.

Gage pulled out his phone with exaggerated slowness. "I have to take this. Pack business."

Trystan didn't stop him, and Keir's rage crackled through the room like lightning before a storm. If looks could kill, both Trystan and Gage would have been nailed to the wall like trophies already.

Gage brushed past Dimitri, bumping his chair with practiced casualness that screamed of purpose to anyone who knew how to look.

I was done with Trystan's bullshit. My chair scraped against wood as I stood, Enzo and Dimitri falling into position behind me like shadows of death.

I fixed Trystan with a stare that had made stronger men crumble. "You have until midnight tomorrow night to produce Serenity." I stood straighter. "If not, I'll order the Santi family to hunt down every single member of your pack."

"Bring it, Santi." Trystan's lips pulled back in a feral grin. "My pack's strong, and it's been a while since we dined on bats."

Keir stood, power rolling off him in waves. "This meeting is over." His fingers curled against the ancient oak table, burning scorch marks into the wood as centuries of magic crackled in the air around him. "I will remind you that no one is to fight on this yacht. Otherwise, Lorcan will order the harpies to attack." The threat was chilling. I'd seen what those winged nightmares could do to supernatural flesh.

One scratch from those talons would kill Dimitri and even leave Enzo and me bedridden for days. I couldn't afford that kind of delay—not when every hour that passed was another hour Serenity remained missing.

I nodded and led Enzo and Dimitri out of the boardroom. The yacht had already glided back alongside the dock; the meeting had been so intense that I am sure not one of us had even noticed our journey around the Mississippi's dark waters.

Trystan and Stark remained in the boardroom, no doubt held back by Keir. His was known for keeping his yacht pristine—not only by maintaining the polished wood and crystal, but also by proactively preventing bloodstains that might never wash out.

Our driver stood at attention as we descended the gangplank, the sleek black limousine a shadow in the New Orleans night. Dimitri slid in first, followed by me, and lastly Enzo—positioning that would help us fight if needed.

"I have a surprise for you." Dimitri's bruised face split

into a predatory smile as he produced a cellphone. "Look what Gage slipped into my jacket pocket."

My hand shot out with vampire speed, wrapping around his throat. "Are you lying?" Power thrummed beneath my fingers, ready to crush his windpipe.

"No, he's telling the truth." Enzo shifted to stand between us, one hand resting on his weapon while his eyes never left my face with the unwavering focus of a guard dog. "I searched him before we left. Thoroughly."

I released Dimitri and flipped through the phone, each swipe of my finger revealing more of Trystan's treachery—meeting locations, contacts, all captured in neat little files proving his betrayal that would burn Trystan's empire to the ground. By tomorrow night, his pack would be nothing but ash and memories.

CHAPTER

THIRTEEN

S*erenity*

BALTHAZAR HAD BACKED me into a corner, and I had been forced to accept his offer: train or watch everyone I love die.

Not much of a choice.

We were in a room in the plantation that was like a large, titanium cell. I couldn't get out. The air was heavy with demonic energy, making my skin crawl and my blood burn.

We'd been at this since this morning, and all I wanted to do was crawl back into bed, but with Angelo's life at stake, I wouldn't give up. Every time exhaustion threatened to overwhelm me, I pictured his face, remembered the warmth of his touch. I'd endure anything—even Balthazar twisting my gift to suit his demonic purposes—to keep him safe.

"Let us try again." Balthazar prowled around me with liquid grace, each step measured and deliberate. "Your healing Enzo was pure instinct—wild, untamed. Like a child playing with matches."

I frowned. "How did you know I healed Enzo?"

"Petar, of course. He's quite the nice little mole. No, more like a rat...always sniffing around for information."

I pressed my lips together tightly and curled my fingers into fists. I imagined all the way a rat could meet its end. Petar would regret sharing Angelo's secrets. He would learn exactly how Angelo dealt with traitors.

He drew the curved blade across his forearm, watching the blood well up with the patience of a master teaching their craft. "I'll teach you to hone that power to an inferno."

He grabbed my wrist, forcing my palm over his wound. It felt...warped. With Enzo, healing him had been like diving into summer sunlight—warm, natural. This was like plunging into arctic waters. Where before my power had exploded through me like wildfire, now it lay coiled in my chest like a frozen serpent, refusing to flow.

"Don't wait for it to come to you," he commanded, his breath ice against my ear. "Reach for it. Grab it. Make it yours."

I closed my eyes, searching for that familiar healing light, but his darkness pressed against my senses. My teeth chattered, not from power this time, but from the cold spreading through my veins. Everything in me screamed that this wasn't right. With Enzo, the power had been pure and instinctive, a gift from my father. This felt like theft.

"Fight it all you want," Balthazar chuckled darkly. "Your blood knows what it wants." His grip tightened, sending icicles through my veins. "Stop resisting, Serenity. Show me what you're capable of."

His darkness surged against my defenses like a crashing wave, and something inside me cracked. Power flooded through the breach—not the warm rush that had healed Enzo, but something ancient, cold and hungry. My skin felt too tight, like it could barely contain this new energy crackling beneath its surface.

"Yes," he hissed. "That's it. Feel how the darkness calls to your light, how they hunger for each other."

I tried to pull away, but his grip was iron. Black spots danced at the edges of my vision as his power and mine twisted together, creating something that was neither light nor dark but something entirely different and highly addictive. My hands began to glow with an eerie purple light, where before they'd shone pure gold.

Balthazar's wound beneath my palm began to heal, but not like Enzo's had. I wasn't just mending flesh now, I was commanding it—forcing it to obey. Each severed vessel, each torn fiber knit itself back together under my will. The rush of power was intoxicating.

"Now you're learning," Balthazar whispered gleefully. "This is true power, little Nephilim. Not the weak healing you've been playing with. Feel how much stronger it is when you take control of your gift instead of simply channeling it?"

He was right—it was stronger. And despite my horror and revulsion, part of me craved more. It terrified me.

When he finally released me, I stumbled back, my legs weak. The room spun, and I could still feel echoes of the dark power still coursing through my veins like poison.

"That's enough for today." His smile was triumphant as he examined his perfectly healed arm. "Tomorrow, we'll try to heal something a bit more...challenging."

I slid down the wall, catching my breath, trying to ignore my power humming beneath my skin. What had he done to me? What had I let him turn my gift into?

Later that night, I still pondered those questions in my bed. I hugged my pillow, thinking of Angelo, wishing he was here to chase away the darkness. A tear slid down my cheek, and I closed my eyes, hoping I hadn't sold my soul to the devil...or, worse, to a demon who looked at me like I was already his...

I was back at Crescent Manor in Angelo's library, but it was different. A golden light shone on the books, making the leather bindings gleam like fallen stars. The familiar scents of old books and Angelo's sandalwood cologne were overlaid with something else now—frankincense, and lightning.

The voice seemed to come from everywhere and nowhere all at once, resonating in my very soul. "Balthazar is leading you down a dark path, Serenity. Stay in the light. The light is what will save not only you, but Angelo as well."

A chill ran through me as the golden light pulsed, revealing shadowy wings on the wall; they weren't the pure wings I'd glimpsed in my dreams before. These were tattered and broken.

"Every time you use his darkness, you tear at your grace," the voice warned. "This is how angels fall, Serenity. Not in one great tumble, but with small slips into the shadows. Each time you let him twist your gift, you lose a piece of yourself."

The light shifted, and I saw my reflection in one of the library's windows. For a moment, my eyes glowed with that same purple light from Balthazar's training—neither divine nor demonic, but something in between. Something corrupted.

"How?" I whispered. "How do I resist his darkness?"

"Remember who you are. Your power comes from love and the desire to heal—not control. When he pushes you toward darkness, hold onto that truth. Light cannot be corrupted unless you allow it to be."

I woke with a start, sweat glistening over my body, the covers nearly drenched. My mind was foggy, as if still in the dream, desperately trying to hold onto the echo of that voice. I recognized it now. It was Angelo's. The sound of it reminded me of his warm, spicy scent—rich, deep, and oh so familiar. Just hearing it made my chest ache with longing. How long had it been since I'd heard him say my name? Since I'd felt safe?

The dream was fading like smoke through my fingers, leaving behind an emptiness that hurt even more than Balthazar's twisted training. I felt something in my palm and I pulled my hand out from under my pillow. I gasped. I was holding a golden feather, glowing with the same pure light from my dream. As I watched, it slowly disappeared like stardust scattering in the wind, leaving behind only lingering warmth where it had touched my skin.

My fingers curled around the phantom warmth, trying to hold it there. Was this really a message from Angelo, or was my mind creating what I needed most? Either way, the words rang true. Love, not control. Healing, not power. It was everything Angelo had taught me about being worthy of my gift...everything Balthazar was trying to corrupt.

I had to fight him. Yes, Balthazar was stronger than me, but maybe it wasn't through strength that I would win. Maybe I could use his own arrogance against him, make him think he was winning me over, and at the same time develop my powers enough to escape and save Angelo. The thought settled in my chest like armor. I might have to walk in the darkness, but I would not let it consume me. And if there was one thing I'd learned from dealing with Freaky Freddie, it was that sometimes the best weapon was letting your enemy think they'd already won.

There was a soft tap at my door. "Get up, sweet Nephilim. You have much to learn today."

Balthazar's husky voice set me on edge, every nerve screaming danger. My hands trembled, and I pressed them flat against my thighs, forcing the shaking to stop. I needed to master more than my powers; I needed to master myself. Taking a deep breath, I practiced the tone in my head first, aiming for something between eager student and a growing embracing of the darkness.

"Don't worry. I'll only be a few minutes." The words came out perfectly—a hint of breathlessness, like I was anticipating our training today rather than dreading it. I caught my reflection in the window, schooling my features into a mask of compliance. Let him think he was breaking me, molding me. Let him think his darkness was seeping into my light.

My stomach churned at the thought of playing along, but I steeled myself. Every moment I spent learning his techniques was a moment closer to being strong enough to escape. Every time he thought he was corrupting me was another chance to understand his weaknesses. I might have to let him think he was winning my soul, but Angelo's voice from my dream echoed in my mind. Light cannot be corrupted unless you allow it to be.

I touched the spot where the golden feather had disappeared, drawing courage from its lingering warmth. I could do this. I could play Balthazar's game while keeping my true self hidden, locked away somewhere his darkness couldn't reach.

For Angelo. For everyone I loved.

Sometimes the greatest act of grace, I realized, was knowing when to let others think you'd fallen from it.

CHAPTER
FOURTEEN

SERENITY. She was in my library, looking as radiant as ever—but there was a purple shine to her now, something that reeked of dark magic. Instead of a dress, she had on a shirt and pair of jeans. I could detect the scent of wolves with my vampire senses.

Not just wolves. Something else too, tainted and foul. Something I hadn't detected for a long time. The stench of true evil—ancient and cold as the void itself.

What had happened to her? Who was Trystan in bed with? I sensed danger, but not from Trystan alone. There was something darker at play.

Suddenly, a voice seemed to come from everywhere and

nowhere at once, piercing straight through flesh and blood to my core. "Balthazar is leading you down a dark path, Serenity. Stay in the light. The light is what will save not only you, but Angelo as well."

Centuries of survival had taught me to fear few things, but that name—Balthazar—made my dead heart clench. And what did the voice mean about saving me? Save me from what?

My blood ran cold as a golden light pulsed, revealing shadowy wings on the wall. They weren't anything like the pure wings I'd imagined Serenity would wear. These were tattered, broken. Just seeing them felt like a stake through my chest. What were they doing to my angel?

"Every time you use his darkness, you tear at your grace," the voice warned. "This is how angels fall, Serenity. Not in one great tumble, but with small slips into the shadows. Each time you let him twist your gift, you lose a piece of yourself."

I reached for her, my vampire speed failing me in this strange dream realm. "Who are you with, Serenity?" My fingers grasped at shadows as my usual powers abandoned me in this ethereal space, leaving me helpless as any mortal.

She didn't appear to hear me. The distance between us felt infinite, though she stood mere feet away.

Then the light shifted and I saw her reflection in one of the library's windows. For a moment, her eyes glowed with a strange, purple light—neither divine nor demonic, but something corrupted. The sight made my fangs descend instinctively.

What was Trystan doing? I'd ripped the bastard apart for hurting her. But this... this felt like something far worse.

"How?" she whispered. "How do I resist his darkness?"

The answer burst from me before I could think, my fingers curling into claws as deep-rooted fury blazed through every immortal nerve. "Remember who you are. Your power comes from love and the desire to heal—not control. When he pushes you toward darkness, hold onto that truth. Light cannot be corrupted unless you allow it to be."

She started to fade away and I lunged for her, my vampire speed finally answering my call. My fingers brushed hers for the briefest of moments before she disappeared, leaving me in agony...

I WOKE up soaked in my sheets with a pounding headache. An empty bottle of wine was on the nightstand.

Balthazar. The name hit me like holy water flooding my veins. An ancient demon who'd been collecting souls since before I was turned. And Trystan had handed Serenity—my Serenity—into his clutches.

I ripped off the covers and released an angry snarl that shook the walls of my room, a snarl to make lesser vampires flee in terror. Glass shattered around me as my power exploded, sending the empty wine bottle against the wall. The scent of my blood filled the air. I'd crushed the crystal tumbler in my hand without realizing it.

A slow, dark smile spread across my face as I took in

the destruction around me. Perfect. Let them hear. Let them know exactly what kind of mood I was in. Blood dripped from my clenched fist, the sting of crystal shards nothing compared to the vicious pleasure coursing through me. The snarl faded to a low, satisfied rumble. I'd held back for far too long, played the civilized creature, kept the monster caged. But sometimes the only answer was letting the beast remind everyone why they feared him.

Balthazar. The demon who'd corrupted angels for sport during the first war. Who'd turned Heaven's warriors into his broken puppets. And now he had his hands on my Nephilim, trying to twist her light into something supremely dark.

I would tear Trystan apart piece by piece for this betrayal. And then I'd remind Balthazar why the Santi family had endured through countless wars while others had crumbled to dust. No one touched what was mine.

No one.

Angry footsteps raced down the hallway to my room and my door burst open. Enzo had the Void Chain and a sword, ready to cut down any enemy. "What happened?"

Well might he ask. Glass was shattered on the floor, not only from the window but the wine bottle. Pictures had fallen. Furniture was overturned. It looked like a tornado had ripped through my room.

Dimitri came up behind him, also holding a sword, surveying the destruction with a dangerous smile that promised violence. "You know, when I said we needed to renovate, this wasn't exactly what I had in mind."

He kicked a piece of shattered crystal with his boot. "That was a hundred-year-old Bordeaux. I'm offended. If you're going to destroy perfectly good alcohol, at least let me have some first." His smirk faded and he turned serious as he caught the murderous look in my eyes. "All right, whose heart are we ripping out? Because this"—he gestured to the destruction—"isn't your usual 'somebody looked at my throne wrong' tantrum."

I dragged my fingers through my hair. "I had a dream. Serenity is trying to contact me. I've never felt anything like it. Her power is growing. She was here in my library, I could feel her." I looked between them as I panted hard. "Trystan, the bastard, is working with a demon. Balthazar."

Dimitri went utterly still at the name, his usual smirk freezing in place. For a split second, his hand went to his wrist— he'd been Balthazar's prisoner once and I could only imagine the horrors he had endured. Balthazar was very good at torture, like begging for mercy good. I had heard the screams from his dungeon, sounds that would have driven lesser vampires mad.

"Nothing like meeting old friends again. I'd rather fly north for the winter." The joke fell flat. "Why, of all the demons in Hell, did it have to be that one? Fantastic." His voice held an edge I rarely heard from him.

I yanked open my closet doors so hard one of them

came off its hinges, clattering to the floor as I reached for my clothes. "Be ready in an hour. We're heading to Trystan's. Fuck this waiting until tonight bullshit."

Enzo frowned, ever the voice of reason. "Are you sure, boss? It was just a dream—"

"Don't push me, Enzo." My hand twitched toward him before I stopped myself. No. Not again. Instead, I seized the broken closet door and hurled it through the bedroom window. Glass exploded outward in a glittering shower as my fangs descended. "We go in one hour."

"Got it," Enzo said quietly, his eyes quietly fixed on the destruction I'd just caused. He backed toward the door, and I caught the slight tremor in his hands—not fear exactly, but wariness.

Dimitri leaned against the doorframe, that sardonic glint back in his eyes. "If we're going demon hunting, I'm going to need a drink. Preferably something that hasn't been hurled against a wall."

Enzo tilted his head. "Good idea. Come on."

After they left, I quickly got dressed and headed down to my special room where I had the tools to kill a wolf shifter. Each step echoed with barely contained violence. Part of me sang with anticipation. Trystan had always been too powerful, too smug, too certain of his place in the hierarchy. And he'd never faced me at my full strength, never seen what I could do when I stopped pretending to be civilized.

Another part whispered caution, reminding me of all

the times my rage had led to consequences I regretted later. But this was different. This wasn't impulsive, blind fury—this was calculated vengeance. And if Trystan had done what I suspected from that dream...if he'd dared to hurt Serenity...then I'd show him exactly why vampires had once been called demons of the night.

FIFTEEN

A*ngelo*

GIANNA STOPPED ME, her face pale. She was visibly agitated. "Angelo, Detective Flanagan's here to see you. There's... There's been another murder."

I cursed under my breath. Chester Flanagan was definitely a thorn in my side. He was Louis DuPont's partner and held me responsible for the murders and his partner's disappearance. He also loved to sniff around my home like a bloodhound. I stared at her. "Who was the victim?"

Tears welled in her eyes. She bowed her head and choked. "My friend Nancee... Nancee Lane."

I remembered her. She was the one that Gianna often

escaped from Crescent Manor to go see. Another young woman dead, another connection to my family. This wasn't coincidence.

"Angelo, there's more. Detective DuPont is with him. He's back, but he's acting…strange."

I froze mid-step, my rage turning to ice in my veins. Another murder. DuPont breaking free. The timing wasn't a coincidence, it couldn't be. Balthazar. I turned back to Gianna, moving with the kind of deliberate slowness that made lesser vampires retreat. "What do you mean, strange?"

She swallowed hard. "His eyes…they're…wrong. And he keeps scratching his arms like something's crawling under his skin—"

"Get everyone out of the main hall. Now." Trystan would have to wait. If what I suspected was happening to DuPont was true, it needed to be handled before the detective became something far worse than just a compromised human. My fangs ached at the thought of what could be nesting inside him, using him like a puppet.

The blood drained from her face. "But Enzo and Dimitri—"

I clasped her arms. "I won't let anything happen to either one of them, but I can't be worrying about you and Elena. Take her and go to my library and lock the door. Don't let anyone in until you hear my voice. Do you understand?"

"I… I understand. I'll take Elena to the library, Angelo."

I waited until I heard Gianna's footsteps fade down the hall, heading toward Elena. Only then did I let my mask slip, letting the beast inside me surface. My power filled the corridor like a living thing, making the crystal chandelier above tremble. Two of my family were in that room with what used to be Detective DuPont. And if anything had happened to them while I'd been upstairs plotting revenge against Trystan...

I moved toward the living room, each step silent. No more displays of temper, no more broken doors or shattering glass. This kind of hunting required stealth. Control. Everything I'd been struggling to master since I stopped being Death's perfect killer.

But Enzo and Dimitri weren't the only ones in danger. Balthazar was trying to seduce my Serenity. So my next move had to be flawless.

I entered the living room where Detective Flanagan, a tall man with glasses, paced impatiently.

Detective DuPont stood perfectly still, and I knew my sister had been right. His eyes were almost black, and beneath his pale, stretched skin, something shifted—like fingers pressing up from inside, testing for weakness. Whatever dwelled within him was growing too large to contain, something dark, something like a demon."

"Cold rage warred with disbelief as ancient memories clawed their way back to the surface. I'd sealed them myself—the twisted bodies, the screams, the way human skin would bubble and stretch as things from the void took possession. I'd buried it all so deep even Death couldn't have extracted them, wrapped each memory in spells of forgetting until they were nothing but shadow and dust. Yet here DuPont stood, his flesh barely containing whatever ancient evil had not only found those buried horrors but had shattered my most powerful spells to possess him. The power it must have taken... I'd seen possession before, but nothing like this. Nothing strong enough to break seals that had held for decades.

The power it must have taken... I'd seen possession before, but nothing like this. Nothing strong enough to break seals that had held for decades. Serenity would ask me to save him—she always believed everyone could be saved. But I knew better. When something this ancient took hold, there was no person left to save. DuPont was already gone.

I wondered if the same thing happened to his son, Steve. Or was he dead? Maybe Serenity's best friend, Joy, had fallen under the demon's possession too.

I kept my movements casual as I crossed the room, deliberately placing myself between the detectives and Enzo and Dimitri. The thing wearing DuPont's skin tracked my every step, its black eyes gleaming with an intelligence that held no humanity. The scent coming off him was pure decay masked by expensive cologne.

Behind me, I heard Enzo's sharp intake of breath. Dimitri leaned forward in his armchair. "Detective DuPont," he drawled. "You're looking a bit...under the weather. Must be something going around." His light tone belied the tension in his posture. He'd caught the rotting scent radiating off DuPont, too.

"Gentlemen." I gave them my best smile, easy and businesslike, one I'd perfected over the centuries of hiding what I really was. "I'm afraid this isn't a good time. I have a rather urgent meeting to attend to." Flanagan might or might not buy the excuse, but as our gazes locked, I let the creature inside DuPont see what lurked behind my carefully constructed mask. Let it glimpse the monster that had made Death himself wary. The thing's borrowed pupils dilated, and for just a moment, DuPont's skin rippled like something was trying to crawl out of it.

"Your meeting is going to have to wait, I'm afraid," Flanagan said. "I assume your sister told you that one of her friends, Nancee Lane, was found at St. Charles' Wharf at approximately three A.M." He pulled out his notepad. "Her body was completely drained, just like Emily Bastion's. Just like all the others."

DuPont's mouth turned up in a cold smile and hunger flickered in his eyes. I could smell the evil. Whatever was rotting in DuPont had been part of that girl's death and set me up to be the villain.

I kept my gaze on DuPont. "What's your point, Flanagan?"

DuPont slipped in front of Flanagan. "Interesting timing, wouldn't you say, Santi? Considering our sources place you and your two associates here at a meeting with

Keir Rankin and Trystan Hunter at that very dock last night. What time was that meeting, Mr. Santi?"

I narrowed my eyes. "Nine o'clock. Why?"

Flanagan pulled out his phone, scrolled through it. "According to the harbormaster's log, Rankin's yacht didn't dock until eight p.m. The meeting lasted until eleven. That leaves plenty of time for..." He glanced up, his eyes flinty. "Other activities."

"We found this near the girl's body." DuPont reached into his pocket and pulled out a gold ring with a ruby. I recognized it immediately. It had been my father's. "This yours, Mr. Santi?"

I didn't answer. DuPont was trying to set me up. How did the foul thing get into him? I gathered my powers of compulsion, let them slide through my mind like ice water, and pushed them toward him. It should have felt like silk against his consciousness. Instead, it hit something rough and ancient, something that shouldn't be there. And in that brief contact, I got a name—Petar Dragan.

Rage exploded behind my eyes. Of course the treacherous bastard would have a hand in this—first Serenity's kidnapping, now this thing wearing DuPont's skin. My fangs ached to descend, my power begging to rip through the room until I had answers. But with Flanagan watching, I could only stand there, centuries of practiced control keeping my mask in place while my mind raced. How deep did Petar's betrayal run? The

DuPonts were old blood in New Orleans, their family tree spreading through the police force like roots. If Petar had given this demon access to one DuPont, he could have given it access to them all. Every officer with DuPont blood could be a potential vessel, waiting to be filled.

Flanagan stepped in front of me, square and solid. "Mind telling me how Ms. Lane fits into this? And you didn't answer my partner's question, Mr. Santi: is that your ring?"

I could feel the noose tightening around my neck, but I remained cool. Not-DuPont had orchestrated this perfectly—the dead girl, the ring, even using these partic- ular detectives. It knew Flanagan already suspected me from the previous murders. More importantly, it knew exactly what I was. I couldn't act against DuPont without revealing myself to his partner.

"It looks like my ring, but mine is locked up in my safe." Each word came out measured, controlled. Behind Flanagan, I saw DuPont's black eyes flash—not out of hunger for blood, but seeing the game we were now play- ing. The thing smiled, and something twisted beneath its skin. "Would you mind producing it?"

"As I told you, I have a meeting." Let the creature think it had me cornered and its little scheme was working. "If you want to see what's in my safe, you'll have to produce a warrant."

"All right, if you want to do it the hard way," DuPont

grinned, his flesh stretching unnaturally over whatever lurked inside him. "We'll get a warrant."

"Very good. Until then, I'll have to ask you to leave my home." I wasn't looking at Flanagan. My gaze was still focused on DuPont, and I let my power surge forward like an arctic wind, invisible to human eyes but unmistakable to the thing wearing the detective's skin.

DuPont's eyes turned pure black and he hissed, too inhuman to pass as normal, but Flanagan was already turning toward the door. In that split second when his partner's back was turned, DuPont's face contorted, flesh rippling as something pressed against it from within. Our powers clashed like steel on steel, and the air between us crackled.

Flanagan stopped as if he had felt something and turned. Instantly, the creature in DuPont contained itself and gave Flanagan an innocent smile that turned my stomach upside down.

Flanagan cleared his throat. "We'll be in touch, Santi." He clearly wasn't buying my story, and he looked at his partner uneasily, as if he realized something was different with him.

He'd better be careful or he'd end up like those girls—drained and dead.

I escorted Flanagan and the thing to the door. After I shut it, I turned to face Dimitri and Enzo. "Trystan is behind this. We're going to end it. No more games. No more politics. It ends now."

I glanced at to Enzo, my voice carrying a lethal edge. "Get Elena and Gianna." He nodded and disappeared down the hall. I looked to Dimitri, who was already on his feet. "Tell me what you sensed."

"Besides the fact that thing was wearing DuPont like a cheap polyester suit?" Dimitri's attempt at humor couldn't mask his tension. "It reeked of old magic. So old that it shouldn't exist anymore. And…" He hesitated, which was unlike him. "It knew things. About us. About you. I could feel it reading everything in the room."

I pressed my palm against the door where I could still feel traces of the creature's power lingering like oil shimmering on water. "Trystan must have been planning this for longer than we thought. He's not just working with Petar—he's found something ancient that can break my compulsions and steal memories." My fangs descended fully now that no humans were present. "Call Keir. I want to know if he knows about a demon playing dirty in the French Quarter and how Serenity fits into the game. And get me whatever you can about Trystan's movements in the last month."

*S*erenity

BALTHAZAR ESCORTED me down to our training center. I glanced at the doors as we passed and wondered if Steven or Louis—or both—were imprisoned here. Each door held secrets—and probably horrors I couldn't imagine. The air grew colder with each step we took deeper into the plantation's belly.

"We're going to continue working on this healing power of yours." Balthazar opened the door with an elegant twist of his wrist. "But today the subject won't be me." There was something close to glee in his tone that made my skin crawl.

I stopped dead in my tracks when I gazed into the room. A young woman was sprawled on the floor, lying in a puddle of blood. Her dark hair was matted with it, her skin so pale it was nearly translucent. One arm was stretching toward the door, as if she'd been trying to crawl to freedom. She wasn't more than twenty, wearing a torn sundress that might have once been yellow. Her chest barely moved with shallow breaths, each one a desperate fight to stay alive.

I looked at Balthazar in horror. "What did you do to her?"

"She's not dead." His voice was casual, like we were discussing the weather. "But she's close. Most of her blood has been drained." He stepped nearer, his breath cold against my ear. "It's a test. Save her, and you prove your worth. Fail…" He let the threat hang over me like a knife suspended on a thread.

I couldn't tear my eyes from her face. There was something familiar about her features—she reminded me of Joy DuPont. She was someone's daughter. Someone's friend. My hands trembled as I clenched them into fists.

"You're a monster. Did you do this? If you didn't, was it Petar?" The words tasted bitter in my mouth. Petar was the only vampire I knew who had turned traitor and chosen to ally with the wolves.

Balthazar leaned closer, and I fought the urge to step back. Being so near a demon made my skin prickle with warning. "Are you quite sure Petar's the only traitor in Angelo's little family?"

Horror struck my heart like ice water. "There's more?" I could hear the desperation in my own voice, hated it, but couldn't hide it. Not when Angelo's safety hung in the balance.

"You'll learn the truth soon enough. Now: let's proceed with our lesson." He gestured casually to the girl as if she was a mannequin rather than a human being, his dismissal of life more terrifying than any show of cruelty.

I stormed past him and rushed over to kneel next to her. Her chest slowly rose, as if she was fighting for every breath. Her lips were crusted with blood, telling their own horror story. "I'm sorry this happened to you." I stroked her hair and glanced up at Balthazar. "If I save her, will you promise not to kill her?"

"Kill her?" His smile was both beautiful and terrible as he gazed down at her without the slightest bit of compassion. "No. That's not my intention."

All I had seen in this place was pain and torture. At least, that's what Gage had shown me in the mirror. The distant, vacant look in Louis' eyes haunted me, and Steve DuPont—once so strong and defiant—now flinched at mere shadows. Whatever they'd done to shatter my friends' minds, I couldn't let them do the same to her. The young woman lay crumpled at our feet, her dark hair spread around her like spilled ink, chest barely moving.

"If I save her"...my voice came out steadier than I felt... "what are you going to do to her, then?"

He reached down and brushed her pale cheek. "You ask too many questions. Heal her and let me worry about the rest."

A chill settled in my heart. The same cold smile he wore now—had Louis and Steve seen it before their minds shattered?

"Heal her like I taught you yesterday." I suspected if I didn't, he'd kill her—and make me watch.

I placed my hands over her heart, feeling it flutter weakly. Balthazar's cold energy pressed against me, urging me to force the healing. But Angelo's words from my dream echoed: *Remember who you are. Your power comes from love and the desire to heal—not control.*

Balthazar was circling us like a shark, his shadow falling over me as he watched. His presence felt like cruel fingers trying to pull me deeper into the darkness. "Take control," he whispered urgently. "Command her body to heal. Make it yours."

I thought back to how gently I'd healed Enzo. That power had flowed from love, not force. I closed my eyes, trying to find balance between what Balthazar demanded and what I knew in my heart to be right. I might have to reach into the darkness, but that didn't mean I had to surrender myself to it.

Tingling sensations moved over my palms, cold and

demanding. I kept my eyes closed, focusing entirely on the feel of my power as it swirled around my fingers like ice water. Balthazar made a small sound of approval, but I wasn't done. Beneath that freezing energy, I let my own power rise up, warm and golden. Not fighting the darkness—transforming it. Where Balthazar's power wanted to command, I used it to guide. Where it wanted to take, I taught it to give.

The two powers danced together beneath my skin. His ancient magic, heavy with the weight of centuries and countless battles, hungered to dominate, to bend, to break. I wouldn't let it. Instead, I wove my warmth through his frost, turning harsh edges gentle, softening iron into silk. It was like teaching a savage lion to purr—dangerous but possible with the right touch.

The woman's body arched slightly as the dual energies flowed into her. I could feel everything—each torn vessel, each dying cell. Balthazar had shown me how to sense these things. Now, instead of forcing them to obey, I encouraged them to heal.

I opened my eyes. The purple light sought out the damage while the gold followed. Warmth filled me and I pushed it toward the woman, wanting to erase all her pain, all her misery. Each broken place inside her called to me like fragments of a shattered mirror desperate to be whole again. With each pulse of healing, I felt her pain lessen, felt life strengthening where death had tried to take hold.

The need to help and to heal burned through me stronger than any magic. Whatever Balthazar ultimately intended for her, in this moment I could at least give her this gift—freedom from pain, a chance at wholeness.

"Come on," I whispered to her, ignoring Balthazar's looming presence. "You can do it." I poured my love and strength into her, remembering every person I'd ever wanted to protect. This wasn't just about power—it was about choice. Choosing to keep my soul while walking through shadow.

I felt Balthazar's tension growing behind me. This wasn't exactly what he'd taught me, but he couldn't deny it was working. The woman's breathing deepened, color returning to her cheeks. My way wasn't as fast as his, but it was just as strong—and it left no scars on my soul.

The light came back into the woman's eyes, replacing that terrible emptiness. I smiled at her, wishing I could promise her safety in this hell. "Do you feel better?"

"Don't let him hurt me again," she whimpered, her fingers digging into my arm. The terror in her voice made my heart clench.

Balthazar clicked his tongue, the sound sharp as a blade. "You enjoyed it well enough before it became a little rough." The woman shrank against me.

I helped her sit up, my arms shaking with exhaustion. "I won't." My promise to her felt hollow—I didn't have the slightest idea how to protect her, especially now that every ounce of energy had been drained from my body. But I didn't have the heart to tell her that.

"You're bleeding," she gasped, her eyes wide with concern. Even after everything she'd been through, she was worried about me.

I touched my nose, and my fingers came away red. "Yes. Sometimes that happens when I heal."

"That's a sign of weakness," Balthazar sneered. "Something we need to work on." He moved closer, his shadow falling over us both. It was clear this lesson was far from over.

I looked at the woman, trying to offer what little comfort I could. "What's your name?"

"Her name is Shannon Bayer. She's a waitress at Crimson Stakes," Balthazar answered, his voice darkly amused.

Oh, god. Angelo was being set up again. Another girl connected to him, another victim to strengthen the police's suspicions. All those women and now this one— all leading back to Angelo.

Maybe Balthazar had something to do with Joy's disappearance too.

The demon shoved me away with supernatural strength, sending me sprawling on the blood-slicked floor. Before I could even cry out, he lunged at Shannon with inhuman speed, his movement a blur of deadly grace.

"No!" she screamed, trying to scramble away, her newly healed body betraying her with weakness. The sound was pure terror, echoing off the walls like a death knell.

Balthazar easily caught her, his fingers leaving new bruises on her pale skin. His beautiful face transformed into something terrible. Fangs descended where there had been none before, longer and more vicious than any vampire's I'd ever seen. He bit into her throat savagely, drinking the blood I'd just restored to her veins. The wet, grotesque sound of his ravenous feeding, nothing like Angelo's controlled bites, turned my stomach.

"No, no, no," I cried as I beat weakly on his back. Each blow was like hitting marble. My knuckles split, adding my blood to the horror around us. Tears streamed down my face as I watched all my healing work undone in seconds.

The woman stopped struggling, her eyes rolling back as her body went limp. He dropped her on the floor like discarded trash, her limbs twisted at unnatural angles, her breathing shallow again. When he turned to me, his face was a mask of blood, his smile crimson and cruel. My legs gave out and I fell to my knees, bile rising in my throat.

He wiped the blood away with elegant fingers, examining the red stains like an art critic studying a masterpiece. "Delicious. Heal her again."

"You're a vampire?" My voice was a broken whisper. But even as I said it, I knew that wasn't quite right. He was something else, something even worse. The darkness rolling off him made my angelic blood scream.

"I can be anything I want, Serenity." His eyes gleamed with ancient malice, shifting from demonic black to vampire red and back again. The sight made my head spin. "Now—heal the bitch."

It was like a light went on in my head, illuminating all the pieces I'd been too blind to see. Every murdered girl, every accusation, every suspicion from the police—it all clicked into place with horrifying clarity. My chest tightened until I could barely breathe. "You... You're the one who's been murdering all these girls in New Orleans and pinning the killings on Angelo."

"True." His smile widened, showing teeth still stained with Shannon's blood. "It's working well. The police suspect him, the wolves circle closer, and his own kind begin to doubt. Even Gianna questions her brother now." He ran a finger through the pool of blood spreading around Shannon's body, drawing patterns like a child playing with finger paints. "The mighty Angelo Santi, brought low by dead prostitutes and cocktail waitresses. Who would have thought it."

He gestured to Shannon's crumpled form. "Now, heal dear Shannon before she bleeds out. We have many more lessons ahead of us." His eyes gleamed. "You, my sweet Nephilim, are going to help me destroy everything Angelo loves."

The threat in his words made my soul shrink. What kind of monster had I been training with? What further horrors was he hiding behind that beautiful, terrible smile?

My heart screamed in my chest as I stared miserably at Shannon's broken body. *Angelo, please. I can't do this alone. I can't fight the darkness without you.* The prayer came from deep within my soul, desperately reaching across the void between us.

SEVENTEEN

*S*erenity

MY EXHAUSTED HANDS trembled as I pressed them against Shannon's wounds. The familiar warm glow of healing magic sputtered weak as a dying candle. Where it had once flowed like a river, now it was barely a trickle.

"Again," Balthazar commanded from somewhere above us. His boots scraped against the stone floor as he circled.

Shannon's eyes fluttered open, glassy with pain. "It's okay," she whispered. "You don't have to—"

Balthazar yanked her away from me and sank his

fangs into her shoulder, making fresh blood bloom across it. She bit back a cry, and I myself couldn't stop my own ragged gasp.

He released her and she fell onto the floor with a loud thud. "Again." His voice was ice.

I gathered what fragments of my power remained, scraping the very bottom of my reserves. The magic came slower now, like honey in winter, and sweat beaded on my forehead as I forced it through my palms. Shannon's wound gradually started to close, but spots danced at the edges of my vision.

Balthazar knelt next to me. "You can't heal her?"

My lower lip quivered as I trembled beneath his gaze, waiting for him to beat me, to hurt me, to do to me what he had done to Shannon. How I hated showing him fear. "I'm trying."

He reached out to touch me and I flinched, jumping back. He flashed me a sad look. "Little Nephilim, I would never hurt you." It was difficult to believe him when he had blood running down his chin.

My arms shook with exhaustion and the room tilted and swayed. I couldn't remember how many times we'd done this now—how many times I'd pulled her back from the brink only for Balthazar to feed again. His demon nature meant he didn't need blood to survive. He was simply mimicking Angelo. But where Angelo could show moments of genuine tenderness, I was beginning to realize that Balthazar's kindness always came with a price. His gentle touches were just another form of torment.

At the same time, I couldn't stop trying to heal Shannon. Wouldn't stop. Each healing took longer, drained me more, but I forced my magic to respond.

Don't fail her Don't fail her Don't fail her.

The mantra pulsed in time with my fading heartbeat as I pressed my hands against Shannon's skin once more.

Please heal her.

A tiny spark flickered deep inside me where my power had almost run dry. I seized it, desperate, pulling at it like a thread in darkness. The spark responded, burning brighter, spreading through my veins like liquid fire. I wasn't sure how I was doing this—it felt different from my usual healing. Wilder.

Balthazar caught my eye. His eyes gleamed intently with something that might have been hunger or fascination. It only made me more determined to heal the poor girl, to prove he hadn't broken me yet.

I gulped in oxygen, focusing everything I had on Shannon. My blood turned molten, racing through my body as my heart thundered against my ribs. Each beat sent a fresh wave of power surging through me, the sensation both terrible and exhilarating, like running a marathon while fever stricken. The magic poured from my hands, no longer a gentle stream but a torrent that threatened to sweep us both away.

Shannon groaned and her eyes fluttered open. Tears streamed down her face. Her hair and her shirt were caked in her own blood. She looked more dead than alive.

Bile rose in my throat as I looked at her. Each wound I'd healed felt like a betrayal, simply preparing her body for fresh pain. My gift of healing had been twisted into an instrument of torture. I wished I could erase her memory so she wouldn't remember what had just happened, or know what was about to happen again.

My magic was diminishing. I felt like a melted down candle with the wick almost out. Each breath felt heavier, the loss of my power a physical ache that spread through my limbs like ice.

"Splendid. You managed to heal her. Even drained and tired, you're powerful," he purred.

He reached for Shannon and she burst into tears, her body trembling.

Her sobs raked across my guilt like glass. Every time I healed her, I was just resetting the canvas for Balthazar's cruelty. The line between mercy and monstrosity had never felt so thin.

I gripped his wrist. "Please, no more. Please," I begged, hating myself for it. But I couldn't bear to watch the girl to be tortured any longer.

He cocked his eyebrow then looked down at Shannon as if she was something under a microscope. Then he picked up a lock of my hair and rubbed it between his fingers. "You've done well, so I'll grant you this one request, but that means we have another test to begin."

A dizzying wave of relief washed over me even as I cringed at his touch. The respite felt poisoned by his final words. Another test. Of course. Balthazar never gave anything without asking something worse in return.

"Please don't let him hurt me." Shannon's fingers dug into my arm, her eyes wild with terror.

Something fiercely protective surged through me. I shielded her body with mine, as if my human frame could somehow protect her from a demon's wrath. I searched Balthazar's face, trying to find the tiniest bit of compassion in his face, knowing there might not be any left to find.

He snatched her up again, fingers digging into her arms like steel claws. Her head lolled back, too weak to resist. When his fangs tore into her throat, blood spilled down in thick rivulets, pattering on the floor like rain.

"Don't, please. I can't... I can't heal her anymore."

He dropped her to the ground next to me and smiled. "As you wish, beautiful." He gave me a big grin. "We'll find another subject."

My stomach swished uneasily and I rubbed my slick forehead. He truly was a monster. How many people would he torture to get what he wants?

He snapped his fingers and the door opened immediately, as if someone had been waiting at his beck and call.

Petar entered the room, swagger in every step like he owned the place. As always, his hair was slicked back with not a strand out of place, and his three-piece blue suit looked freshly pressed despite the lateness of the hour. The red tie screamed for attention—as obvious as a rooster in a chicken coop. Everything about him felt carefully chosen to project an image of power.

But true power didn't come from silk suits or practiced struts.

It was Angelo's quiet smile before he showed his teeth.

It was Balthazar's casual cruelty, his absolute certainty that no one would dare stop him.

Petar was just playing at being one of them. He'd studied their movements and learned their mannerisms, but it was like watching a child playing dress up. No one would ever truly fear or admire him. He could wear the finest suits and practice that swagger for centuries, but he'd never be more than what he was: nothing.

A shadow of a shadow, desperate to be seen.

Petar wasn't alone. Steven DuPont trailed behind him like a ghost. His amber hair hung loose over his shoulders, lacking its usual careful styling, and the absence of his signature bandana and sunglasses left him looking vulnerable. But what chilled me most was his face—blank and empty, his usual sharp intelligence replaced by a vacant stare. He moved like a wind-up toy, each step mechanical and lifeless.

My throat closed up at the sight of him. I wanted to run over and fling my arms around him, shake him until that terrible emptiness left his eyes. This wasn't my Steve—Joy's older brother who'd treated me like a second sister despite his gang ties. The guy who'd taught me how to survive the streets, shown me how to throw a punch, how to use a knife in a fight, who'd cleaned my bruises after Freddie had beaten me. Seeing him reduced to this hollow shell felt like watching someone befoul a sacred place.

I forced myself to stand. The room swayed, but I locked my knees. "Balthazar, no. Please. Not Steve." My voice cracked on his name.

Balthazar's sweet, deadly smile spread across his face. "You think I'm going to torture your little friend?" He tilted his head, studying me with predatory interest. "More importantly, does Angelo know how you feel about him?"

I stepped in front of Steve, ignoring how the movement made the room spin. "Yes, damn it. Don't hurt him." My voice was raw, desperate. I couldn't watch Steve suffer like Shannon had. Not after everything we'd been through.

Balthazar's hand found my cheek, his palm still wet and sticky with Shannon's blood. The touch was gentle, almost loving, and all the more terrible for it.

"Tsk, tsk. Angelo would be most disappointed." Petar smirked as if he'd just discovered a secret weapon.

Something snapped inside me. The room stopped spinning as rage topped exhaustion. I whirled around, putting every ounce of hatred into the slap that I cracked across his face. "Shut up, just shut up, you bastard."

His hand clamped around my wrist like an iron shackle, twisting my arm behind my back with savage force. Raw fury was in his voice. "Don't ever touch me, bitch." His breath was hot in my ear, his voice trembling with rage and—was that fear? "I'm your future king."

King? The idea was so absurd it almost made me laugh despite my pain. This pathetic creature who could only feel powerful by hurting someone already weakened? Who had to announce his own importance to everyone?

I turned around, not able to take my eyes off Steve. He stood motionless, his vacant eyes fixed on nothing. Whatever they'd done to him was worse than any physical torture. They'd removed everything that made him Steve, and I had a sickening feeling I knew exactly why Balthazar had brought him here.

Shannon pressed against my legs like a cornered animal, her terror a stark contrast to Steve's emptiness. Her fingers clutched at my jeans, silently begging for protection I wasn't sure I could give.

I wasn't just meant to heal bodies anymore. I was to heal minds.

"Steve?" My voice stumbled over his name. I searched his face for any sign of the protector who'd taught me to throw a proper punch in a grimy alley behind Freaky Freddie's favorite club and who'd shown me how to break holds just like the one Petar had me in now.

"You're my second little sister," he'd always say, ruffling my hair affectionately after I managed to land a hit during practice. "Ain't nobody gonna mess with you when I'm done teaching you." He'd worn his past like armor—ex-gang member turned guardian, street-smart and loyal to the bone. No one could lay a hand on me when he was around. He'd made sure of that.

Today, Steve didn't move. Didn't blink. Just stared straight ahead like a mannequin in a shop window.

That's when I put my finger on what was wrong with his eyes. The familiar blue—the color of summer skies, he'd once joked—was gone. In its place was nothing but darkness, black as tar pits, infinite as a starless night. Whatever looked out through those eyes wasn't Steve anymore.

"You've got ten seconds to let her go, Dragan— starting now. Ten." Balthazar's voice cut through the room like a blade.

Petar's grip on my wrist tightened.

"Nine." Balthazar stepped closer, his shoes leaving bloody footprints on the floor. "Eight."

Petar's breath caught.

"Seven." A meditative smile spread across Balthazar's face. "Six. I wonder if your blood tastes as bitter as your ambitions, little king."

"Five." He was close enough now that I could smell Shannon's blood on him. "Four."

Petar's hands began to tremble.

"Three." Balthazar's fangs gleamed. "Two—"

Petar shoved me away so hard Shannon lost her grip on my legs and I stumbled into Steve. His body felt rigid and cold. It was like running into a statue.

The Steve I knew would have caught me, steadied me, cracked a joke about my clumsiness. This Steve just stood there, those horrible black eyes staring into nothingness while I regained my footing.

My throat tightened. What had they done to him? And could I bring him back?

Balthazar pulled me next to him, his touch surprisingly gentle. "Are you all right?" His voice held the same tender concern he'd had before torturing Shannon.

"I'm fine." The lie tasted bitter on my tongue. My arm throbbed where Petar had twisted it, and I could already feel the bruises blooming on my skin.

"Let me see," Balthazar murmured quietly, as if soothing a frightened animal. He pushed up my sleeve with careful reverence, nothing like the brutality he'd shown Shannon.

Ugly red marks wrapped around my arm like serpents; Petar's fingers were mapped out in angry crimson. Balthazar ran his palm over the wounds, leaving trails of Shannon's drying blood on my skin. Tingling warmth flooded over my skin and spread through my veins. The welts faded, the pain dissolved—and Shannon's blood was left smeared across my arm like a macabre bracelet.

He flashed me a smile that would have melted most

women's hearts, all perfect teeth and practiced charm. But I'd seen those same lips stained with Shannon's blood. Seen what lurked behind that polished mask.

"As you can see, I can have a gentle touch when I want to." His words dripped with double meaning. "I can heal or harm as it suits me."

I forced my lips into a smile, though it felt like stretching a wound. "So you won't hurt Steve?"

"No." His eyes glittered with amusement. "I have another mission for him."

The blood drained from my face. "Mission?"

"Yes." He snapped his fingers like he was calling a dog. "Here, Steve. Find another girl that works for Angelo and bring her to me." His gaze cut to Petar, sharp as broken glass. "You. Go with him."

I looked between the three of them—Balthazar's smug satisfaction, Steve's empty eyes, Petar's barely contained fear. The pieces started falling into place, but I didn't want to see the picture they made. "Wait." I grabbed Steve's arm, feeling nothing but cold flesh beneath my fingers. "What are you doing?"

Balthazar's smile widened, savoring the moment like fine wine. "My darling Nephilim, surely you must realize that Steve is the one who has been supplying me with my toys."

"Toys?" I gestured at Shannon still crumpled on the floor, her blood drying brown on her skin. "You mean like her?"

"Yes. Steve has been playing fetch."

A gasp tore from my throat as I clapped my hands over my mouth. The room tilted as realization hit. "Did he..." The words felt like broken glass in my throat. "Did he take Joy?"

"That he did."

My knees gave out and I collapsed, sobs wracking my body. The Steve I knew would have died protecting his sister. Would have fought armies bare-handed to keep her safe. That Steve was gone, replaced by this hollow-eyed puppet. "Is she... Is she dead?"

"Not at all." His soft voice crashed through my head like a thunderclap. "Don't you see? She's the big carrot." He paced around me in a slow circle, a shark scenting blood in the water. "So long as you do what I want, she lives. I've forbidden the one who summoned me from killing her."

"Summoned you? You mean like a person?" Hope flickered—a name meant someone I could fight.

"More like one of the four mafia kings of New Orleans."

My heart slammed against my ribs. "Which one?"

He waggled his finger like he was scolding a naughty child. "Ah, ah, ah. That would be telling."

Behind him, Steve and Petar slipped out the door to go procure another victim. And somewhere in the city, Joy was alive but imprisoned, her fate tied to my obedience.

The horror of it all twisted my soul, each revelation another burden I somehow had to bear.

I looked at Shannon's broken form, then at the blood Balthazar had left on my skin. How many more would die before this game of his was done? And which mafia king was pulling the strings like a twisted puppeteer?

CHAPTER

EIGHTEEN

ngelo

I SLIPPED Moonfall inside my suit jacket, the sacred dagger's weight comforting and familiar against my ribs. Such a beautiful, elegant thing, designed solely for one purpose—ending wolf shifters. The silver runes running along its hilt and blade burned cold through the fabric, a reminder of what I intended to do. Trystan would feel that cold soon enough, right before I drove it into his heart—but not before he told me where he and Balthazar were keeping Serenity.

Enzo lounged against the wall outside my secret room.

He was trying to look casual, but I could smell the anticipation rolling off him, acrid as gunpowder. "Got it, boss?"

I pulled my jacket back, revealing the blade. "Trystan's a dead man." The words tasted like a sweet promise on my tongue.

Satisfying thoughts of cutting out Trystan's heart kept clawing at my focus, but I forced myself to keep my mind on what needed to be done. I gave Enzo a fierce stare. "Are Elena and Gianna safe?"

"Yes. They are in the library. Luigi is guarding them."

"Good."

The library was one of the most secure rooms at Crescent Manor. No windows, just one heavy door, and layers of my strongest wards woven into every wall. They'd be fine.

Dimitri appeared, smirking as usual. "Sooo... We're walking into what's probably a trap with a demon who likes to play torture games probably waiting in the wings?" He cocked an eyebrow. "Sounds like a fantastic way to spend the evening. Should I bring snacks?"

Let him come, I thought, hunger and violence singing in my blood as my fingers caressed Moonfall's hilt. Tonight wasn't about clean, elegant kills. Tonight was about sending messages. And nothing says "stay out of my territory" quite like a dead wolf and a demon who has finally learned his place.

I glanced at Dimitri. "You still have the burner phone that Gage slipped you?"

He patted the bulge on his jacket. "Right here."

"This could get ugly, boss," Enzo muttered as we headed out of the house to the limousine. "You don't think we should have more men?"

I shook my head. "No, this is a sneak attack. Trystan won't be expecting that. It will be the last mistake he makes. Once again—is Crescent Manor well-guarded?"

"Guys at all the entrances. No one's getting in," Enzo said. "Not even that thing that's taken over DuPont. I made sure it's warded against demons. And I've even got Solomon's Seals placed at seven points around the property." He pulled out one of the ancient coins, its surface etched with symbols. The metal had the old-blood patina that only came from centuries of use.

"You're telling me those little trinkets actually keep out demons?" Dimitri's voice was heavy with skepticism.

"Regular demons, yeah." Enzo flipped the seal between his fingers. "Even powerful ones can't cross once it's activated. But DuPont"—he shrugged—"well, he's something else entirely, isn't he?"

I studied the seal, noting how it pulsed to absorb the shadows around it. "And Balthazar hasn't noticed?"

"That's the beauty of it." Enzo's grin turned predatory. "Demons don't even sense the barrier until they hit it, and by then it's too late. Like walking into a wall of holy fire."

Perfect, I thought. Balthazar couldn't interfere if he couldn't reach us. And Trystan? Well, he'd learn what happened to dogs who strayed into the wrong territory.

The three of us exited Crescent Manor. Pascal got out of the driver's seat and opened the limousine door for us. Dimitri was well enough to start driving again, but he was actually proving more useful as one of Enzo's men.

The bruises I'd left on him were fading like watercolors washing away—purple melting to green, green dissolving to yellow, yellow barely visible against his skin. The split lip had knit itself closed, though he still ran his tongue over it occasionally, like testing a memory. Only the shadow of a bruise around his eye remained, and even that was disappearing—faster than it should have, frankly. Vampire blood worked fast, but not this fast. Then again, Dimitri had always been different, though I hadn't really noticed until I'd had cause to mark him.

He caught me studying him and flashed that familiar cocky grin, though there was something new behind it now—respect, or perhaps a better understanding of boundaries. Amazing what a thorough beating could do. The bruises might have healed, but the lesson would probably last much longer.

Pascal's worried eyes met mine in the rearview mirror. "Sir, we're being followed."

I tensed, cursing under my breath. The black Mercedes, three cars back, kept a discreet distance. Keir Rankin, meticulousness as always. My phone rang, his name lighting up the screen.

"Rankin." I already guessed why he was calling, why

he was tailing us. This was how he operated—show what he knows, then deliver the real intel.

"I have some news about Balthazar." His voice was clipped, professional.

I sat straighter in my seat. "And?"

"Word is that one of the four mafia kings conjured him. I know it wasn't me, and I'm pretty sure it wasn't you, so that leaves either Hunter or Barone."

Maximo Barone. The human king played his role perfectly—all legitimacy and custom-tailored business suits. But I'd seen what lay beneath that polished veneer. He could have made a deal with Balthazar just as easily as Trystan Hunter could. But that burner phone pointed in the wolf king's direction.

"Anything else?" In the mirror, I watched Rankin's Mercedes maintain its discreet distance. He'd shadow us all the way to Trystan's if I let him, gathering intel while keeping us in sights.

"Whoever conjured him has DuPont's daughter Joy. Rumor has it she might not be human. I can't confirm or deny that, but someone wants her badly enough to send a demon. She might have an unleashed power like your Nephilim."

"Not human?" My mouth went dry. I'd seen enough supernatural being to know how devastating their power could be. This complicated things. It could explain why it was important that she go missing. Her power could rival Serenity's. If she had angelic blood...

Tension crept my neck like icy fingers. "You think she's another Nephilim?"

"Like I said, it's only a rumor."

"Well, find out if it's true."

"Working on it already. You on your way to see—"

"You know exactly where I'm going, Rankin," I snapped. "You wouldn't be three cars back if you didn't." I watched his Mercedes signal for the same turn we'd just made. "Keep your distance. I'll call you afterward."

I could hear the smile in his voice. "Of course. Happy hunting."

The call ended, but Rankin's Mercedes remained—close enough to observe, far enough to deny any involvement if things went sideways at Trystan's. Perfect positioning, as always. I had to admire his technique, even if being watched irritated me.

Enzo ran the Void Chain through his palm, the black metal links whispering against his skin. "You think he's going to stay outside Trystan's compound?"

I shrugged, watching Rankin's Mercedes settle into position with military efficiency. "Depends on what happens at the front gate." I could feel Moonfall's cool presence against my ribs. "Rankin doesn't want a war, but if things get ugly, he'll move in. He's our insurance, too—everyone's witness that whatever happens next, Trystan started it."

We finally pulled up to the front gate. The compound's high walls loomed over us, multiple cameras tracking our every move. One of Trystan's guards approached—a young wolf, trying too hard to look tough in his tactical gear. Please. I could smell his nerves from here.

I nodded and Pascal rolled down the window.

"Do you have an appointment?" The guard's hand rested on his sidearm. As if bullets could stop me.

I pulled out my phone, dialing Trystan's private number that he'd given me back when we were pretending to be civilized. "Open the damn gate, Trystan. We have business to discuss." My voice held the kind of power that didn't need to shout to be threatening.

"Meeting's not until tonight," he growled, but I heard the tension underneath. He knew what my early arrival meant.

"If you don't open the gate..." I let each word fall like a stone. "Then I'll assume you have something to hide and are declaring war." It was a simple threat. Clean. The kind that couldn't be misinterpreted.

The silence stretched out. I could almost see him weighing his options, calculating risks. His breathing was heavy through the phone—the wolf in him desperate to challenge, the king in him knowing better.

Finally, a growl. The line went dead.

The gate swung open with a mechanical whine. Trystan's guard bared his teeth as we rolled past him. His attempt at menace was pathetic, barely a ripple in the ocean of threats I'd weathered.

Behind us, Rankin's Mercedes pulled forward slightly,

smooth as a shark following blood. He positioned himself for a clear view of whatever came next.

Enzo's fingers tightened around the Void Chain. Dimitri's smirk took on a hard edge. Even Pascal's habitually impassive face showed a hint of anticipation.

Time to see if Trystan was smart enough to give up Serenity's location, or if New Orleans was about to witness exactly what happened when someone took what belonged to me.

NINETEEN

I FORCED myself to stay seated, though every instinct screamed to leap out of the limo. Control was everything in my world—it was what separated kings from rabid dogs. But with Serenity missing, my control was slipping through my fingers. My fingers drummed against my thighs, betraying the beast I was barely keeping caged.

"Well, well." Dimitri's lips curved into a smirk. "Look who's decided to crash our little party. And here I thought Rankin had better things to do than follow us. Like, oh, I don't know—run his own territory." He lounged back in his seat, radiating that particular brand of dangerous amusement. "Should we send him an invitation next time? Maybe a fruit basket?"

Sarcasm dripped from his every word, but I caught the calculated gleam in his eyes as he watched Rankin's car. Dimitri's jokes had teeth sometimes.

Pascal parked the limousine in front of Trystan's plantation mansion. The white Corinthian columns rose like bones against the sky, the whole place reeking of old money and territorial pride. He got out and opened the door for Enzo, who emerged with the Void Chain coiled in his hand like a sleeping snake.

I didn't wait for the clearance ritual and scrambled out right after Enzo. My patience had died somewhere between Serenity's disappearance and the discovery of Trystan's betrayal. The beast in me was clawing at my control, demanding blood and revenge. One wrong move, and every shifter on this property would learn exactly why vampires had ruled New Orleans for centuries.

Dimitri slid out the other side, his usual smirk gone. Even he knew when to dial back the jokes.

Gage, Trystan's enforcer, and Stalker, another of Trystan's men, were waiting at the top of the stairs like particularly grim sentries. Their faces had that unique look reserved for men who knew they were guarding the wrong side but were in too deep to back out now.

Poor bastards.

Another car door whispered shut behind us and Keir and Lorcan materialized from their vehicle, moving with that predatory grace that marked the truly dangerous. My eyes snapped to the sky, searching for Lorcan's harpies. The blue expanse looked clear except for a scattering of white clouds—which unfortunately was the perfect cover for those winged nightmares.

"This is a private party," I said, fixing Keir with a glare that would have sent smarter men running.

"Apologies. Consider it officially crashed." Keir met my gaze without flinching. Always did have more balls than sense.

"Why are you here, Rankin?"

He shrugged, the gesture too casual to be anything but calculated. "This little war of yours could threaten my empire, Santi. I'm here to make sure my interests are protected."

"Bullshit. You want to know if Trystan is working with Balthazar." I didn't bother framing it as a question.

"Let's just say I have a vested interest in the matter."

I nodded, weighing his words against what I knew of him. Keir played his own game—always had. I wasn't naive enough to think he was on my side, but at the same time, he surely wasn't stupid enough to trust Balthazar. The demon's reputation for betrayal was as legendary as his cruelty.

Trystan was about to learn a hard lesson about dealing with demons. By the time this was over, his little power play would explode in his face—and I'd make sure to be standing far enough back to enjoy the show, but close enough to twist the knife.

Gage narrowed his eyes that went from brown to gold. "You don't scare me, vampire."

"Oh, that's adorable." Dimitri touched the last trace of a bruise on his jaw. "I said something similar just last week. Spoiler"—he gestured at his healing face with a theatrical flourish—"it didn't end well. But hey, knock yourself out, keep poking the homicidal vampire. I'll just stand back here and watch. Anyone bring popcorn?"

The gold in Gage's eyes flickered, his gaze darting between my cold smile and Dimitri's fresh bruises. Keir sighed heavily, like a teacher dealing with a particularly obtuse student. "You're not really that foolish, are you, wolf? Santi's one step from declaring war and you're acting like he's a kid in a mask. Would you like me to list the body count from his last territorial dispute, or shall we skip the history lesson and move on to the part where you fucking take us to Trystan?"

"Trystan did say to let them in, Gage," Stalker muttered as he opened the door.

I brushed past Gage. One false move, and forget the Moonfall blade, I'd just drain him dry. I didn't bother waiting for Trystan's men to show me to him. I knew where the little puppy held court.

Two guards flanked the study door, hands on their weapons. I didn't bother with ceremony. One moment I was standing outside the door, the next I'd torn through it with a crack that echoed through the mansion like a gunshot.

Trystan sat behind his mahogany desk, playing king. Above him, a massive painting of his white wolf dominated the wall—all fangs and fury, intended to remind visitors what lurked just beneath his tailored suit. Cheap theatrics. My black wolf was equally as massive and deadly when I chose to transform into it, and I didn't need wall art to advertise it.

"Santi." His lips curved into that insufferable smile that had started wars before. "Why so impatient?"

The room reeked of arrogance and lies. I was done playing these games, pretending at civility. I moved around the desk in a blur of vampire speed, hands already reaching for his throat.

Steel-strong fingers locked around my arm, yanking me back. Fae strength, face speed. Both surprising and infuriating.

"Not yet," Keir gritted between his teeth, his usual diplomatic mask cracking. When Fae or Dark Fae moved, they moved like lightning. Right now, luckily for Trystan, Keir was the only thing standing between the wolf king and a very messy death at my hands.

I wrenched free of his grip, my fangs aching to descend. But Keir was right—we needed to play this smart. "Show him, Dimitri."

"A little present." Dimitri's smirk had hardened into something darker as he tossed the burner phone onto

Trystan's desk. It landed like a thousand accusations. "Next time you decide to make secret calls to demons, maybe don't do it in vampire territory."

The phone sat between us like a loaded gun. Trystan's smile didn't waver, but something flickered in his eyes—calculation, maybe, or fear. Either way, he knew the game had just changed.

Trystan stared at the phone, his face a mask of practiced neutrality. "Where did you get that?"

The Moonfall blade whispered against silk as I drew it from my jacket. The sacred steel caught the light, hungry for wolf blood. "Never mind. How about you tell me where Serenity is."

Keir stepped forward, his voice poison. "I suggest you tell us the truth, Trystan." His eyes fixed on the wolf king. "Is that phone yours?"

Trystan flipped through the messages with the casual air of a man reading a dinner menu, not evidence that could start a war. But there were tells—a slight tightening around his eyes, a finger hesitating over certain texts.

Stalker's face had drained of color, the blood abandoning ship before the storm hit. But Gage wore a smirk that spoke volumes. It was the kind of expression a man gets when he finally sees his boss cornered and doesn't hate it. Interesting.

"Bring Ivan to me." Trystan's eyes flicked to Gage, cold as winter steel.

The smirk vanished from Gage's face like it had been

slapped off. He left without a word, his footsteps just a little too quick.

I let Moonfall dance between my fingers, the blade catching the light with each turn. The weapon's presence made the air heavy, charged with the promise of violence. "Are you saying that burner phone isn't yours?"

"No." Trystan's voice was steady, reasonable. Perfect for a lie. "But I paid for it. It belongs to one of my enforcers —Ivan Toser. He said he lost it." His eyes met mine, a clear challenge in them. "How did this fall into your hands?"

Dimitri glanced at me, one eyebrow arching, clearly asking permission to drop the bomb.

I nodded, curious to see how the wolf king would handle hearing about the rats in his court.

"Gage slipped it into my pocket as an early Christmas present." Dimitri delivered the line with theatrical flair, but his eyes were sharp, watching for a reaction. "I'd have preferred a gift card, but hey—"

The words hadn't even finished leaving his mouth before rage transformed Trystan's face. His aristocratic blue eyes blazed molten gold, the wolf beneath his skin clawing to get out. "Get. Gage." The words came out midway between human speech and animal growl.

Stalker bolted from the study like Death itself was on his heels. Given the fury radiating off Trystan, maybe it was.

The change rippled through Trystan and the careful facade of civility peeled away as he emerged from behind his desk—hair sprouting thick and wild down his head and arms, fingernails extending into curved daggers, his canines lengthening into razors and splitting his perfect politician's smile into something savage.

Stalker burst back in, twisting a third man's arm behind his back.

"Let me go," the man gasped—Ivan, I presumed. Perfect. Almost all the players were finally on stage. But Gage's absence nagged at me. Trystan had sent him to retrieve Ivan, yet here was Stalker instead.

I sat quietly, waiting for the real show to begin.

Clearly, it nagged at Trystan too. His glare shifted from Stalker to the empty doorway. "Where's Gage? I sent him to get Ivan."

Stalker shoved Ivan at Trystan's feet. "Dunno. I found Ivan scaling down the wall. No sign of Gage."

"Ivan." Trystan's voice dropped low. "Did Gage tell you to come down here?"

Ivan's Adam's apple bobbed, his face draining of color. "No."

A lie. Fear rolled off him in waves—if I could smell it, Trystan certainly could.

I watched Trystan's rage was a tangible force as he snatched Ivan off the floor and slammed him against the wall. The plaster cracked, sending a spiderweb of fissures racing up to the ceiling. "You. Betrayed. Me."

"What?" Ivan's feet kicked uselessly against the wall, his hands scrabbling at Trystan's grip like a mouse caught in a trap. "No, I didn't—I swear. I—" His protests devolved into a choked gurgle.

The wolf king's control was slipping. I could smell it. His eyes flared with unholy yellow light as he hurled Ivan across the room. The desk splintered under the impact, papers scattering like confetti. I didn't move to help either of them. Let them tear each other apart; it would save me the trouble.

"Why did Gage give Dimitri Dragan your phone?" Trystan's voice had dropped to that register that made small animals freeze.

Blood painted Ivan's lips as he crumpled to his knees. Each word came out between desperate gasps. "Gage...forced me. He wants... He wants to be king." His head bowed in submission—too late for that now. "If I didn't do what he said... he would kill my mate."

My fingers tightened on Moonfall's hilt. Gage. The pieces were falling into place.

Trystan's hand shot out, taking Ivan's head back by the hair. "They have Shannon?"

"He gave..." Ivan's voice broke like shattered glass. "He gave her to the demon."

I caught Dimitri's eye. Balthazar. Of course the demon would be involved in this coup.

"Where are they?" Trystan twisted harder, and I heard tendons creak as his control finally snapped. His fangs sank deep into Ivan's shoulder, eliciting a scream that could have wakened the dead. The scent of fresh blood filled the air, sweet and metallic.

"Shadowmoon," Ivan sobbed. "Your grandfather's old place."

Blood dripped from Trystan's mouth as he released his bite. I smiled. His grandfather's abandoned den. I knew the abandoned den—every vampire in New Orleans kept tabs on old wolf territory. It was the perfect hole for traitors to hide.

And now we knew exactly where to find them.

TWENTY

S *erenity*

BALTHAZAR LEFT to get Shannon and me food, as if we were guests at some twisted dinner party rather than his prisoners. I sat on the floor next to Shannon and leaned back against the wall. I doubted she would even be able to eat. My own stomach churned like a storm-tossed sea, each revelation making me sicker. He was methodically dismantling my world piece by precious piece, stripping everything away with surgical precision.

Petar Dragan wanted to be king. The thought sent ice through my veins, because the only one way that crown would ever touch his head would be through Angelo's death. Raw panic clawed up my throat at the mere thought of losing him. He wasn't perfect—he could be cruel, possessive, and dangerous—but he had become my anchor in this supernatural storm. In his arms, I felt invincible. Protected. Like all the darkness in New Orleans couldn't touch me as long as he held me.

But it wasn't just Angelo. Balthazar's poisonous influence had also reached Steve DuPont—my protector, my brother in all but blood. Now he moved like a marionette on demon strings, his eyes black and empty where warmth once used to live. Trapped in some hellish trance, dancing to Balthazar's music.

The pieces clicked together with horrible clarity. That's why Angelo's compulsion had failed. He couldn't break what was already broken. Balthazar had gotten there first, turning Steve into something worse than dead —a puppet who helped murder the very people he once would have died protecting.

Steve, who'd once growled at anyone who looked at Joy wrong. Steve, who'd been our shield, our protector. The thought turned my stomach to ice. If Balthazar ordered him to hurt Joy...to make her the demon's next toy...

I had to get out of here.

Angelo, please find me. Please. Find Joy. Save her.

Shannon slumped against the wall beside me, more corpse than girl. Tears cut clean trails through the blood on her cheeks, the only pure thing left in this nightmare. I watched every shallow breath she took like a hawk, terrified that it might be her last.

Please hurry, Angelo. Before there's nothing left of us to save.

My hand trembled as I reached toward her. I could heal her—but Balthazar would only hurt her again. And again. Still, my fingers stretched out, power gathering at my fingertips. What kind of healer was I, if I allowed her to suffer?

I placed my hand on her skin, searching for that familiar spark of power, but it was like trying to draw water from a dried-up well. My healing powers had abandoned me when I most needed them.

A sudden crash came like thunder, shaking dust from the ceiling—something massive had just hit the building with devastating force. Footsteps pounded down the hall, a stampede of panic punctuated by screams that froze my blood, each cry cutting off more suddenly than the last.

My heart slammed against my ribs as I leaped to my feet. Whatever was coming, we absolutely could not be here when it arrived.

Shannon dissolved into gulping sobs, her entire body trembling. She looked so small, so fragile—Balthazar's latest broken toy.

I rushed to her, grabbing her arm. "Something's happening. We need to get out of here." *Now. Before whatever's causing those screams finds us.*

She sagged against my shoulder, dead weight. "I can't. I'm too weak." Her voice faded away.

"No, you're not." I hauled her upright, ignoring her whimpers of pain. Gentle wasn't going to keep us alive. "Come on—walk."

"Where?" Her arm swept over the windowless room in a gesture of defeat. "There's no place to go."

Another crash, closer now. The screams had taken on a wet, gurgling quality that turned my stomach. Metal clashed against metal, punctuated by sounds of bodies hitting walls—heavy thuds that spoke of broken bones and worse.

My eyes darted around our prison. No windows. The door might as well be a death sentence. There—the ventilation grate. Old buildings like this always had oversized ductwork. It might be wide enough.

I lowered Shannon to the floor, her confusion clear. She clung to my leg like a cat, her fingers trembling where they gripped my jeans. "What are you doing? Don't leave me. Please." Her skin was paper-white where Balthazar had fed, blue veins stark against her neck.

I squared up to the vent, channeling all the self-defense lessons Steve had ever taught me into my every kick. The hardwood creaked beneath me.

"Trying—"

BANG

"to find—"

CRASH

"a way—"

CRACK

"Out of here!"

Each impact sent pain shooting up my leg, but the metal was beginning to give.

The grate finally tore free with a shriek of protest, sending me stumbling backwards. My heart slammed against my ribs—part terror, part wild triumph. Stale air rushed out, bringing with it the musty promise of escape. I braced myself against the wall, legs trembling from the repeated kicks, my right shin screaming where I'd connected with the metal. Worth it. Every bruise would be worth it.

The tunnel was narrow, but it would do. One person at a time, at crawling speed—not ideal, but infinitely better than whatever horrors were closing in behind us. Those screams were definitely getting closer, although on the plus side the confined space would slow down anything bigger than us. I flexed my foot, ignoring the throb. We'd have to move fast, injury or no injury. Whatever was coming down that hall, whatever was causing those screams—it would have to catch us first.

"You first." I grabbed Shannon's arm and shoved her toward the vent opening. The screams outside were getting closer.

"I can't." Her voice quivered, exhaustion and terror warring in her eyes.

"Those things out there could be more demons. Do

you want them to find you?" The words came out harsh, but fear had stolen any softness from my voice. "What do you think they'll do to you if Balthazar hands you over to them?"

Terror flashed across Shannon's face. She glanced over her shoulder at the door, then back at the dark, gaping maw of the vent. The hope of survival finally won. She dragged herself forward with trembling arms, each movement punctuated by soft groans of pain. I crawled in after her, the cold metal pressing against my palms, my knees. The vent felt smaller now that I was inside it, the walls too close, the air too thin.

"Faster," I whispered, trying to keep my voice steady. "Please, Shannon, try to go a little faster."

The door exploded inward with a sound like a thunderclap. Wood splintered, metal shrieked, and my heart stopped.

"Serenity?" Balthazar's voice rolled through the room like black smoke. "Where are you?"

My whole body locked up, ice flooding my veins. That voice. That falsely tender voice that promised such beautiful things only to ripped people apart. My lungs seized up, and I had to press my fist against my mouth to contain the panicked sound trying to escape. Sweat slicked my palms against the metal vent, and for a horrible moment, I was back in his grasp, drowning in sulfur-sweet darkness.

No. No. Keep moving. Don't let him in your head.

Shannon froze ahead of me and let out a soft, muffled

cry. Her entire body started trembling, her ankle quivering under my warning grip. I could hear her ragged breathing echoing in the metal tunnel, too loud, too fast. She was hyperventilating.

Through the darkness, I saw her shoulders hunch, making herself smaller and more vulnerable—exactly what he wanted. His voracious feeding had left her too weak.

I could picture him standing there, probably still wearing that pleasant smile, Shannon's blood dried on his chin. Surveying the empty room. Seeing the broken vent. Knowing exactly where his prey had gone.

Crawl. Crawl. Crawl. My mind screamed at my body to move faster, but there was nowhere to go but forward, nowhere to hide in this metal tunnel. If he reached in with those long arms...

Shannon's harsh breathing echoed off the metal walls. My own pulse roared in my ears. Behind us, silence, the kind that comes before a storm. Then—

"How did you get in here?" Balthazar's angry voice echoed through the vent.

"Where is she?" The voice sounded exactly like Angelo's, that perfect mix of ice and rage. My heart clenched painfully. Balthazar was such a master of deception. This could easily be another of his games, another way to toy with my emotions, a trick to make me turn back.

"Someplace you'll never find her. She's mine."

The words bounced off the metal walls, trapping me in

their threat. my stomach lurched, hope crumbling to ash in my mouth. I pressed my back against the cold vent, nowhere to run, nowhere to hide from this horrible uncertainty. This was exactly how Balthazar operated—letting you believe rescue was at hand before tearing all hope away. But god, it sounded so like Angelo, that protective rage I'd trusted with my life before.

My fingers scraped against the metal as I fought to keep myself from coming apart. One wrong choice in this metal coffin and Shannon and I were both dead.

CHAPTER

TWENTY-ONE

S *erenity*

LOUD SCREAMS WERE STILL ECHOING outside the vent, vibrating through the metal against my spine. But I forced my racing mind to ignore them and focus instead on every nuance of the two voices arguing beyond our metal prison. Each word could mean life or death. Balthazar was a master of disguise. My skin crawled at the memory of how many times he'd twisted his voice into something familiar, something safe, only to tear hope away. It could be him out there right now, spinning another beautiful lie to lure me out like a spider drawing a fly into its web.

"I have something for you, demon." Metal clinked against metal.

My heart stuttered in my chest, hope and terror warring for control. I bit down hard on my lower lip, the taste of copper flooding my mouth as I fought to stay silent.

That voice—god, it sounded *exactly* like Angelo, right down to the dangerous edge he got in his voice when protecting someone. Even the way he spat the word 'demon' was pure Angelo. But Balthazar had fooled me before, had wielded my memories like weapons. Each perfect inflection could be another carefully crafted lie, designed to make me crawl out of safety and right into his hands.

Arrgggh!

The scream that ripped through the vent walls now wasn't like the others. This one was raw, savage, cut off abruptly like the speaker's throat had been slashed. But was it real? Was any of this real?

I froze mid-crawl, my hands pressed against the cold metal, doubt churning in my stomach. Every instinct screamed at me to keep moving. I couldn't risk going back, couldn't risk being trapped by Balthazar again. The memory of his tortures, of being forced to heal Shannon over and over, made my skin crawl. No. Even if that really was Angelo, I couldn't risk being caught. Freedom was too close.

Tears slid down my cheeks as I forced myself forward,

following Shannon through the darkness. Real rescue or cruel trick—it didn't matter. This was our chance to escape, and I was taking it. I'd rather die in these vents than spend another moment as Balthazar's plaything.

Footsteps echoed behind me, each one making my heart stutter. Every instinct screamed at me to shove Shannon forward faster, but she suddenly stopped, her body sagging against the metal.

"Serenity," she whispered, her voice thick with terror. "It's a dead end. Another vent. Gage's men. They're on the other side." Her eyes found mine in the dim light, wide with desperation. "I don't want to die, Serenity." Her voice was heartbreakingly small.

The world tilted sideways. Trapped. We were trapped between Balthazar and Gage's wolves. My chest constricted, each breath coming shorter than the last as the metal walls seemed to close in. Shannon's face blurred in front of me; all I could see was her terror reflected back at me. Guilt consumed me. I'd led her right into this death trap, promising safety, promising escape—

No. Focus. *Think.* There had to be a way out.

I glanced over my shoulder. A long shadow stretched across the vent entrance like reaching fingers. Trapped. We truly were trapped.

Shitshitshitshit

My muscles screamed as I wriggled in the narrow space, turning to face whatever was coming. If Balthazar wanted us, he'd have to fight. I'd die before I let him touch Shannon again.

Someone peered into the vent. "Serenity? Are you in there?"

Everything in me froze. That voice. That silhouette. It looked like Angelo, sounded like Angelo, but Balthazar was a master of illusions. How many times had he played with my mind already? Made me see things, believe things, only to twist the knife deeper when he revealed the truth?

I wanted so desperately to believe it was really Angelo. My body ached to move toward the voice and to safety. But fear held me in place like thick iron chains. I crouched there in the metal tunnel, trembling like a rabbit in a snare, caught between hope and terror. One wrong choice could doom us both.

Suddenly, the figure shifted—bones cracking, form expanding—into a massive black wolf. The beast filled the vent entrance, its breath fogging on the metal as it sniffed. Then it began squeezing into the tunnel, massive shoulders scraping the sides.

Oh god Oh god Oh god

Hope shattered in my chest, leaving nothing but jagged shards of terror. Not rescue. Not safety. Just another monster in this nightmare. My mind screamed at my body to move, to run, to do something other than freeze like a deer. The scraping of fur against metal sent shivers down my spine as I scrambled backward, colliding with Shannon.

The impact knocked the air from my lungs, but my hands found her shoulders, pushing her back, trying to put as much distance between her and those gleaming teeth as possible.

She gasped, her fingers digging into my arm. "What are you doing? Oh shit, what is that thing?"

"Get back, get back," I hissed between my teeth.

"I can't. There's no place to go." Her terrified whimper shattered what was left of my hope.

Stupid. So stupid to think anyone was coming to save us. Now Shannon was going to die because I'd let myself believe in rescue, let myself hope that we weren't alone.

The wolf's breath came steamy on the metal, closer now. My muscles coiled tight as I dropped into a crouch, desperately channeling every fighting instinct I had, like a cougar facing down a bigger predator. Dumb, maybe—what could I really do against those teeth, those claws?—but I'd die before I let it reach Shannon. The metal walls pressed in around us as I watched death crawl closer in our prison of steel.

The creature was inches from my face now, close enough to tear out my throat. I squeezed my eyes shut, my whole body seizing with terror. Balthazar. It had to be Balthazar. Any second now and I'd hear that silky laugh, feel that cold grip on my skin. My heart slammed so hard against my ribs I thought they might crack. The memory of his touch, his hunger, sent bile rising in my throat. Not again not again not again. I couldn't survive another round of his tender cruelty, his sweet poison.

Angelo, where are you?

"Serenity. I finally found you." The voice was rough with emotion.

That spicy scent I knew so well hit me like a punch to the gut, flooding my senses with memories of safety that felt like home. My body responded instantly—pulse racing, skin tingling, every cell reaching for him. Warm breath against my skin. The metallic tang of fresh blood. A violent shudder ran through me. Could it really be...? My hands shook as I forced my eyes open, heart nearly stopping in my chest.

The wolf was gone, replaced by Angelo, his crimson gaze, his long dark hair falling around the face I'd dreamed of seeing again for what seemed like forever.

My fingers twitched forward, aching to touch him, to prove he was real and not another cruel trick of my desperate mind. But Balthazar's deceptions had taught me the cost of hope. Trust meant death in this nightmare. Yet every instinct screamed that this was indeed Angelo—my Angelo—his scent wrapping around me like a familiar embrace, calling to something deep in my soul.

"Is it... Is it really you?" The words scraped past the tightness in my throat. My body trembled with the effort of holding back, caught between the desperate need to throw myself into his arms and the paralyzing fear that he'd transform into Balthazar the moment I did so.

"Take my hand." He extended it toward me, patient, waiting.

I placed my shaking hand in his. If this was indeed Balthazar's final cruel trick, at least I might buy Shannon some time. But that touch—I knew that touch. Warm, calloused fingers wrapped around mine, nothing like Balthazar's icy caress that left poison in its wake. My whole body responded, a wave of recognition so powerful it nearly brought dropped me to my knees. Where Balthazar's touch brought numbness and terror, this... this was life flooding back into a frozen limb. Painful and beautiful and real. Every point of contact burned with memories of safety, of nights spent wrapped in strong arms that protected instead of imprisoned.

He drew me out with careful movements, like I was something fragile and precious, not the broken, scrambling thing I'd become. Metal scraped against my back as I crawled toward the exit. When I looked up at his hard face, I saw the evidence of his path to me—blood staining his chin, his shirt torn and soaked crimson. He'd carved his way through anyone who stood between us. And his eyes...god, his eyes...held that mix of fury and tenderness that no one, not even Balthazar, could fake.

"Is it really you?" The words scraped out of my raw throat. I'd asked this question a hundred times in a hundred dreams, only to watch his face twist into Balthazar's cruel smile. My fingers clutched his shirt, anchoring myself to this moment, this reality. "Please be you."

"It's me." His voice cracked on the words. Then his arms were around me, pulling me against his chest with a desperation that matched my own. His heart thundered against my ear—that powerful, inhuman rhythm I'd grown to trust. I breathed in his scent, sharp, metallic and predator-sweet, searching for any trace of Balthazar's evil coldness. But where Balthazar's touch had always felt like ice seeping into my bones, Angelo's embrace burned with fierce protection, with a warmth that made me want to weep.

"You found me." The words came out broken, half-sob and half-prayer. After endless wandering, I was finally home.

His arms tightened around me, and when he spoke his voice held that dangerous edge that had made empires kneel. "I would have torn this city apart brick by brick to find you. Every person who helped hide you will beg for death before I'm done."

"I love you." The words ripped from my chest, raw and desperate. Through all the nightmares, all Balthazar's lies, every moment of terror—our connection had helped me through the darkness.

He was my life, my savior.

His hand cupped my face, thumb brushing away tears I didn't realize I'd shed. The gesture was achingly gentle, even as blood dripped from his sleeve. This was my Angelo

—ruthless king, tender protector, the monster who'd kill for me and the man who'd die for me.

"My light." His voice was rough with emotion as he pressed his forehead to mine. "In all this darkness, in all this blood and death, you're the one thing that keeps me from losing my humanity entirely."

The crash of a door being broken down somewhere in the building shattered our bubble of reunion. But for once the sound of violence didn't make me flinch. I knew those footsteps.

Sure enough, Enzo and Dimitri burst into the room, their presence confirming this was really happening. Like Angelo, blood dripped down their chins and stained their shirts. Behind us, Shannon still huddled in the vent, but she was safe now. We both were.

I cupped Angelo's rugged face in my hands, feeling the familiar angles beneath my fingers. "It's really you. I didn't think you'd ever find me." A sob broke free, releasing all the fear and doubt I'd been holding.

"I'll always find you, Serenity." His voice carried the weight of an unbreakable vow. "You're mine."

TWENTY-TWO

S *erenity*

I CURLED my fingers into his bloodied shirt, hanging on as tight as I could, tears blurring my vision. I leaned against his chest, wanting to inhale his scent and listen to his heartbeat forever. The events of the last few days had left me shaken, and each breath was ragged with exhaustion.

"Angelo, please take me home."

He kissed the top of my head, his lips lingering there for a moment. "I will." His voice was soft but carried a hint of steel that made me feel safe for the first time in days.

The door burst open with enough force to make me flinch. A man with long hair and a beard rushed in, his wild appearance making Angelo's arms tighten protectively around me. The newcomer's shirt was also splattered with blood, and purple bruises bloomed across his visible skin. His eyes darted around the room with desperate intensity.

"Shannon? Where is she? Is she alive?"

"I've got her." I looked over Angelo's shoulder to where Enzo stood, cradling a small form wrapped in his jacket.

"My god." The man ran across the room in three long strides, his hands trembling as he took Shannon from Enzo. "What did he do to you?" His strong voice broke on the last word, thick with emotion. He cradled her like she was made of glass, his fierce appearance contrasting sharply with his gentle touch.

Fear pricked at the back of my neck. "Angelo, who is that?" I whispered against his chest. I refused to let Shannon be tortured again.

"Ivan Toser. He's a wolf." Angelo's chin brushed against my hair as he observed the scene. "Shannon's his mate."

A burst of anger gripped me, my hands clenching into fists against his chest. "They practically killed her." My stomach dropped as I realized what Gage's betrayal meant —he'd sided with Balthazar against Trystan, helped take Shannon. In the mafia world, disloyalty meant death. "Trystan won't punish them, will he? Shannon's been through hell."

"Trystan knows who the real traitor is," he said, his voice carrying that lethal edge that reminded me exactly who and what he was.

I didn't want to think about mafia justice anymore. Shannon and I were both safe and all I wanted to do was stay next to Angelo. My muscles felt like lead, and I snuggled closer to him, seeking warmth and comfort. "Take me home. I never want to see this place again."

The world became a blur of motion, and before I knew it, Angelo was settling me into the plush leather back seat of the limousine. He pulled me onto his lap, one arm wrapped securely around my waist while the other hand smoothed my tangled hair gently.

A thought nagged at me, impossible to ignore despite my exhaustion. I looked up at Angelo, meeting those intense red eyes that seemed to glow in the dim interior of the car. "Can Balthazar..." I swallowed hard, forcing myself to continue. "Can he get inside Crescent Manor?"

Angelo's expression hardened, but his touch remained gentle. "No. It's warded."

The tension in my shoulders eased slightly, but questions still swirled in my mind. Where were Balthazar and Gage? Gage might well be dead, but the real danger to Angelo was Petar, trying to steal his crown—as if Petar could ever walk in Angelo's shoes.

The smooth movement of the limousine and Angelo's steadying presence slowly lulled me into a daze. As my eyes grew heavy, I listened to his breath and his heartbeat.

They were like music to my ears—a sweet rhythm that promised safety, promised home.

The city lights streaked past the tinted windows like shooting stars, and Angelo's thumb traced soothing circles on my shoulder. As I relaxed into the comfort of his embrace, I couldn't forget the look in Ivan's eyes when he'd seen Shannon—a mix of relief and rage that spoke of a love fierce enough to tear the world apart.

It was the same look I always got from Angelo. I knew he would find me. The surety of that knowledge was like a warm blanket around my shoulders—Angelo would always come for me, no matter what.

Enzo and Dimitri sat on either side of Angelo and me, making me feel like I had a wall of protection inside the limousine. All three vampires were on the alert, eyes scanning the darkness outside. Blood stained their clothes and skin, testament to the violence they'd unleashed to get to me. I didn't recognize the driver, but I assumed he was one of Angelo's men. He had blood dripping down his chin as well, the metallic scent of it filling the air.

I couldn't imagine the carnage back there. They must have killed dozens of wolves to get to me. No one had ever fought for me like that before. For the first time in my life, I truly belonged somewhere. Tears pricked my eyes at the realization, and I quickly blinked them away.

They must have killed countless wolves to get to me. No one had ever killed for me before. Steve had fought for me when we were kids, but this was different. Guilt and gratitude warred in my chest, making my heart feel too big for my ribs. My heart ached for the wolves who'd been forced to follow Gage and Balthazar, enslaved by circumstances like I had been. As for their willing followers—ice crystallized in my veins and I couldn't find any mercy in my heart.

I was humbled that Angelo and his men had carved such a bloody path to reach me. I wasn't just another disposable piece in someone's game - I was as important as Gianna or Elena.

I glanced closer at Dimitri. He had faded bruises on his face, as if he had recently received a severe beating. Dimitri caught me looking at him. His lips curved into that trademark smirk, but his eyes held a shadow of something darker—pride mixed with defiance, maybe even a hint of shame. "See something you like, princess? Trust me, you should see the other guy." His tone was light, playful even, but there was an edge underneath that suggested he knew exactly what I was thinking.

Angelo tensed beneath me and flashed his fangs at Dimitri.

"Your problem is you just don't know when to quit, Dragan," Enzo muttered.

That made me think Angelo had done this. Why? What had Dimitri done to deserve it?

But I didn't want an interrogation right now, I just wanted to get home. I was so excited to see Elena and Gianna again. They'd become like family to me.

Crescent Manor was warded, but the limousine was not: out here, we were vulnerable. Every shadow that passed over the windows made my heart jump, terrified that Balthazar and his men were following us. I shrank closer to Angelo, drawing comfort from his solid presence while silently urging the limousine to go faster.

The driver finally pulled into the driveway and got out to open the door. Enzo exited first, scanning the limousine and the surrounding area for threats.

Dimitri got out next, then after a brief minute he ducked his head into the car. "It's safe."

Angelo stepped out, still holding me in his arms like I was something precious. Dimitri held the back door open —watchful, eager to prove his renewed loyalty with every small service.

Elena and Gianna were waiting for us in the foyer, as if maintaining a vigil. Just the sight of them brought tears to my eyes and a lump formed in my throat. Gianna was like the sister I'd never had, who'd welcomed me into this dark world without judgment. Meanwhile Elena was the grandmother I'd always dreamed of—all warm hugs and kitchen wisdom, healing my wounds with comfort food and soft words.

"*Ma pauvre chérie.*" Elena's cool hands clasped my tear-stained cheeks. Something inside me melted at her touch, like always when she mothered me. After what seemed like weeks of cruel hands and crueler hearts, her gentle touch was like a balm to my battered soul.

Gianna embraced Dimitri fiercely as he crossed the threshold, not caring that her designer dress was getting covered in bloodstains from his shirt.

"I've got to get Serenity upstairs." Angelo's voice was quiet and authoritative as his gaze found Enzo. "Find out where Gage, Petar, Balthazar and the others disappeared to. Make sure to bring Petar to me alive."

I buried my face in Angelo's shirt, shuddering to think what would happen to Petar even though he'd stolen me from my home and tossed me to a psychotic wolf and a cruel demon. I would never forget the feel of their hands on me, their cruel laughter. Some nightmares didn't fade with waking.

Once again, the world turned to a blur and the next thing I knew we were in our room. Angelo set me down gently and closed the door with a soft click. The familiar sight of our sanctuary—the bed with its silk sheets, the leather-bound books on the shelves, the tapestries and paintings that spoke of his centuries-old existence—broke something inside me. I burst into tears.

"Shh." He pulled me into his embrace and just held me, his arms a cocoon around my shaking body. His voice was rough with emotion, something rare for him. "I'm sorry I wasn't there to protect you, Serenity."

I pulled away and wiped my tears, needing to see his face. "All I could think about was you. I kept calling out to you." My voice caught, remembering how desperately I'd screamed for him in my mind, praying he would somehow hear me.

"I know. I heard." His red eyes held mine, intense and serious.

It felt like the floor had dropped out beneath me. "What?"

"Every time you called for me, I felt it here." He touched his temple. "At first, it was just whispers, like fragments of a dream. But then they got louder, and with them came headaches. Images, too—flashes of where you were and what you were seeing." His fingers traced my cheek, and I could feel the slight tremor in them. "The plantation. Balthazar. That horrible room they kept you in."

I caught his hand, holding it against my face. "But how? Was I really calling out to you or was I just..." I swallowed hard, remembering those terrible moments of desperation. "Praying, hoping somehow you'd find me?"

He slipped his fingers through my hair, drawing me closer until our foreheads touched. "All I know is you've marked my soul, Serenity. I never stopped looking for you. No one can keep you from me. I'll always find you."

I pulled away reluctantly. "I want to take a shower. I need to wash off everything from that place—the bayou, the wolves, and especially Balthazar and his friends." My skin crawled at the memory of the demon's presence, of the wolf's rough hands. I needed to scrub away every trace of their touch, every moment in that plantation.

"Go ahead. Take as long as you need."

"No." I held out my hand, surprised at how much it still trembled. "I want you to join me. If you have time, I mean..." The words came out small and uncertain. Even after everything—the bond we shared, him coming for me and hearing my calls—part of me still feared he'd pull away and retreat into his role as the vampire king with more pressing matters to attend to than taking a shower with me.

Angelo's eyes softened with that rare gentleness that only I saw. He took my outstretched hand, his thumb brushing over my knuckles. "The only thing that matters right now is you." He drew me closer and I could feel the tension in his body, the careful way he held himself. "Let me take care of you, *cara mia*."

My breath hitched at the Italian endearment. Even now, still shaken and afraid, something warm bloomed in my chest at his tenderness. This was the Angelo that only I got a glimpse of—not a ruthless king, not a feared, ancient vampire, but the man who could bring me back from the edge with no more than a gentle touch, a loving word.

CHAPTER

TWENTY-THREE

S *erenity*

ANGELO CARRIED me into the bathroom that had a sunken marble tub and shower big enough for three. I stripped off my jeans and the shirt that Balthazar had given me. The bastard hadn't given me any undergarments—another sick way to make me feel vulnerable and exposed. The clothes were caked with Shannon's blood and I threw them into a corner, never wanting to wear or even see them again. The blood had soaked through in places, leaving rusty stains on my skin that sickened me. Shannon's blood. I could still hear her screams. I wrapped my arms around myself, trying to hold back the tremors those memories triggered. Even here in Angelo's bathroom, the sounds wouldn't leave me alone.

Angelo watched me silently. There was nothing sexual in his gaze—just a fierce protectiveness that steadied my shaking hands. His eyes tracked each bruise and scrape on my exposed skin, and although his expression remained carefully neutral, I saw his jaw tighten. The marks were a reminder of everything he hadn't been able to prevent, everything Balthazar and his men had done.

His eyes turned to midnight as his gaze locked on mine. "Who hurt you?" The words came out soft, lethal—the kind of quiet that preceded bloodshed.

I looked down, trying to hide the bruises around my neck. The same shame washed over me, hot and suffocating, just like when Freddie used to hurt me. "Gage," I whispered, the name bitter on my tongue. "He did this when I couldn't heal the Luparion Crystal."

I flinched when Angelo reached for me, my body reacting instinctively before my rational mind could catch up. The hurt that flashed across his face was quickly replaced by something darker and more lethal.

Angelo lifted my chin, his touch gentle but his eyes promising death. "He'll never hurt you again. I protect what's mine."

"I know," I said through my tears, wanting Angelo's hands and lips on my body. He'd be the one to erase my nightmare, not just wash away the physical traces of that place but replace every cruel touch with his gentleness, every fearful moment with his love.

I stepped closer to him, my fingers finding the buttons of his shirt. They were stained with blood, too: blood he'd spilled coming for me. "Touch me," I whispered, my voice breaking. "Make me forget everything except you."

His eyes darkened, but he caught my trembling hands in his. "Serenity…" My name was a prayer on his lips. He brushed away my tears with his thumb, his touch so tender it made fresh ones fall. "Let me take care of you, cara mia. Let me make you feel safe again."

I gave him a mischievous smile. "Perhaps you should take off those stained clothes, my king."

I heard his clothes rustle and fall as I turned on the hot water, its force pelting against the white tile walls. Angelo's hands gently turned me to face him, and I couldn't help but admire his sculpted body—the well-defined muscles of his arms, the broad expanse of his chest, the narrowness of his hips. My eyes were drawn to his bulging cock, and my cheeks flushed with desire.

He took my hand, pressing it to his lips. Without breaking his gaze, he led me to the shower and checked the temperature. Steam curled around us as we stepped inside together. The warm water ran down in rivulets between us as he drew me closer, until nothing existed but his eyes and the heat of his body against mine.

I closed my eyes, letting the water cascade over me in sheets, soaking my hair and washing down my body. Each warm drop carried away another fragment of fear, another moment of pain from the past few days. Angelo had found me. Had saved me. My protector, and my salvation.

When I opened my eyes again, Angelo had turned around, his muscular frame now between me and the spray as he faced me. Water traced a path down his chest, highlighting every powerful line of him. My trembling fingers followed one droplet as it trickled down. This was the man who'd torn through armies to reach me, who'd painted the world in blood to bring me home. His muscles tensed under my touch, a reminder of the lethal strength he contained—although he had never been anything but gentle with me.

Desire pooled low in my belly as his hands slid up my arms, leaving trails of heat in their wake. I belonged to him, body and soul, and right now I needed him to remind me of that. Needed him to chase away the memory of other hands with his touch. My fingers curled against his chest as he drew me closer, our bodies molding together perfectly.

He picked up a bottle of shower gel and squeezed some into his hands, creating a thick lather. Something in his eyes darkened.

"I can feel your need to be clean of them," he murmured. "Let me help with that."

I froze, staring up at him. "You can feel what I'm thinking?"

His lips curved slightly, but his eyes remained intense. "Of course. You're part of me now, Serenity."

My heart stuttered as pieces clicked into place. All those desperate nights in captivity, when I'd felt less alone, less broken… "When I was in that cell," I whispered, "sometimes I felt… safer. Protected. Like someone was watching over me." Tears pricked my eyes as the truth sank in. "That was you, wasn't it? You were there with me somehow."

"You're powerful, Serenity. You were able to contact me. Unfortunately, I couldn't contact you." His kiss against my neck held a hint of regret, as if the memory of that one-sided conversation still tormented him. "But it's how I found you."

His hands moved gently as he massaged the suds over my breasts, each touch replacing violation with worship, sending shivers of pleasure through me. Without hesitation, I opened my mouth and he bent down to me, our lips meeting in a fervent kiss. My tongue tasted the metallic tang of blood, but all I could think about was Angelo— vampire…king…and mine.

My fingers traced a path down his chiseled chest, eliciting a sharp intake of breath from him. As I wrapped my hand around his throbbing length, his gaze met mine intensely.

"You're playing with fire, Serenity," he warned, his voice low and husky. But the desire in my veins was undeniable as I continued to slide my hand up and down his velvety shaft, aching to feel every inch of him.

"Maybe I want to get burned," I breathed, my body on fire with need.

He guided me back until my legs met the shower bench. His hands settled on my hips, easing me down onto the marble. He knelt in front of me, water cascading over his powerful shoulders as he trailed kisses down my neck, and I arched my back, surrendering to his touch. His sharp fangs grazed my skin, making me shiver with both fear and excitement. He moved a hand lower, caressing my stomach before plunging a finger into my wetness. I gripped his shoulders and groaned, the combination of pleasure and pain overwhelming me and making my blood boil with desire.

With a gentle touch, he trailed his tongue along my neck, sending shivers down my spine. As he moved lower, his mouth found my breast and he pulled one nipple between his lips, causing pleasurable tingles to spread throughout my body. His skilled tongue danced along the most sensitive parts of me, igniting a fire that threatened to consume me. I tangled my fingers in his wet hair, pulling him closer as I moaned wantonly in response to his touch.

The steady rhythm of the water, the subtle movement of his lips, the calculated flicks of his tongue... It all sent me spiraling into a state of pure ecstasy, driving me closer to the edge with each passing moment. The warm, refreshing water droplets cascading over my skin added to the overwhelming sensations building inside me. My senses were heightened as I was consumed by his touch, lost in the rhythmic dance between our bodies. It was like being tossed on a tempestuous sea, with waves crashing and winds howling, but I wouldn't want to be anywhere else but here.

He gently parted my legs, his warm breath caressing the sensitive skin of my inner thighs. Slowly, his skilled tongue left my breast and made its way down to my most intimate place. His dark hair glistened, water plastered to his skin as his head settled on my blond curls, eagerly exploring every inch. My hands gripped the marble bench, my body trembling with anticipation as he continued to tease and please me with his wicked tongue. With each lick and kiss, I felt myself further consumed by pleasure and losing myself more in a world of sensation and desire.

"You taste exquisite," he murmured, his voice like a dark promise.

"I need you," I whispered, feeling the blood rushing between my legs.

"And you'll always have me," he replied, his tone possessive yet tender. "Just me, nobody else."

Every nerve in my body sparked at his words, like matches being struck against sandpaper. "Take me," I pleaded, unable to deny the overwhelming pull towards him.

With a sudden burst of strength, he lifted me off the

bench and pressed my back against the cold, wet wall. My thighs quivered under his firm grip, his throbbing erection pressing against my leg. Then with one stroke he thrust inside, stuffing me completely with his thick cock. The sensation was overwhelming, flooding me with pleasure mingled with a slight sting of pain.

My entire body was ablaze with desire as he slid in and out. Every nerve in my body was alight, sending sparks of ecstasy coursing through me. Each thrust drove me closer to the edge, building a tsunami of pleasure that threatened to consume me entirely. This was what I yearned for—his control, his touch. It banished any lingering shadows from the past few days and replaced them with pure, unadulterated bliss. The intensity of our union left me breathless, lost on a sea of pleasure.

His scent marked every inch of me, erasing every trace of Balthazar like holy water burning away corruption. His toned and powerful body pressed me firmly against the marble shower wall, trapping me in his embrace, keeping me from falling. His touch as his fingers held my trembling thighs was both gentle and possessive. We moved together in a wild and primitive dance, each thrust of our hips sending sparks of pleasure through my entire being.

I trusted him. He was the light I would always reach for, the light that would chase away every shred of darkness.

He plunged deep within me, claiming me utterly. The hot water cascading down our bodies only added to the intense sensation of being consumed by his desire. I was lost in a sea of bliss, completely surrendering to him—mind, body, and soul.

Our slick skin slid against each other's desperately. The scalding water rained down on us like a torrential downpour, swallowing our moans and cries. My hips collided with his, the impact echoing off the walls intensifying our desire.

He threw his head back, revealing sharp fangs dripping with hunger. Without hesitation, he sank them into my quivering flesh. Fire erupted through my veins, igniting every nerve in an explosive wave of pleasure.

I screamed out his name. My fingers dug into his broad shoulders. He responded with one final thrust, driving deep inside of me and releasing his hot seed. I let out a ragged breath and collapsed, my body trembling with pleasure and exhaustion, reveling in his arms holding me against his hot flesh.

He smiled down at me as his hips still pulsed against mine. "The water's turned cold."

"Funny, I didn't notice." I kissed his wet chest and smiled as he drew in a quick breath. "Thank you. You don't know how much I needed this."

"I do, in fact." He kissed me deeply. "Remember, I can read your mind now. For the record, Nephilim, I wanted this as much as you."

I gazed up at him lovingly, my heart overflowing. "Then you also know how much I need you."

He chuckled. "Indeed I do."

My fingers traced patterns on his chest, the steady rhythm of his heartbeat soothing me. Our eyes met, and in his gaze I saw a reflection of all the love and devotion we shared. "I love you," I whispered again, the words a promise and a declaration. There was nowhere else in the world I would rather be than in the shower with him, sharing this moment, with him deep inside me—even if the water had run cold.

TWENTY-FOUR

ngelo

I GAZED DOWN AT SERENITY, at her blue eyes so full of passion. For centuries, I'd ruled with ice in my veins. Now this woman had done the impossible—made me feel warm and human again.

I would never let anyone take her from me again. She was mine to possess, to take care of. The thought of Gage touching her, of Balthazar keeping her locked away, turned my blood to acid. They would pay for every mark on her skin, every moment of fear in her eyes. I'd ensure their deaths were slow, particularly Gage's. The wolf had dared to lay hands on what was mine.

She still had black and blue bruises on her fair skin. Each one meant a death sentence I would personally deliver. The other families might view Serenity as my weakness, but they'd soon come to learn she was my strength, and my enemies would understand that hurting her meant signing their own death warrant. No territory, no amount of power, compared to having her safe in my arms. The king of New Orleans had finally found his queen, and God help anyone who tried to come between us.

I gently lowered her legs and withdrew from her, my breathing slowly returning to normal. The bathroom lights cast a warm glow on her skin, radiant from our intense passion. She reached for the bottle of gel and lathered it onto her skin before rinsing it off, each movement stirring a deep hunger inside me.

"Shall I wash your hair?" My voice was husky with desire.

She laughed, a sound that brought a smile to my face. "Yes, if you want."

I poured the shampoo onto her scalp, my fingers gently massaging as she purred like a contented cat. The scent of coconut and vanilla in the air added to the sensual atmosphere. I rinsed away the suds, admiring the way her hair shone under the water, reflecting the sunlight streaming through the bathroom window. It was a simple act, but in that moment, it felt as intimate as our lovemaking.

"I'm so tired," she mumbled as I rinsed her hair again. Her body swayed slightly against mine, exhaustion evident in every line of her body. The events of the last few days, the fear, the trauma—all of it was catching up with her.

I cursed myself. I shouldn't have taken so much blood from her. But the way she'd offered herself to me without hesitation had made my fangs ache. And I'd selfishly wanted to erase every trace of her captivity with my touch. I should have shown more restraint.

I patted the towel over her body and dried her blonde hair. She was like a weary goddess. I slipped her robe on, my movements gentle, as if she might shatter. Her skin was too pale, her pulse slower than I liked. The dark circles under her eyes stood out like bruises. She'd been missing for almost ten days, nearly driving me mad. She must not have slept these past few days, especially with Balthazar haunting her. She needed rest to replenish what I'd taken. What kind of protector was I if I couldn't control my own hunger?

But that had to wait. She'd been taken when my back was turned, and Gage had gotten to her far too easily. I had to prevent that from ever happening again, needed to understand every weakness he'd exploited.

I fingered the blue silky robe that matched her eyes. "How did Gage kidnap you?"

She yawned, tying the robe's belt around her slim waist. "You don't know?"

"No."

She sighed heavily. "Petar told me that you and Joy were in a van outside and that Joy was wounded." Her voice caught, heavy with self-recrimination. "I was so foolish! I believed him. He's crazy, Angelo. He wants to be king."

King? Ice crystallized in my veins as rage exploded through me. Petar. My own lieutenant. The betrayal gutted me, leaving nothing but murderous rage, making my fangs elongate. He hadn't just betrayed me—he'd used Serenity's compassion against her, knowing she would rush to help Joy. The fool dared to challenge my crown by stealing my queen. My vision edged with red. He would beg for death long before I finished with him.

"None of this is the least bit your fault." I lifted her chin and stared into her eyes.

A weak smile curved her lips before she yawned again, swaying on her feet. I caught her against my chest, steadying her exhausted body. Even half-asleep, she curled into me like she belonged there. Trustingly. After everything she'd been through, she still trusted me completely. The weight of that trust sat heavy in my chest.

I lifted her into my arms, carrying her to our bed. She murmured something unintelligible, her face pressed into my neck. The scent of fear still clung to her even after the shower. How many nights had she lain awake in that plantation, terrified of what dreams might come? How many times had she called for me while that demon tormented her?

Balthazar would pay for every hour of sleep he'd stolen from her. And Gage would die for hurting her. But right now, she needed me here, needed to feel safe enough to finally rest. I could hunt later.

I pulled the cover over her. "Please don't leave me." she mumbled.

"Never." I crawled in naked next to her and pulled her close, her body fitting against mine perfectly like she was created for this space. She spooned herself into me, seeking my protection even in sleep. The weight of her trust humbled me —after everything she'd endured, she still turned to me like I was her sanctuary. I resisted the temptation to take her again, though my body ached for her. She was exhausted. After what she'd endured, peace was the best thing I could give her now.

Her blond hair cascaded over her pillow like a halo, and the beast within me quieted at having her here, safe in my arms. My mate. My light. The other half of my damned soul. The days without her had been a special kind of torture—sensing her pain and her terror but being unable to reach her. Each scream that had echoed through our connection had shredded what was left of my humanity. Only her presence now, warm and real, kept the monster inside from painting the world red.

I knew this peace was temporary. This business with Balthazar, Petar, and Gage had to end. If not, Serenity would never truly be safe. I had too many enemies circling, waiting for another chance to take her. If they hadn't learned their lesson from the bloodbath I'd created finding her, and they dared to try again, I wouldn't just kill the perpetrators—I would dismantle their entire world. Anyone who even thought about touching her would suffer until they begged for death.

Serenity's soft snores told me she was asleep. I could still taste her sweet blood, so pure and willing, mixed with the blood of Gage's whimpering curs, taken in violence and terror before they died. They had all been expendable. Not one of them knew where the coward had fled.

Pathetic. Gage hadn't even trusted his own men with his escape route. Although, considering how easily they'd broken under questioning, I suppose it was smart of him. It still wouldn't save him. New Orleans was my city. I had eyes everywhere, and Gage would need more than Balthazar's protection to survive what I had planned for him.

Business demanded I meet with Enzo and Dimitri to plan our next move regarding Petar, but the thought of leaving Serenity, even for a moment, made my blood turn cold. Petar had played his role perfectly—earning my trust, infiltrating my organization, waiting for the perfect moment to steal my queen. That serpent had wormed his way into my empire, and I had allowed it. Dimitri had seen through him, had warned me, but I had ignored his counsel. A king's mistake. One that would be paid for in blood.

Someone softly knocked on my door. No one would

dare disturb me unless it was important—they knew better than to test my patience when I had just reclaimed my queen.

I slipped from the covers, unconcerned with my nakedness. The door opened silently beneath my careful touch—Serenity deserved her hard-won peace.

Enzo stood outside my door. Of all my men, only he would risk my wrath in this moment.

I glared. "What?"

Enzo met my gaze, unflinching—another reason he was my second. "Trystan can't find Gage. Neither can Keir."

My jaw clenched. So Gage was still out there, still hunting my queen. The bastard had already proven he could breach my defenses, first by killing one of my men, then stealing Serenity from what was supposed to be an impenetrable fortress. Crescent Manor's security had failed twice now, but this wouldn't happen again. I would turn this place into a bloodied fortress if that's what it took to keep her safe.

Soft footsteps came down the hall and Dimitri approached us with a glass of bourbon in his hand. He eyed me up and down dubiously. "I hear birthday suits are all the rage these days."

I gave him a sharp look, not in the mood for any of his games.

He took a swig of bourbon, unperturbed by my silent warning. "You know what's funny? Keir just called." He swirled the bourbon in his glass, drawing out the moment like he always did when he had particularly lethal information. "According to him, while we were all playing hide and seek with our little princess, Steve DuPont was keeping himself busy." His lips curved. "Another girl's gone missing. And word is, he's the one that's been collecting them and leaving clues to lead the police to you, boss. Isn't that just...fascinating?"

Anger gripped me and. Steve had been setting me up, using my distraction with Serenity's kidnapping to play his games. No one double crosses me and lives to enjoy it.

I narrowed my eyes. "Why did Keir call you and not me?"

He shrugged. "He did call you. I guess you were busy with other business and didn't answer your phone."

I snagged my phone off the nightstand. Damn—a missed call from Keir. He must have tried to get in touch while I was in the shower with Serenity.

Dimitri's expression turned grimmer. "There's something else. Balthazar's been riding Steve's meat suit."

My jaw clenched as I considered this new information. Possession by a demon only ever resulted in death. Demons rode humans hard and discarded the broken remains like empty bottles. The kindest thing to do was to put them down. But why was Balthazar specifically targeting the DuPont family? The demon never made a move without careful consideration. There had to be a reason he'd chosen this particular piece to play.

I put my hands on my hips. "Contact Keir and Trystan. Find out why Balthazar is targeting the DuPont family. Every demon has a weakness—if we find his connection to the DuPonts, we find his vulnerability."

"Angelo?"

I turned around and saw Serenity sitting up in bed, her golden hair tousled, still wearing the blue silky robe. Her arms were wrapped around her waist like she was trying to hold herself together.

I frowned. "Serenity, go back to sleep. I'm sorry we woke you. I'll be back in a minute."

"No...I mean... I heard what you said about Steve DuPont. I saw him at the plantation." Tears filled her tired eyes. "Dimitri is right. Balthazar is possessing Steve, forcing him to kidnap women that knew you."

I motioned to Enzo and Dimitri. "You have your orders."

Dimitri and Enzo nodded and left. I shut the bedroom door softly and stared down at my queen, then slid into bed next to her and slipped a hand around the back of her neck. "You're exhausted." I kissed her full lips. "Don't worry about Steve or Louis."

She put her palm to my chest. "You don't understand. I can heal Louis and Steve, same as I did Enzo." Her voice wavered with exhaustion. She didn't mention how healing Enzo and Shannon had left her drained and vulnerable, but I could tell. This would be what Balthazar would want. A Nephilim's greatest weakness was their own compassion.

I sighed, memories of similar choices flooding back. Serenity didn't understand this dark path of possession— a path I needed to protect her from at any cost. I would do anything to keep her safe, even if it meant killing two people she considered family, even if it broke her heart.

I looked at her gently. "Enzo was bleeding and dying. He wasn't possessed by a demon. That's completely different. It's not something that can be mended like a physical wound."

She scowled, hurt flashing in her eyes. "You're saying I can't heal them?"

"You really can't, I'm sorry." My voice turned to steel. "Neither Enzo nor Shannon was possessed. Possession is extremely dangerous, Serenity. The demon has taken hold of Louis. Balthazar commands a host of demons and these demons are powerful and very dangerous. I forbid you even to try." The memory of finding her in that abandoned plantation was still too fresh, her bruises still too visible on her skin.

She narrowed her eyes, that familiar stubbornness rising. "Louis is like a father to me and Steve is like a brother."

"I know, Serenity. But I'm sorry, that's my final answer. I won't risk losing you again, especially to a demon." I gripped her chin, making her meet my gaze. "If you tried to heal Louis and Steve, that thing wearing their faces would rip you apart without blinking, and I'd have to make an example of the men who protected you, who gave you a father's and a brother's love. Don't ask me to do that."

She went still under my grip, her eyes filling with tears. "So you'll kill them instead?" The words came out barely above a whisper. "The men who kept me safe, who loved me when I was alone?"

"If it meant keeping you safe, yes."

She stared at me as if trying to decide whether I was telling the truth. The vampire king who'd slaughtered entire families without remorse, now struggling with the thought of killing two men?

Love had made me weak. Or maybe it had made me stronger.

"I thought you said you believed in me," she said softly.

"I do. But my job is to protect you. Balthazar is targeting the DuPont family for a reason, and I don't think it will end well."

She swallowed hard. "Do you think he intends to kill them? Don't lie to me, Angelo. Tell me the truth."

"People that are possessed are never the same, Serenity. Evil taints their soul. Even if you healed them... They wouldn't be the people you remembered." The truth felt like ash in my mouth. "A demon's corruption goes deeper than flesh and bone. He'll use their love for you to destroy them from the inside out."

"But how long have they been possessed?" she pressed. "Maybe it if it's not that long, then I can heal them." She was refusing to give this up. I needed to distract her and take her down a different path.

I rolled on top of her, pressing her back onto the bed. I wanted to erase this path from her mind. "No, Serenity. You can't. This is Balthazar. No one survives a possession from him. Trust me on this. Louis and Steve are now our deadly enemies."

"But—"

I opened her robe and placed my mouth on her breast, driving away her questions, taking her down a path of bliss and away from danger. Her protests dissolved into soft moans, her fingers threading through my hair as she arched into my touch, finally surrendering to the distraction I offered.

CHAPTER
TWENTY-FIVE

S *erenity*

FORTY-EIGHT HOURS after I'd been rescued, Angelo, Dimitri, and Enzo were hunting my captors. Gage had made the mistake of thinking he could break me, and with a demon like Balthazar backing him, the wolf shifter had gotten bold. Too bold. I knew Angelo wouldn't rest until he made them pay—my vampire mafia king wasn't exactly known for his mercy.

Meanwhile, I was stuck at Crescent Manor, feeling more like a prisoner than Angelo's queen. I leaned back in my chair in the library, trying not to think about the marks Gage had left on my skin. Luigi Bruno, my newly appointed guard, stood near the doorway, his usual stoic expression on his face. He might as well have been a statue for all the conversation he offered. Angelo's orders were clear—I wasn't to leave the grounds. Luigi took that directive with unwavering seriousness.

If only Angelo had assigned Enzo or Dimitri instead. They would have talked to me while I pored over these endless books, searching for anything that might help. The whole situation with Louis and Steve consumed my thoughts. Everyone, from Angelo to Balthazar, claimed they were possessed, but Balthazar had also said I was powerful. Maybe, just maybe, Angelo was wrong about my inability to heal them. If there was even a chance I could...

I had been poring through the angel books, especially the ones discussing telepathy. Apparently, I had sent Angelo messages without even realizing it. If I could do that unconsciously, what might I be capable of with actual practice?

I traced my fingers over the ancient text, studying the illuminated manuscript. According to this, angels could purify corrupted areas, create shields of holy energy, banish evil entities, and enhance strength against dark creatures. They could also have visions of truth and sense dark curses. My heart beat a little faster as I read. Angelo and his men hadn't been able to determine where Gage, Balthazar, and their men had gone, but maybe I could.

Maybe if I concentrated really hard, I'd be able to find Joy as well—the sister I'd chosen, the one person who'd always been there for me. The thought of her being possessed too, her soul trapped while something else pulled her strings, made my stomach turn.

Luigi shifted by the door, and I resisted the urge to sigh. Despite what Angelo thought, I wasn't some delicate flower that needed constant protection. I'd survived living in the same house with my monstrous stepfather, Freddie. I'd endured being sold at auction like a piece of property. I'd even endured being kidnapped by a demon. And each time, I'd come out stronger.

My fingers tingled whenever they touched the book, as if the mere thought of these powers was awakening something inside me. I understood Angelo wanting to protect me, but I couldn't just sit here doing nothing. Not while Steve was trapped behind those soulless black eyes, Balthazar pulling his strings like a puppet. And Joy... God, if they'd done the same thing to her, if that demon had taken her as well... The idea of my two closest friends suffering made my chest so tight I could barely breathe. I had to find a way to help them. I had to.

But first, I needed to figure out how to practice without alerting my ever-watchful guard. Angelo had said he didn't want me practicing my powers unless he was here to supervise, claiming it would attract Balthazar's attention, even with Crescent Manor's wards protecting us. But what was the point of playing it safe when the demon already had Steve and possibly Joy, and had proven he could get to any of us?

My gaze drifted to the silver bracelets Luigi kept at his belt—magical bindings that would lock away my powers if I disobeyed. I'd seen his hand hovering near them whenever I got too quiet or still. As if he could sense my desperation building.

The smell of something spicy drifted into the library and my stomach growled. I glanced at my watch. It was nearly three o'clock and I had only had a piece of toast at breakfast.

"*Excusez-moi, monsieur.*" Elena's soft voice drifted into the library.

Luigi growled, "Angelo said…"

"She needs to eat. You don't want me to tell him that you refused to allow her to eat, do you?"

Luigi turned sideways with a grunt and allowed Elena into the library. She carried a tray with a crock of French onion soup and a loaf of French bread with some butter. There was also a small salad with goat cheese, some cut up apples, and a few olives.

"Elena, that looks wonderful." I pushed away the book I'd been studying, trying to casually flip away from the page about angelic essence tracking. As I moved to close it, that same tingling sensation I'd been practicing with earlier sparked through my chest.

Elena gasped softly. "*Mon Dieu*! You're glowing, *ma petite*!"

I quickly clamped the feeling down, but Luigi was already moving forward, alert. Elena, however, didn't seem alarmed—if anything, her eyes sparkled with interest.

"No sir, nothing like this onion soup in that terrible place, I can assure you," I said with a laugh, trying to redirect attention to the food. My heart was pounding, but Elena's curious look made me wonder just how much she understood about what I was.

Elena smiled and headed toward the door, not before giving me a subtle wink that Luigi didn't see.

"Is Angelo back yet?"

She sighed and shook her head. "Not yet, *chérie.*"

Luigi stepped aside to allow Elena to pass, his suspicious gaze lingering on me longer than usual. I focused on the soup, pretending I didn't notice, but my mind was racing. Elena hadn't seemed surprised by the glowing—just how much did she know about Angelo's and my world? More importantly, would she keep my secret?

The soup was long gone, but I couldn't focus on my book anymore when I returned to my reading. The words about angelic shields kept blurring together, even as they nagged at me. I closed my eyes, pretending to be resting. Power hummed beneath my skin, different from the visions I'd sent Angelo. The book had described divine shields as extensions of grace, like a bubble of pure light. Was that what I was feeling now?

Steve's possessed face flashed through my mind—those black eyes, that twisted smile that wasn't his. I had to find a way to save him.

Without considering that Luigi might be watching, I reached for that tingling energy inside me. Light blazed beneath my closed eyelids as I imagined pushing it outward, pictured creating a barrier of pure grace around myself. The air crackled with energy.

"*Santa Maria!*" Luigi's sharp exclamation made my eyes snap open.

A dome of shimmering golden light surrounded me, rippling like sunlight on water. For a moment, triumph surged within me—and then the drain hit. It felt like all my energy was being siphoned away at once. The shield flickered, and a dark presence flashed through my awareness, distant but distinct. Balthazar. He was somewhere north of here—

The shield collapsed. I slumped forward, my vision going dark at the edges. My hands trembled as I gripped the armrests to keep from sliding out of the chair.

"*Fermatevi!*" Luigi had his phone out, frantically dialing. "Angelo, sir, she's doing something with her powers—there was light everywhere, and she almost passed out." He hesitated, his hand hovering over the silver bracelets at his belt, and he whispered low. "Should I put on the bindings?"

I blinked in surprise. Was that actually reluctance in Luigi's voice? Maybe my stone-faced shadow wasn't as cold as I'd thought.

"Wait," I tried to say, but my voice only came out as a whisper. The room wouldn't stop spinning, either. But through the exhaustion, hope flickered. For just a moment, I'd sensed Balthazar's location. If I could do it again, get better and stronger at it...

Maybe I could find him. Maybe I could save Steve.

But first, I had to figure out how to stand up without falling over.

Running footsteps came down the hall. "Serenity, Serenity." Elena ran over to me. "*Mon chérie*, what has happened to you? You're so pale."

"I don't know... Maybe the last few days are catching up with me." I hated lying to her, but I needed to be strong enough to save the people I love.

She put her arm around my shoulder and took my arm, helping me to my feet. "*C'est assez*. Enough. You need rest. The books can wait until tomorrow."

My legs buckled, and I sagged against her like a marionette with cut strings even as heavy footsteps approached, thundering down the hall.

"*Capo*..." Luigi's shoulders hunched with nervous deference. "I was watching her like you ordered, but—"

Angelo shouldered past him into the library, his presence filling the room like a black storm cloud. Enzo and Dimitri materialized in the doorway, their chilling stillness more threatening than any drawn weapon.

"What happened?" Angelo crossed the room in three swift strides and lifted me into his arms, his face hard with barely contained fury. "Report, Luigi. Now."

"She started glowing, *Capo*," Luigi said, standing at

attention. "Never seen anything like it. The whole room was lit up like St. Peter's Square at Christmas."

I frowned at Angelo, trying to focus through the fog in my head. "How did you get here so fast?"

"We were already on our way back when Luigi called." His voice was softer when he spoke to me, but I could still feel tension thrumming through him. Someone was going to pay for this—I found myself hoping it wouldn't be Luigi.

Angelo carried me up to our room, cradling me against his broad chest. "What were you doing?"

I stiffened at his patronizing tone.

"Angelo, I'm not a fragile porcelain doll. I need to be helping." Even as I said those words, I fought to keep my eyes open.

He kissed the top of my forehead. "What you need, sweet Nephilim, is rest."

He laid me down on our bed. Too tired to argue, I stared up at the ceiling, my vision still swimming with images of Balthazar. Telling Angelo would mean watching his face darken with that dangerous fury, might even mean those silver bindings clicking around my wrists. But keeping secrets from him... God, hadn't we learned the hard way that secrets got people hurt? Got them killed?

I opened my eyes and stared up at him. I clasped his rugged cheek, steeling myself. "Angelo, I saw him."

His eyes narrowed. "Who?"

"Balthazar."

His eyes widened. "Here at Crescent Manor?"

"No. I had a vision, like I did with you. He's nearby. Not in the bayou. North of here. I can sense him. Evil. So full of hatred."

"Are you sure?"

I nodded. "Yes. Angelo, I created a shield around me. I can protect us when we go into battle. We won't be defenseless."

He stretched out beside me, his body warm and solid against mine. With a gentle hand, he tilted my chin up to meet his gaze. His eyes were intense, filled with determination and something else I couldn't quite place. "You're not going into battle," he said firmly.

I opened my mouth to speak, but whatever protest I'd planned died as his lips found mine. His kiss was soft yet demanding, and I melted into him despite my best efforts to resist. His arms wrapped around me, pulling me closer as the kiss deepened, until there was nothing left in my world but him—his warmth, his touch, his taste. Everything else faded away like smoke in the wind.

As always, he had a way of possessing me completely and igniting a passion that burned hotter than any battlefield.

CHAPTER
TWENTY-SIX

S*erenity*

I SHOULD HAVE STOOD my ground and begged him to listen to me, but Angelo had a way of sweeping me up in his fervor. His touch ignited a fire within me that was more than just desire. It was pure energy surging through my veins. My depleted powers sparked back to life wherever his skin met mine, filling me with a dangerous mix of strength and need. My heart raced as I let him take control, lost in the chaos of it all, knowing I should fight this but craving both his touch and the restoration of my power.

The smooth strands of his jet-black hair cascaded down onto my cheek, tickling it ever so slightly. His lips trailed along my throat and the hollow of my neck, sending shivers down my spine. I moved my leg against his, aching for more contact. He brushed his sharp fangs against my skin, causing me to gasp with pleasure. Fire burned bright within me, ignited by his touch.

I slipped my hands under his shirt hungrily, desperate to feel the warmth of his bare skin against mine. The low growl that escaped from his throat only fueled my desire further, and I could feel his body tensing as our bodies pressed together. The feel of his hard, throbbing cock against my thigh sent waves of arousal through me, mixing with the heat already coursing through my veins.

As his lips brushed against the sensitive skin of my neck, his low voice rumbled through my body like a warm caress. "What were you researching, little one?" he murmured.

My mind struggled to keep up as his hand slowly slipped down to trace a path over the curves and planes of my body. I slipped my hands into his pants and squeezed his firm buttocks. My research felt very unimportant now, overshadowed by the searing pleasure that radiated from his touch.

His fingers reached their destination, igniting every nerve ending in my body. I could barely form words as I gasped out, "Powers...angel powers." All thoughts and desires had melted away except for the exquisite sensation of his hand stroking my secret curls so expertly.

With a gentle yet insistent touch, he lifted my shirt up and placed feather-light kisses down my chest. As his warm lips traced their way across my skin, a trail of fire followed behind. Anticipation built within me as he pressed his mouth against the fabric of my bra, sucking harder with each passing moment. My heart raced as I pulled him closer to me, feeling the heat and desire between us.

His voice broke through the haze of pleasure, reigniting my mind. 'What kind of powers?' His words were like sparks, kindling a flame within me. Was he interrogating me? If so, he was doing it with such prowess and elegance that it felt more like a seduction than an interrogation. He directed me toward his desires without even uttering them aloud, leaving me wanting more with each passing moment.

"I... I wanted to see if I could protect you and the others...from demons." It wasn't exactly a lie. I couldn't tell him about trying to expel demons, though. He'd lose his mind if he knew I was thinking about confronting Balthazar.

"That's not quite true, is it?" Angelo's voice went dangerously soft. "We're connected, remember. I can read your mind." His grip tightened. "You can't expel a demon, Nephilim. You're not that powerful—Balthazar would only toy with you. Break you."

He swirled his tongue down to my belly button, sucking it, driving me crazy. I thrashed on the bed as he made his way lower. He pulled down my pants and underwear, then tossed them onto the bed.

Cool air brushed over my hot skin and I stared down at his dark head. He glanced up at me as he kissed my mound. "Mi vita, listen to me. Your power, your fierce fire—they're what made me fall for you. But Balthazar is not just another demon. He harvests souls like others collect trinkets, and the thought of him getting anywhere near you..." His voice turned rough. "Promise me you'll be careful. I can't lose you."

My throat tightened at the raw emotion in his voice. This was the Angelo few people ever saw—the one who could be tender, who loved with the same intensity he ruled. His fear for me was real, and it made my own deception cut deeper. But how could I turn my back on Steve and Joy when they needed me most? When every moment I delayed could mean losing them forever?

His hot tongue flicked against my sensitive clit, and I couldn't help but cry out in pleasure.

"I promise, I promise," I panted, even as my heart ached with the lie.

"You can't save them on your own," he murmured against my skin.

I stiffened. I kept forgetting he could read my mind.

"I know what you like, Nephilim. Not just saving the people you love, but how you want me to pleasure you."

His words sent heat racing through my veins. Even now, with Steve and Joy in danger, Angelo could make me forget everything but the feel of him, the need for him. It wasn't fair how well he knew me—both my desperate need to protect and my desperate need for him.

With a firm grip, he spread my trembling thighs even wider, exposing me completely to his eager mouth. My breathing became erratic as he worshipped me, his skilled tongue exploring every inch of my core. Each stroke and lick sent shivers of pleasure through my body, building up a pressure that threatened to consume me. I screamed his name as I reached the peak of ecstasy, my entire body quivering and writhing under his touch. The intense sensations left me panting and gasping for breath as I slowly came down from my euphoric high.

With a quick tug, he unbuckled his pants and shoved them down below his hips. I could feel the heat radiating from his body as his rigid cock pressed against my thigh. His breath was hot in my ear as he whispered, "Turn over. Get on your hands and knees."

My heart raced with anticipation. "What?" I forced the word past frozen lips.

"I'll bring you pleasure like you've never known," he continued, his hand sliding down my back to rest on my hip.

The world narrowed to just his touch, his voice, the fire he ignited in my blood. This was Angelo's real power over me—not the protection, not any rules, but how easily he could make me forget everything else. One touch and I was lost, my body betraying every resolution I'd made to stay focused on saving my friends.

Trembling, I slowly got on my hands and knees, feeling exposed and vulnerable. He grabbed my hips firmly in his hands before suddenly shoving inside me without warning. A gasp of pleasure escaped my lips as he buried himself deep. With each powerful thrust, I could feel him hitting all the right spots, bringing me to heights of ecstasy that I had never experienced before. The sound of our bodies slapping together echoed through the room, mixing with our ragged breaths until we were both lost in the heat of passion.

A tidal wave of pleasure cascaded over me, roaring like a mighty river. His touch was electric as he slipped his hand around and stroked my clit, sending spirals of tingling sensations through my body. My senses were overwhelmed as another orgasm ripped through me, leaving me blind to everything except the intense waves of pleasure coursing through me. It was as if every nerve ending in my body had exploded, dancing and pulsating with ecstasy.

Angelo, dark eyes blazing, bent over me. His fangs grazed my shoulder before piercing my skin with a sudden bite. My body tingled with waves of arousal that surged through me, intensifying the already feverish sensations.

Power radiated out from me, pulsing through my veins as a bright light filled the room. Our bodies trembled in unison, causing books to topple and fly across the room as I let out another scream of pleasure and release.

My legs trembled and threatened to give out, but his strong arms wrapped around my waist, holding me close to his muscular body. He thrust into me with a final, powerful stroke, releasing his hot seed inside me.

The pierce of his fangs that came next made me gasp —not in pain, but pure pleasure. This was what I'd been craving, what only Angelo could give me. Each time he took my blood it awakened something wild in me, fed my powers until they hummed beneath my skin like lightning. His bite was a drug, dangerous and addictive, making me feel more alive, more powerful than I'd ever felt without him. It felt like he was branding me, marking me as his and no one else's.

This was more than mere feeding—it was a declaration. Every pull of his mouth screamed that I belonged to the vampire king, and God help anyone who tried to take me from him. I arched into him, wanting more, craving everything he could give me.

With gentle care, Angelo lowered me onto the soft bed, still buried in me. My breath came raggedly as I gazed over my shoulder at him. His lips met mine in a searing kiss, both of us panting with desire. I could taste my own blood, and somehow that made it even more thrilling.

"I never want to leave you," I whispered against his lips.

His deep gaze held mine as he replied, "Nor I you. And I will do whatever it takes to keep you safe. You belong to me."

My heart swelled with love for this fiercely devoted vampire who had claimed me as his own. In that moment, I knew that I belonged to him completely, and would do anything to protect him, even it meant I had to break my word.

Slowly, deliberately, Angelo pulled out of me and ran his tongue along my shoulder. A shiver of pleasure shot through me, followed by a wave of strange sensations that flowed from the point where our bodies had connected. I looked up at him in confusion.

"What are you doing?" I asked breathlessly.

"Healing your wound," he replied softly, pulling me into his arms. I snuggled into his chest as he stroked my hair with gentle fingers. "Just rest now."

I closed my eyes and let myself relax against him, feeling the warmth of his body seep into mine. The faint scent of sandalwood hung in the air, adding to the soothing atmosphere. The steady sound of his heartbeat lulled me into a peaceful state, and before long, I drifted off into a deep sleep...

· · ·

MOONLIGHT OOZED *through the shattered stained glass like liquid mercury, casting twisted shadows across the sanctuary. Glass shards glittered like teeth on the putrid floor, crunching under my feet. The pews lay scattered like broken bones, their wood splintered as if something inhuman had torn through them in a murderous rage. The altar wasn't just damaged—it was desecrated, its ancient bricks stained with something dark that made my stomach turn. The massive crucifix hung upside down, swaying slightly even though there was no wind.*

Cobwebs thick as burial shrouds draped from the ceiling. Footsteps echoed on stone – slow, deliberate, savoring my fear.

Please be Angelo. Please be Angelo. Please, God, let it be Angelo.

But I knew it wasn't. Something ancient and evil pressed against my mind, and my soul recognized its jailer. Balthazar.

I commanded my legs to run and my throat to scream, but my body betrayed me. I stood frozen, a puppet waiting for its master, while my heart slammed against my ribs like it was trying to escape without me.

Balthazar spread his arms in a disgusting mockery of Christ's embrace. "Serenity, my love. How I've missed you." His voice held the soft menace of a snake's belly sliding across stone.

The blood didn't just drain from my face – it felt like it crystallized in my veins.

"Such delicious fear," he purred, moving closer. "You are smart to be afraid, my dear. Running from me was...most unwise. Though I must admit, I was intrigued when you reached out to me."

Terror exploded through my chest as his eyes ignited—not just red, but the wet crimson of fresh arterial spray. A whimper caught in my throat.

Contacted him? I never—

Then the memory came rushing back: the library...practicing with images...Balthazar's face materializing in my mind.

Shitshitshitshit

"Ah, now she understands." His smile revealed teeth too sharp, too numerous. "I felt you there, in that vampire's pathetic sanctuary. A mere baby, playing with powers you barely comprehend." His hand clamped around my arm like a steel trap. My muscles, my very will, belonged to him now.

"Let me show you, little Nephilim, what happens to those who think they can escape me."

My lungs burned with each ragged breath as I waited for death's mercy.

He caught my chin, claws pricking skin. "Death? Oh no, precious little one. I want you to live. Live, and remember." His face drew closer, sulfur on his breath. "I'm going to hunt you. And when I find you—not if, when—your vampire king will watch helplessly as I claim what's mine."

He broke into a sinister smile. "And then it will be your turn to watch as I rip out his heart."

His nails lengthened into obsidian razors.

The first slash came faster than a blink.

$\sim$

I BOLTED AWAKE, my scream echoing off the walls. Angelo was gone. Where was he? The agony was molten metal under my skin. With trembling fingers, I touched my arm.

Three cuts wept fresh blood onto the sheets.

They spelled a word:

Soon.

TWENTY-SEVEN

A*ngelo*

SERENITY'S SCREAM shattered the silence like a bullet through glass. I never should have left her. The ancient tome slipped from my fingers, hitting the floor with a dull thud that echoed my dropping heart. Every protective instinct I possessed roared to life. My mate was in danger.

I moved faster than shadows, the world blurring around me. Behind me, I heard Enzo and Dimitri's pounding footfalls.

The door splintered under my hand as I burst into our bedroom. My fangs descended, ready to tear apart whatever dared threaten what was mine.

"Serenity?" The word was a feral growl. Luigi was already there, sword drawn, methodically sweeping the shadows of our sanctuary. The second time. This was the second fucking time he'd failed to protect her on his watch.

"*Capo,*" Luigi stuttered, his face pale as moonlight.

I picked him up and tossed him across the room like a piece of garbage. The impact split the mahogany-paneled wall, sending splinters cascading to the floor. The sound of breaking wood echoed through the mansion's hallway. "What happened?"

"I—I don't know." He looked up at me with horror etched across his face, a thin line of blood trickling from his split lip. His designer suit was crumpled, dusted with debris. "She... she just started screaming, then locked herself in the bathroom. I swear on my life, *Capo*, I swear on my mother's grave—"

I grabbed him by his silk shirt, lifting him until his feet dangled and kicked. The fabric strained under my grip. "Was anyone with her?"

He frowned, sweat beading on his forehead. "No, *Capo*. No one. She was alone in the bedroom, sleeping. Everything was fine until—"

I dropped him, not caring how he landed. My boots echoed against the marble floor as I hurried to the bathroom, the scent of fear and blood growing stronger with each step. I slammed my fist against the ornate door, the wood creaking under the impact. "Serenity, open this door."

I could hear her soft tears on the other side—a sound that nearly shattered my centuries-old heart. Each quiet sob was like a silver dagger twisting in my chest. The beast within me stirred, sensing her distress. Someone had hurt her.

And I would rip out that someone's throat. Slowly. Painfully. They would learn why the other mafia families feared the name Angelo Santi.

"Open this door right now, Serenity, or I'll rip it off its hinges." My voice was deadly calm, but the threat was real. Nothing would keep me from her.

"Angelo, what's going on?" Enzo's voice came from behind me, tense with concern.

I didn't answer. All my focus was on the damn bathroom door that stood between me and Serenity. Between me and whatever had caused her pain. My fangs lengthened involuntarily, pressing against my lower lip.

A soft click was my answer.

I ripped open the door, the handle crushing under my grip. Serenity stood there, trembling slightly, a white bandage wrapped around her arm. The metallic scent of her blood filled my nostrils, making the predator in me stretch awake, snarling. But there was something else— something strange about the smell. Something that made my instincts scream.

"What happened?" I forced the words out through clenched teeth, fighting to maintain control.

"Nothing. I cut myself, that's all." She tried to move past me, her blue eyes avoiding mine, but I blocked her path with my body. The large marble bathroom suddenly felt suffocating, despite my lack of need for breath.

"You're lying." I clasped her wrist firmly but gently, my pale fingers cold and stark contrast against her warm skin. "Don't ever lie to me, *cara mia*. Not you." I softened my voice, though the rage still simmered beneath the surface. "Whatever this is, whoever did this—they won't see tomorrow's sunset. But I need to know the truth."

The overhead lights flickered, casting shadows across her tear-stained face. She looked up at me then, fear and something else—was it shame?—swimming in her eyes. "Angelo, please... Some things are better left in the dark."

"Nothing stays in the dark from me, sweet Nephilim. I've lived in shadows for four hundred years." I brushed a thumb across her cheek, wiping away a tear. "Now tell me who hurt you, so I can paint these walls with their blood."

She lowered her head. "I can't tell you."

I narrowed my eyes. "Why not?"

She stood there, crying quietly, still refusing to answer. I could use compulsion on her, but that was a very last resort.

"Enzo."

Serenity looked up at me wildly as Enzo approached, like a trapped doe sensing the wolves closing in.

"Hold her," I told him simply.

"N-no. Please, don't." She shook her head vehemently and pulled on her arm, but I held it in an iron grip, forged from centuries of existence.

"Sorry, princess," Dimitri drawled from the doorway, his signature smirk playing at his lips. "If there's one thing I've learned in my far too eventful life, it's that secrets have a way of getting everyone killed." He moved with preternatural grace to block Elena, who was trying to push past him. "Not this time, Elena. Some things require a... heavier hand."

Enzo clasped Serenity's arms, his grip firm but not cruel.

Serenity stared up, her big blue eyes filled with tears and fear. Each drop that fell from her lashes was like acid on my skin. "Angelo, don't do this."

"*Mon Dieu*, what's going on?" Elena cried behind me, struggling against Dimitri's restraining arm.

"What's going on," Dimitri answered, ice-blue eyes hardening, "is that someone decided to play with what belongs to a very old, very powerful vampire. And unlike my brother Valentin, I'm completely on board with the bloody aftermath that's about to unfold." He turned to Elena, his voice dropping to that dangerous velvet tone he reserved for serious moments. "Stay out of this one, Elena. Your heart of gold isn't needed here."

Gianna burst into the room, power crackling around her like static electricity. "Don't talk to her like that," she snapped. "Elena's the only one who makes this place feel like a home instead of a fortress. We need her kindness, especially now."

I barely registered their exchange. My focus remained laser-sharp on Serenity's bandaged arm. Not even Elena's humanitarian protests could stop me. I was going to find out what Serenity was hiding, even if I had to tear apart every secret in this city.

"Last chance, *tesoro*," I murmured, reaching for the bandage. "Tell me willingly, or I take what I want to know."

"*Dio mio*," Enzo breathed, gaping at something behind me.

I turned, following his gaze to the king-sized bed visible through the connecting door. The word "*SOON*" was already written across the white Egyptian cotton sheets in dark, crusted blood. Fresh crimson droplets were bleeding up through the fabric like macabre raindrops in reverse, forming new letters beside the original message.

"Balthazar," I growled, centuries of power thrumming through my veins. The demon who dared to think he could challenge the vampire king.

"No!" Serenity suddenly thrashed in Enzo's grip, her eyes wild and desperate. "Please, you don't understand. He'll kill you! That's the whole idea—he wants you to come after him!" Tears streamed down her face. "He said... He said he'd make me watch while he tore out your heart."

The world went red. My fangs descended as rage

exploded through me, a fury so ancient and primal it made the windows rattle in their frames. The demon dared to threaten my mate with my death? Would make her watch? I could feel my power rolling off me in waves, turning the air arctic. Even Enzo took a step back, though his grip on Serenity never loosened.

"He threatened to make you watch?" The words came out in a deadly whisper, each syllable dripping with centuries of violence. My hands curled into fists. Balthazar had crossed every line—taking her friends, marking her for his sick game, threatening to break her with my death. The demon thought he knew what a monster was? I'd show him what a real monster looked like. I'd show him what happens when he threatens what is mine.

"Yes." She sniffed, her eyes glistening with tears.

Demons versus vampires were never pretty. "That's why you're not going to the battle."

The fresh blood continued its macabre dance across the sheets:

PRESTO... IL TUO SANGUE SARÀ MIO

Gianna murmured, translating with growing dread. "Soon... Your blood will be mine." Her eyes widened. "What does that mean?"

"He plans on possessing Serenity," I said grimly, rage coiling in my gut like a serpent. "Blood possession—one of the oldest, darkest forms of demon magic."

To take control of another's blood was to own their very essence, to make them a puppet dancing on crimson strings. It's what he'd already done to Louis DuPont. I refused to allow him to do the same to Serenity.

"Someone's feeling theatrical tonight," Dimitri murmured coldly, eyes fixed on the forming letters. "Though I have to admire the dedication to interior decorating."

Serenity's knees buckled, and Enzo slowly released his grip. "Angelo, please. You don't know what he's planning. Everything...kidnapping me, sending this message... It's all part of his twisted game."

I caught her before she could fall, my grip gentle despite the fury coursing through my veins. The same hands that had thrown Luigi against the wall for failing to protect Serenity.

"Look at me, *tesoro*." When she wouldn't meet my eyes, I tilted her chin up. "Balthazar made one critical mistake."

"What's that?" she whispered.

"He forgot who rules this city." My voice was soft, but it carried all the weight of my sovereignty. "I didn't become king by showing mercy to traitors."

More droplets began to surface on the sheets, bleeding upward against gravity to form new words with deliberate, taunting slowness:

CHALLENGE ACCEPTED

"Angelo." Serenity clutched at my shirt, her fingers trembling against the silk. "The others—"

"Let them come," I cut her off, wiping a tear from her

cheek with a gentleness that belied the murderous rage in my veins. "Every last one of them. Balthazar needs to be reminded why even the oldest vampires kneel in my presence."

"Well then," Dimitri drawled, his eyes darkening with bloodlust as he watched the blood letters shimmer in the dim light. "Shall we find out where this big party is going to be held?"

I studied Serenity but she avoided my eyes. "You know where, don't you?"

"No, I don't." She yanked her arm away from me and I released her, noting how her pulse had jumped at the lie.

"Serenity." I lifted her chin, my thumb gentle against her jaw. "He showed you, didn't he?"

"No—yes—but you can't go there, Angelo! I won't let him kill you." Her blue eyes filled with fresh tears, confirming my suspicions.

"The confrontation is coming whether you like it or not, Serenity. He wants you just as much as the other kings do—as much as I do," I said softly, remembering my own obsession when I first saw her. "He might even want you even more. That's what I have to find out."

She stared at me for several heartbeats, conflict warring in her lovely eyes. "He said... He said he knew my father. Do you think that's true?"

I shrugged, though the implications sent ice through my veins. "Possibly. Demons and angels are aware of each other." She gave me a puzzled look and I drew in a deep breath. "Serenity, surely you know your father has to be an angel. Which one, I'm not sure."

"Do you think Balthazar's plan has anything to do with my father?"

I drew her into my arms, breathing in her scent—sunshine and something otherworldly that even all my centuries of existence couldn't identify. "I don't know, Serenity. That's what I have to find out. If I knew his plan, then I'll know how better to protect you." I stroked her hair, feeling her tremble against me. "Please. Tell me."

She braced her shoulders, that stubborn light I'd come to both love and fear entering her eyes. "If I tell you, you have to take me with you."

"Never." The word came out like a growl.

She gripped my shirt, her knuckles white with desperation. "Listen to me, Angelo. I was able to make a shield in the library—"

I wasn't going to let her be a hundred miles near Balthazar. "Yes, and you also contacted Balthazar unknowingly." The memory of finding her in that hysterical fit after the dream terrified me.

"But—"

"Ah, you two might want to look at this. Balthazar sent has another secret coded message," Dimitri said, his voice tight with tension.

I glanced at the bed, where fresh blood was seeping through the sheets. Balthazar never did play fair.

BRING HER OR JOY DIES

The words were like a death sentence, and I felt Serenity go rigid in my arms. Joy—Serenity's best friend, whom we'd been hunting for weeks—was snared in Balthazar's web.

"Fuck. Fuck. *Fuck.*" Enzo slammed his fist into the wall repeatedly, cracking it. Each impact echoed his failure to find her before the demon did.

The choice wasn't really a choice at all. And Balthazar knew it.

TWENTY-EIGHT

S*erenity*

"*No!!!*" I screamed and arched my back as anger soared through me, hot and wild and uncontrollable. My power unleashed like a tsunami—the bed, dresser, television, and end table shot toward the ceiling as if gravity had reversed. The chandelier shattered, raining crystal daggers that suspended mid-air, catching the light like deadly stars.

Then everything crashed to the floor with devastating force. Wood splintered into thousands of pieces. The mattress caught fire, blue flames eating through the blood-stained sheets, devouring Balthazar's threats.

Something screamed. No, shrieked—an inhuman sound that made the windows vibrate, that drove even the ancient vampires to their knees. The sound of something ancient and terrifying awakening.

Black smoke burst from my skin, writhing like living shadows. Electric blue flames crawled up the walls and across the ceiling, consuming everything in their path. The air crackled with power that tasted of defiance and destiny.

Then the flames imploded with a final thunderclap, disappearing into nothingness and leaving in their wake the scent of burnt feathers and lightning.

Pain sizzled through my veins like holy fire, a battle of light versus darkness that tore a scream from my throat. Every cell in my body felt like it was being purified and purged as good and evil warred beneath my skin. The scratches on my arm didn't just fade—they burned away in agony, Balthazar's dark magic fighting against whatever divine power coursed through me. Where his mark had been, my skin now glowed with a faint, pearl-like luminescence, the last evidence of a war between Heaven and Hell fought in my own flesh.

Angelo grabbed my arms, nearly lifting me off the floor, his expression savage with worry. His fingers dug into my skin with barely contained strength, as if he feared I'd vanish if he didn't hold on tight enough. "Serenity. Damn it." His muscular arms were like iron bands around me as I contorted, writhing as another wave of holy fire scorched through my blood. The pain was beyond screaming now—it was a white-hot supernova burning away everything dark and corrupt, threatening to consume me entirely. My skin blazed with a light that made the vampires hiss and shield their eyes, but Angelo wouldn't let go, even as the divine power singed his body and smoke rose around us as if we were in the middle of a bonfire, thick and black and writhing with otherworldly power.

Enzo cried out. "Angelo, release her!"

"Never." His face turned dark, as if he was burning from the inside. A roar of pure agony tore from his throat, a sound that ripped right through me.

This was my fault. I was burning him. I breathed deeply, trying to rein in my power.

Calm down Calm down Calm down

My heart thundered against my ribs as I fought for control. The power coursed through me like a rushing river, resisting every attempt to dam it. Angelo's arms tightened around me even as his skin blackened, and I could feel him trembling with the effort to hold on.

"Please," I whispered, tears streaming down my face. "Please stop." I wasn't sure if I was begging my power or Angelo. The smoke swirled faster, hungrily searching for something to consume. Divine energy crackled through the air like lightning, and I could taste Heaven's fury sharp and bright on my tongue like the sharp bite of centuries-old whiskey.

Control it Control it Control it

A surge of energy exploded from deep within me, pure white light that cut through the black smoke. The windows shattered outward. Angelo's grip finally broke as he was thrown across the room. My feet left the ground, suspended in air as wings of light unfurled from my back, casting shadows that danced like living things on the walls.

A voice that wasn't mine tore from my throat, ancient and terrible: *"ENOUGH!"*

The room froze. Even the smoke seemed to pause mid-swirl.

Then everything imploded.

The light collapsed inward, a vacuum of power that sucked all the chaos back into my body like a black hole devouring stars. The energy that had been coursing through me vanished, leaving nothing but bone-deep exhaustion in its wake. The smoke dissipated, taking the last remnants of my strength with it. I dropped to the floor like a marionette released from its cross, my knees cracking painfully against the hardwood. Every breath I took felt like I was inhaling shards of glass, my lungs burning as if I'd been underwater for hours instead of minutes.

Silence fell, broken only by the sound of glass tinkling to the floor and my ragged breathing. My arms trembled as I tried to push myself up, but my muscles had the consistency of warm jelly. Sweat dripped from my temples, each drop carrying a piece of my remaining energy with it. Even my eyelids felt heavy, threatening to close despite the danger I knew still lurked.

"Angelo?" Fear clawed at my throat as I scanned the settling dust. My vision swam, but I forced my eyes to focus, to find him. The room was a war zone of my own making. Then—movement in the corner. Angelo. My heart lurched at the sight of his healing skin, the evidence of what my power had done to him. But his expression... I'd never seen him look at me quite like that before. Like I was something both magnificent and terrible.

"What am I?" The question slipped out before I could stop it.

"Something that Balthazar should be very, very afraid of," he said softly, reaching for me despite everything that had just happened. He pulled me into his arms, cradling my shaking body against his chest as my legs threatened to give out completely.

Enzo emerged from the smoke, his usually immaculate suit covered in debris, a thin trail of blood running from his temple where he had been struck. His eyes were wide with a mix of awe and wariness as he steadied himself against the wall.

Dimitri rose where he had been protecting Elena and Gianna in the far corner, his broad shoulders smoldering slightly where divine energy had caught him. He must have thrown them on the floor then shielded them with his body when the power exploded. Both women were pale but unharmed, clutching each other as they stared at me with newfound terror—or was it reverence? The vampire's usual calm demeanor had cracked, revealing raw amazement beneath.

Luigi crawled out from underneath what remained of the bed, scowling as if personally offended by the debris. His face was ashen, hands trembling as he brushed dust and splintered wood from his clothes with sharp, angry movements.

Angelo stroked my hair. "That wasn't demonic power, Serenity. I've seen demon power, and it burns red and black, corrupted and tainted." His voice carried the weight of centuries of knowledge. "But blue flames? That was angelic power. Pure celestial energy. Holy. The kind that could burn a dark creature like Balthazar to ash."

I looked up at him. "I've never felt anything like that before. What's happening to me?"

"Your power is strengthening. Maybe Balthazar had something to do with that, but he couldn't corrupt it. You're too strong. Your father must be extremely—" He broke off, studying my face as if seeing me in a new light, connecting pieces of a puzzle he'd been trying to solve since we met.

"You mean I could kill Balthazar?" Even saying his name took energy I didn't have. Weariness wound around me even tighter, making my thoughts as heavy as my limbs.

He shook his head, his expression grave. "No. Balthazar is only one level under Satan. Not even Michael the Archangel could kill him. But you might be able to banish him to Hell." His voice carried the dark wisdom of countless lifetimes. "That's why he wants your blood—angelic power as strong as yours could force him back to the Pit. He wants to possess you and corrupt that power before you learn how to use it against him."

My stomach lurched at the word "possess". The room spun slightly as the true weight of Angelo's words hit me. I wasn't just some random target—I was a weapon. One that could send a demon prince back to Hell. No wonder Balthazar had been so intent on binding me to him. "So that's why he—" I couldn't finish the sentence, the memories of what he'd done still too fresh—forcing me to heal Shannon again and again.

"I felt the darkness trying to consume me," I whispered, my voice shaking. "But I fought it. I think it was my love for you that kept me from going darkside, Angelo. Even in my weakest moment, it was you who bound me to the light."

His arms tightened around me, and I felt a low growl vibrate through his chest. "You fought off a demon prince's corruption. For me." His fangs descended, possessive hunger darkening his eyes. "Let Balthazar come. Let him try to take you away from me." He pressed his lips to my forehead, the gesture both tender and fierce. "He'll see what happens."

Enzo looked at Angelo. "But Balthazar will try and

steal her. He's not one to give up. Neither is Gage." His voice hardened. "He desperately needs her to heal the *Luparion Crystal*, especially now that Trystan is on the hunt for him."

"I know." Angelo's voice was heavy with grim certainty.

Dimitri glanced between us, his sardonic smirk deepening. "Well, this is a delightful plot twist. A demon lord teaming up with a wannabe wolf king. Gage wants to overthrow the current alpha, and Balthazar... what? Decided to play supernatural kingmaker for shits and giggles?" His eyes narrowed thoughtfully. "Unless there's something about wolf blood that our friendly neighborhood demon needs for his master plan."

Angelo met his gaze. "My guess is that Gage summoned Balthazar and sold him his soul in exchange for his help in becoming king."

I rubbed my slick forehead. "But Balthazar said that it was one of the four mafia kings who summoned him, not Gage. He just wouldn't tell me which one."

"Then we'll have to find out which king bears the mark of a demonic pact," Angelo said, his eyes fixed on me with new understanding. "Your angelic power—it can sense dark magic."

"Finally," Dimitri smirked, though his eyes tracked the swirling smoke with barely concealed unease. "Some concrete answers in this supernatural soap opera."

My heart picked up speed despite my exhaustion. The

air around me felt different now, and I tasted corruption on my tongue. A wave of darkness hit me, an oily slick sensation that made my skin crawl and my stomach swirl uneasily. I moistened my lips. "Something's happening. I taste something foul, and I feel like I'm going to be sick."

"Your angelic blood has gotten stronger," Angelo said grimly. "Strong enough that it can detect demonic magic. The mark of Hell can't hide from Heaven's power."

I looked around the room wildly, my heart hammering against my ribs. Everything felt heavy: my arms, my legs, even my eyelids. My powers, so overwhelming just minutes ago, were now as useful as a dead battery. "Demonic magic? Does that mean Balthazar came back?"

Pascal burst into the room out of breath. "We got trouble. Rankin and Hunter are here."

As if one crisis wasn't enough. Angelo's expression darkened as he looked at Elena and Gianna. "You two go down there and greet them. Offer them refreshments. I want everything to look normal."

"But Angelo—" Gianna protested.

He snapped his fingers. "Now."

Elena clasped Gianna's arm. "Come, *ma chérie.*"

Gianna grumbled and threw up her arms as she followed Elena out of the room. I envied their steady steps —even standing was becoming a monumental task.

Angelo turned to me, power radiating off him in waves that made my weakened knees want to buckle. "You, however, are staying put."

I pushed my shoulders back, ignoring how much effort that simple movement took. The room might be spinning, but I met his fierce gaze anyway. "But you just said that my angelic blood can detect demon magic." I swallowed against the lingering taste of corruption. "I need to be there when you question the kings. I'm the only one who can sense if any of them have made a pact with Balthazar."

His fangs descended, centuries of protective instinct warring across his face. The air grew heavy with his power, making Dimitri and Luigi exchange uneasy looks. Even in my drained state, I could feel the predator rising in him.

Enzo took a step forward. "You need to stay in control, boss. You don't want Rankin or Hunter suspect you're losing control."

"You're weak as hell." He grabbed my arm, gentle despite his harsh tone. "You don't want either Rankin or Hunter sensing you're weak right now. You're not going."

Pride made me square my shoulders again. "I'm not weak." The lie tasted bitter on my tongue.

"Please. You can barely stand." He pointed at Luigi. "Move her to the library. She gets hurt again and you and I are meeting in my interrogation room. Do I make myself clear?" The temperature in the room seemed to drop at his words.

Luigi swallowed, his Adam's apple moving up and down like he was trying to dislodge ice. "She won't."

I gritted my teeth and clenched my fists, fighting both

exhaustion and frustration. I wanted to argue, but if I did, he'd probably have Luigi tie me up. Angelo didn't make idle threats when it came to my safety. The thought of what his "interrogation room" might contain was enough to make even my sluggish mind wince in sympathy for Luigi.

Then again, if I was lucky, there might be a book in the library about angelic blood that could help me understand what I was becoming—even though right now just walking there felt like it would take whatever scraps of energy I had left.

TWENTY-NINE

ngelo

I HOPED I wasn't making a mistake allowing Luigi to guard Serenity. If he failed me again, he wouldn't leave my interrogation room alive.

Enzo and Dimitri flanked me as we headed to the living room.

Pascal trailed behind, guarding the rear.

"No, I don't want anything to drink," Trystan was growling in the living room when we walked in. He and Keir were seated on the couch. Elena held a tray loaded with sweet tea and cookies, her hands trembling slightly as she stood before them. Southern hospitality, even in the face of supernatural tension.

Anger rose in me like a tide of black ice as I entered the room. The wolf king thought he could come into my home and threaten my people? In New Orleans—my city, my territory? I let my predator surface, feeling my fangs descend. The temperature plummeted as darkness gathered around me like a cloak of shadows. "I hope you're not threatening my staff in my own home, wolf." My voice carried four centuries of lethal authority. The last person who'd threatened my people in my territory now fed the gators in the bayou.

I let my fangs descend. "I hope you're not being rude to my staff, wolf." My voice carried four centuries of lethal authority.

Keir glanced between Trystan and me. "Gentlemen, please. We have far bigger problems than any petty differences between you two." His expression was grim. "We found Gage and Balthazar at St. Christopher's Church. They're performing some kind of ritual that could threaten all three of our families. The power readings are off the charts." He hesitated. "Petar was there, too."

The rage that exploded through me turned my vision red. Petar. The traitor who'd helped Balthazar and Gage take Serenity, who'd betrayed loyalty for power. The marble fireplace cracked under the force of my fury. I could still see the marks Gage had left on her, still smell her fear from when she'd been their captive.

"There's something else," Keir said. "A dark power. It's not demonic, but it's extremely powerful."

A power that wasn't demonic?" I thought of Serenity's blue flames of holy power, and Balthazar's demonic corruption. If some other force was at play here, something neither angelic nor demonic... "Explain."

Keir ran a hand through his hair distractedly. "I've never seen anything like it. It's... ancient. Cold. Like staring into a void. When it pulses, it's like all the light gets sucked out of the air. Even Balthazar looked to be wary of it." His eyes met mine. "Whatever they're doing in that church, that power is at the center of it. And it's growing stronger."

"He's telling the truth, Angelo. I can feel it." Serenity's soft voice behind me made every muscle in me stiffen.

I groaned and turned around. Through our connection, I felt only exhaustion from her—none of the visceral reactions her angelic blood had to demonic presence, like the nausea she'd experienced when Balthazar's blood message had triggered her powers. That meant Keir and Trystan were clean. But I didn't want them knowing about her ability to detect demon magic—they'd be too tempted to try and steal such a powerful weapon for themselves.

Pascal's face paled. "I'm sorry, boss. I didn't see them coming."

Idiot. I should have known. Gianna had my blood and could be quieter and move quicker than Pascal.

Serenity stood behind us with Gianna supporting her.

My sister shouldn't have brought her here—not when she was this weak, not when we didn't know who to trust.

Keir's eyes narrowed, studying Serenity with cold calculation. "What does she mean that she can feel that we're telling the truth?"

"Nothing," I growled. "Gianna, take her back upstairs. She's exhausted."

"But she can help you, brother." Gianna's chin lifted in defiance.

"Take her back up. Now." My voice dropped to a dangerous whisper.

"But I can help." Serenity started, meeting my angry gaze.

"You're not fooling us, Angelo." Trystan rubbed his chin thoughtfully, his eyes never leaving Serenity. "It's her Nephilim powers, isn't it? She can sense deception." His lips curved. "Or is there even more to it?"

"Angelo," Serenity rubbed her forehead tiredly. "I felt something. Something outside."

I focused on our connection, letting her sensations flood through me again. Whatever she'd detected wasn't demonic—there was none of that oily darkness that had made her sick earlier. This was different. Through her, I felt something ancient stirring, like a distant storm gathering power.

I poured all my power into our connection, forcing my thoughts through our mental bond. *Serenity, don't share anything in front of these two. You'll only make yourself more vulnerable.*

Her response came immediately, exhausted but stubborn. *Understood, but you can't hide me.*

I ignored her plea and focused instead on Keir and Trystan. "Did you see anything out of the ordinary outside?"

Keir met my gaze, a predatory gleam in his eyes. "She *is* powerful, Santi. Being able to sense dark magic or a dark presence is something we can use against Balthazar and Gage and whatever they are conjuring at St. Christopher Church."

My power surged through my tensed muscles, making the air crackle with barely contained violence. The mere suggestion of using Serenity as a tool made my fangs itch to descend. "She's not going anywhere near there." I forced my voice to stay steady. "I'll ask you again—you didn't see anything out of the ordinary outside?"

Trystan shook his head. "No, not unless you consider seeing King Nico and the headmaster of Red Rose Academy out of the ordinary. They were walking down the street in a heated discussion."

"Well, isn't that interesting?" Dimitri drawled, swirling his bourbon. "Our dynamic duo having a lover's quarrel. Those two are usually joined at the hip." His smirk didn't quite hide the calculating look in his eyes.

I thought about it for a minute. "They might be

concerned about what's going on at St. Christopher's Church."

Enzo met my gaze. "They might also suspect it has something to do with the murdered girls."

Trystan cocked his eyebrow. "According to Ivan's mate, Shannon, Balthazar admitted he's been killing the murdered girls. You didn't tell King Nico?"

I sighed heavily, feeling every year of ruling this territory in my bones. "I didn't think he or Headmaster Tarus would believe me. They have already convicted me."

Trystan leaned back on the couch and rubbed his chin. "Interesting." Behind his casual pose, the wolf king's eyes glittered with deadly purpose.

Keir, always logical, drummed his fingers on the armrest. "We need to move fast. We don't want Balthazar, Gage, and Petar to grow stronger. And this thing, whatever it is, might soon become more powerful than us." It was the first time I heard a slight tinge of fear in his tone.

He wasn't looking at me. He was looking at Serenity, who had remained silent during the exchange. I had enough of the Unseelie king's obvious focus on her. She sagged against Gianna, her exhaustion a reminder of how vulnerable she was right now. She needed time to heal.

"Gianna." My voice dropped to a deadly whisper. "I am only going to say this once more. Take her back to my room now."

Gianna opened her mouth to protest, but Dimitri shook his head almost imperceptibly and she clamped her mouth shut. For once, Serenity didn't argue with me either. She understood this wasn't the time or place to challenge me in front of Trystan and Keir.

Gianna escorted Serenity out of the living room. I tilted my head and Enzo moved into position to guard the hallway that led to the stairs up to mine and Serenity's bedroom. He held the Void Chain in his fist.

Trystan glanced at Enzo then at me, incredulous. "You're seriously not going to use her? She could be our greatest weapon against our enemies."

I growled, my fangs descending. "Absolutely not. She was taken from me once. No one is going to take her from me again."

Trystan rolled his eyes. "You're hiding our biggest asset. According to Shannon, Balthazar fed on her repeatedly, and each time, Serenity was able to heal her. We need her."

Anger surged through me, my power threatening to explode. It took every ounce of control I'd mastered in centuries of ruling not to hunt down Balthazar right now and tear him apart for torturing my mate. My hands curled into fists as the truth sank in. That sick bastard had forced Serenity to heal Shannon over and over, knowing her compassion wouldn't let her refuse. He'd used her own kindness as a weapon against her soul. I refused to let her go through that again, no matter what advantages Trystan thought it might give us.

Dimitri and Enzo looked to me. Their pointed states

carried unspoken questions about how much I would reveal.

I stated bluntly, "We need to do this without her."

My vision tinged red as centuries of carefully controlled power threatened to explode. The temperature in the room plummeted. How dare they try to use my mate like this? Serenity wasn't some magical detector they could deploy at will. She'd already suffered enough at Balthazar's hands.

THIRTY

THE TENSION in the room thickened until the air felt like steel against skin. My power rolled off me in waves, a reminder of why I ruled these territories. Trystan shifted uneasily and Keir lowered his gaze. They'd all seen what happened to the last person who threatened my mate.

Keir stopped thumping the armrest. "We need to have a plan of attack. I don't believe an ambush would work this time. We did that at the abandoned plantation. They will be expecting it."

Trystan glanced at him. "What do you suggest, then?"

"Sneak attack at dawn," he said simply. "I'll have

Lorcan bring the harpies. And let me be clear…" Trystan leaned forward, rage emanating from him. "No one kills Gage except me."

I locked gazes with Dimitri, centuries of blood debt in my voice. "Petar is mine."

Dimitri raised his glass with a dark smirk. "By all means, have at Daddy Dearest. I'll even gift wrap him for you. Betrayal's kind of a family specialty, isn't it?" He took a deliberate sip of bourbon. "Just do me a favor—make it hurt."

The words hit like acid, burning through old scars. Betraying the Santi family and kidnapping my mate— each offense alone warranted death, but together? I'd make it legendary. "Trust me," I said, ancient malice coloring my voice, "what I have planned will make my other punishments look merciful."

Keir pulled out a map of St. Christopher's Church and spread it open across the coffee table. "The church sits in the middle of one of the oldest graveyards in New Orleans. Look at how the oldest crypts are positioned—the Nightshade crypt, the Dixon tomb, and the old DuBois mausoleum. They form a perfect triangle around the church."

"Three of the oldest crypts in New Orleans," I murmured, tracing the triangle on the map. "Two of them built by the most powerful witch families in the state. Balthazar chose this church deliberately. He must be using the church as a focal point, with the three magically charged crypts surrounding it. Perfect setup for whatever ritual he's planning."

"What about wards?" Dimitri swirled his bourbon. "I'm betting our friendly neighborhood demon prince has the place locked down tighter than a nun's habit." His usual smirk faded. "The Nightshade crypt might give us an advantage, though. My sister-in-law's family didn't build it there by accident. Every magical current in New Orleans runs through that graveyard."

Keir's eyes narrowed. "Of course—your brother married the Nightshade witch. What can you tell us about the crypt?"

"Oh, somebody didn't do their homework." Dimitri's dangerous smile widened as he lounged back. "That crypt isn't just your average spooky family vault, believe me. My sister-in-law's family has centuries of nasty surprises stored in there. We're talking grimoires that would make your hair curl, artifacts that could level half of New Orleans..." He took a deliberate sip and chuckled. "Thanks to my brother's excellent taste in wives, I know exactly where all the really fun toys are kept."

Trystan pointed at the other two crypts. "What do we know about these?"

"The Dixon crypt's a dead end," Keir said. "High Priestess Abigail Dixon died not too long ago. But Peyton Storm, the new High Priestess at Goody Magic Academy, has been tracking dark power surges coming from St. Christopher's Church."

Trystan gave him a puzzled look. "She can sense them all the way from Salem?"

"The Dixons were clever," Keir noted. "They built their tomb on a natural convergence point. That's why Peyton can sense disturbances all the way from Salem. Their crypt acts like a magical antenna."

I was trying to remember everything I knew about the witches in New Orleans, but I was drawing a blank. All my focus was on keeping Serenity safe. "And the DuBois family?"

"According to my sister-in-law, the DuBois family made quite the habit of marrying into both families over the centuries," Dimitri drawled, his smirk widening. "Created one hell of a magical dynasty until they died out fifty years ago. But their crypt?" He raised his glass in mock toast. "Still holds enough combined power to make your average family feud look like a kindergarten spat. When witches do family drama, they do it with a bang. Literally."

I pointed at the Nightshade crypt on the map. "Since we can't get into the Dixon or DuBois crypts, we'll start here. Balthazar might want something inside—or we might find something to use against him." I glanced at Dimitri. "Call your sister-in-law. She might know what we're looking for, and we need to know what magical defenses her family built into that crypt.

"The crypts are surrounded by tombs and mausoleums," Keir pointed out. "Perfect cover for an ambush from either side."

Trystan scanned the map thoughtfully. "My wolves can take the grounds. We know Gage's scent—he won't slip past us. But all those graves..." He frowned. "Could be a problem if Balthazar decides to raise anything."

"That's the thing," Dimitri said, pulling out his phone. "My sister-in-law says the Nightshade crypt was heavily warded against evil, including demons. Some old family grudge about a deal gone wrong."

Keir glanced at each of us. "I suspect the other two crypts are warded against evil as well."

Trystan had a puzzled look. "So Balthazar can't enter any of the crypts?"

"No. He'll have to use someone else to enter for him," I said. "Someone that can get past the wards."

"Gage?" Trystan suggested.

"Please." Dimitri's smirk turned sharp. "A wolf shifter? The Nightshades didn't mess around with their wards—he wouldn't make it past the first one without getting his tail singed." His expression darkened. "Though I should suggest some creative additions to their defenses. Nothing says 'keep out' quite like a few specially crafted torture spells. My bad for not thinking of it sooner."

I stared keenly at Dimitri. "He might not be the only one that Balthazar plans to force to open the crypt. When was the last time you spoke to your brother or sister-in-law?"

The bourbon glass froze halfway to his lips. For the first time tonight, Dimitri's carefully crafted mask of sarcasm slipped. His fingers flew over the phone keys as he dialed his brother. Each unanswered ring chipped away at his composure. "Come on, Val, pick up the damn phone." He tried another number, then cursed. "They're not answering. Not Rose, not Valentin."

This wasn't what I wanted. Balthazar was one step ahead of us, building his arsenal. If he couldn't use Gage to get into the crypts, he had a plan B while we were still trying to form a plan A.

I looked at his stricken face. "Balthazar has them."

"Balthazar won't just kill them." Keir's quiet words fell like stones in the silence. "He'll break them piece by piece until they give him what he wants. He knows exactly how much pain a vampire can take before their mind shatters, and witches…" He let the implication hang in the air. "He'll use one to break the other."

"No. Neither of them would cooperate," Dimitri snarled, but the fear in his eyes betrayed him. His hand clenched the phone so hard he cracked the screen. "Val's too stubborn and Rose would rather die than—" He stopped, the implications hitting him.

I understood his terror all too well. I didn't know Rose and Valentin well, but they had fought Balthazar before. This would be sweet revenge for the demon prince. Balthazar didn't just kill his enemies—he made examples of them. He'd force Valentin to watch Rose suffer, or Rose to watch Valentin break. The demon would weaponize their love, like he was trying to do with Serenity and me.

"Think about it, Dimitri. He would threaten to kill one of them to force the other one to do his bidding."

Dimitri went absolutely still as the words hit home. Then his composure shattered.

"Well, isn't this just perfect." Dimitri's laugh was pure venom as he hurled the ruined phone across the room. It shattered against the wall like his composure. "Dear old Dad's really outdone himself this time. Teaming up with a demon prince? Kidnapping my brother?" He poured another bourbon with shaking hands and downed it in one go. "Don't worry, Angelo, Petar's all yours—but I'll gladly help make his last moments memorable. Nothing says goodbye quite like a family reunion from hell."

My vision turned red. But I couldn't let fury cloud my judgment—not with Serenity still recovering upstairs, not with her powers likely being what Balthazar really wanted all along. Even with the Solomon's Seal coins warding Crescent Manor, Balthazar was a crafty bastard and might find a way to penetrate the protection spell using someone else.

"Luigi!" I called. When he appeared in the doorway, I fixed him with a lethal stare. "Take Serenity to the spare bedroom. Double the guard." I grabbed his arm then lowered my voice. "Give her something to help her sleep. No one gets near that bedroom. If Balthazar's willing to take Valentin and Rose to get into that crypt, he might try for her next."

The doorbell rang, then Elena came into the living

room with Detective Flanagan trailing her like a blood hound. Power erupted through me, turning my vision red. That demon-loving bastard had outmaneuvered me again —using a police detective as his puppet to breach my defenses. I couldn't touch Flanagan without bringing down the entire department. Rage shook me to the core as I realized how perfectly Balthazar had played this move.

"I'm sorry, Angelo." She wrung her hands.

Detective Flanagan pushed past her and handed me a piece of paper. "I have a warrant to search your premises for the ring that you claimed was in your safe. If it isn't there, I can only assume that the one found with Nancee Lane was indeed yours, and I'm placing you under arrest for her murder. Detective DuPont is standing guard outside to prevent anyone from leaving."

My fangs itched to descend as the trap became crystal clear. DuPont couldn't cross the wards, but he didn't need to. He was waiting outside like a spider, ready to snatch anyone trying to escape this web of human law enforcement. And if they arrested me, Serenity would never let herself stay behind. She'd walk right into Balthazar's trap, trying to save me.

The demon prince had orchestrated this perfectly. He'd found a way to use my own power against me. One wrong move, one flash of supernatural power, and I'd have the entire New Orleans police force down on my head. And Serenity would be left vulnerable.

THIRTY-ONE

EVERY MUSCLE in my body coiled tight enough to snap. The paper crumpled in my fist as I fought back the urge to let my power explode, to show this human cop exactly what happened to those who threatened what was mine. But that's exactly what Balthazar wanted. I forced my voice steady, though my fangs ached to descend.

Three officers entered my home behind Detective Flanagan, their boots tracking human stink across my floors. They wouldn't find the ring since Petar had obviously stolen it. Not that Flanagan or New Orleans' finest would believe me.

Detective Flanagan looked between Trystan and Keir, his instincts clearly unsettled by the predatory energy rolling off the wolf king and the otherworldly chill emanating from the Unseelie. "I take it I'm interrupting something important. Why are you three meeting?"

Keir gave him a tight smile as he folded up the map, frost crystallizing on its edges. "Family business."

Flanagan's hand drifted toward his gun. "What kind of business?"

Trystan's lip curled, a low growl threading through his words. "The kind that doesn't concern human law enforcement." His eyes flicked to me, heavy with meaning. "Detective Flanagan was just leaving."

Flanagan puffed up his chest. "You will tell me what this is about. I'm conducting a murder investigation and I'm beginning to suspect that all three of you are involved somehow."

I bit back a smirk. If he knew the full truth—what really prowled the streets of New Orleans and what kind of creatures he was threatening right now—he would crawl back to the precinct on his belly and hide under his desk.

I looked at Trystan. "Go check out DuPont."

Flanagan reached for his gun as Trystan headed for the door, but I was already there, my fingers locked around his wrist like steel bands. The bones beneath my grip felt delicate as bird wings. "I wouldn't do that if I were you, Detective."

"Pol—" His cry cut off as I caught his gaze. My power surged forward, crystallizing in his mind like frost creeping across a window. I watched his pupils dilate, his mouth go slack as the cold darkness of my will seeped into every corner of his consciousness.

"You found the ring." Each word dropped like an icicle, sharp and inevitable. "You will leave the premises. Now."

The three other police officers reached for their guns, but supernatural speed made their movements look like slow motion. Enzo caught the first officer's wrist in an iron grip, his compulsion already threading through the man's mind. Dimitri had his target pinned against the wall, moving with the fluid violence of a born predator. Keir's power manifested in waves of arctic cold, freezing the third officer in place as tendrils of dark fae magic wrapped around him like living shadows.

"I wouldn't," Dimitri purred, his casual tone belied by the deadly grip he maintained. "Guns make such a mess, and Elena just had the carpets cleaned."

I headed over to Enzo's captive. The officer's pupils dilated as my power poured into his mind, wiping it clean like a blank slate before I painted new memories across it —the ring, gleaming under evidence lights, case closed. When I released him, he swayed slightly, caught in the web of false memories..

I glanced at Dimitri. "You can let go of him. The compulsion's complete."

"Aw, but we were just becoming friends," Dimitri

drawled, releasing his grip on the officer with exaggerated care. "I was about to teach him the finer points of supernatural etiquette. Rule number one: never pull a gun on creatures who can snap you like a twig. It's just..." He straightened the officer's collar with mock solicitude, "...bad manners."

Keir stepped back from his man, frost still crackling in the air around him. "He won't remember anything or why he was here. Unseelie glamour is...exceptionally thorough." A cold smile played at his lips as he regarded the officer, who swayed on his feet, eyes glazed with fae magic.

Power exploded through me, making the lights flicker. That demon bastard had orchestrated every detail. The warrant. The kill team. All of it designed to either end with my death or force Serenity to leave the safety of the wards to save me. My fangs descended as centuries of carefully maintained control threatened to snap. Balthazar wasn't just playing with law enforcement; he was playing with my mate's heart. Using my death to draw her out.

Tell me," I snarled, power lacing every word with enough darkness to make even Enzo take a wary step back, "who gave the order?"

Enzo's gaze flickered between the glazed-eyed officers. "The orders came through headquarters, but..." He shook his head. "The trail goes cold there. Someone made sure to cover their tracks."

Snarls and growls suddenly erupted outside, followed

by human screams that cut off too quickly. I raced to the front door, power crackling around me. The scene that greeted me made even my centuries-old blood run cold.

Snarls and growls erupted outside, followed by human screams that cut off too quickly. I raced to the front door, power crackling around me. The scene that greeted me made even my centuries-old blood run cold.

Trystan had shifted into his wolf form—massive and white as arctic snow, terrible in his fury. His victim lay beneath massive paws, a middle-aged man in an expensive suit now soaked with blood. I recognized him with disgust. Detective Whitehead, one of my most reliable contacts in the police force, a man I'd kept well-paid for decades to look the other way.

The demon's possession had twisted his familiar features into something inhuman: blackened veins spiderwebbing across gray skin, eyes like burnt coals until the last moment. Now his throat was torn out, blood staining Trystan's pristine fur crimson. Black smoke rose from the corpse, the demon's essence wailing as it disappeared into the ground, leaving behind the shell of a once-useful ally. The wolf king's golden eyes blazed with predatory satisfaction, red droplets stark against his white muzzle. But DuPont—the one who mattered, the one who could lead us to Balthazar—was nowhere in sight.

My men had formed a perimeter, keeping curious eyes from witnessing the carnage. But even with all the guards around the house, this was still too public.

Keir stepped in front of me, his Unseelie glamour already permeating the air, hiding both the dead body and Trystan's massive wolf form from mortal eyes.

"Get inside that hedge and shift back," I ordered the wolf king. Branches rustled as the massive white form disappeared behind the foliage. A moment later, Trystan's voice came from behind the thick leaves, tight with fury. "DuPont reeked of demon magic before he fled. But that's not all." His hand thrust through the greenery, something silver catching the light. "He left this."

My throat went tight. Valentin's pendant, its delicate chains dripping fresh blood.

"Said to tell Dimitri this is just the beginning." Trystan's voice hardened. "Balthazar's only just started with Valentin."

Keir took the medallion, frost spreading across the silver as he examined it. "There's old magic in this. Power tied to blood and family bonds." His eyes gleamed with otherworldly light. "The kind demons love to corrupt."

Dimitri snatched it out of Keir's hand. He pulled an identical medallion from within his shirt, murder in his eyes. "Mom gave us these last Christmas. She said it was to celebrate her boys being together again." His fingers closed around both pendants. "Touching family moment, really. But if Balthazar thinks he can use my baby brother as leverage..." Dark veins crawled beneath his eyes as his power surged. "Well, let's just say I've got some ideas about where to stick this pendant."

He blurred toward the steps, but I caught Enzo's eye with a slight nod. He instantly materialized in front of Dimitri, catching him by the throat and lifting him off his feet.

Behind us, Trystan dragged the bloody corpse inside, still naked but focused on the task. My men moved with practiced efficiency—they didn't need orders for this kind of cleanup anymore. The body would disappear into the bayou's depths, another secret the swamp would keep for me.

"Get a hold of yourself," I growled at Dimitri. "You can't run off half-cocked. That's exactly what Balthazar wants."

"Right, because your plans are working out so well." Dimitri's voice dripped sarcasm even with Enzo's hand wrapped around his throat. "Let me guess—you think we should sit around drinking bourbon and strategizing, meanwhile my brother could be bleeding out somewhere. Thanks for the advice, but I think I'll stick with my plan of immediate, excessive violence."

My power filled the room like a desert wind, making even Dimitri's smirk falter. "Your brother's only alive because Balthazar needs him to be. The moment you rush in without thinking, that changes." I stepped closer, letting centuries of ruthless authority color my voice. "I've spent four hundred years dealing with creatures like him. You want violence? Fine. But it'll be calculated, precise, and exactly when I say. Or I'll have Enzo chain you in my interrogation room until this is over."

Gianna burst into the entryway, her power crackling around her. "What's going on? Enzo, release him. Now."

Enzo cocked his eyebrow at her demand as Dimitri smacked at his hand, feet still dangling. He looked to me for orders.

I grabbed Gianna's arm. "He's out of control. I won't have it. Enzo, lock him in the interrogation room until he calms down."

"No!" Gianna whirled on me, eyes blazing. "That's my husband, brother. You can't just—"

"I can, and I will." Ice filled my voice. "This isn't a request, sister. Challenge my authority again, and you'll join him."

Enzo dragged a snarling Dimitri down the hallway, Gianna's fists pounding on his back. I caught Enzo's eye. "Chain him up. If my sister can't control herself, have a second set waiting."

Trystan yanked on the clothes Elena brought him. "And the cops?"

"Compel them to forget everything and send them on their way." I turned to Pascal. "Follow them. Make sure they go straight to the station. Anyone who deviates— handle it." The implied threat hung in the air. We didn't leave loose ends.

Keir circled the entranced officers. "The ones orchestrating this may have infiltrated the police department. We need to see who has corrupted the force."

"Balthazar first." My tone ended all discussion. There was a reason I'd ruled New Orleans for decades. "These humans are disposable pieces. I want the demon who thinks he can play games in my territory. We move as planned. We'll meet at midnight tonight."

Keir vanished in a shimmer of dark fae magic – he would be gathering his Unseelie warriors, preparing them for the hunt through the shadows. Trystan straightened his suit jacket, already back to his elegant human form. He would be rallying his pack, positioning them throughout the Quarter. The wolf king's hunters were unmatched at tracking prey.

I had more pressing matters to attend to. I headed upstairs to the guest room where Luigi stood guard. "Status?"

"All quiet, *Capo*." Luigi straightened. "Everything good downstairs?"

"Flanagan and his men won't be a problem. Compulsion's holding for now." I nodded to the bedroom door. "She awake?"

He shook his head. "No movement since the sedative took effect."

I opened the door. Serenity lay still and vulnerable, the sight stirring both predator and protector in me. "Hold your post," I ordered. "No one enters. No exceptions."

"Yes, *Capo*." Luigi closed the door with silent efficiency, leaving me alone with her.

I gathered Serenity in my arms, pressing my lips to her forehead. The drug would keep her under until this was finished. She'd be angry at me when she woke, but her fury was a price I'd gladly pay to keep her safe. And alive.

CHAPTER

THIRTY-TWO

S erenity

I WAS *in the same decrepit church again, where stained glass windows let in barely enough moonlight to be able to see anything. Balthazar stood with a strange glow around him, like a twisted halo, studying me with ancient eyes.*

"You didn't believe me about Joy," he said. Not a question.

The name ripped through me. Joy—missing for weeks now, her disappearance haunting every waking moment. My best friend since childhood, vanished without a trace despite Angelo turning New Orleans upside down searching for her. My throat closed around a scream of rage and grief. "Don't," I choked out. "Don't you dare speak her name."

He snapped his fingers and the world spun away, leaving me stumbling in darkness. When everything stilled, I found myself in an abandoned house. Wooden boards covered the windows, but slivers of light cut through the gaps.

The soft glow appeared again, illuminating Balthazar as he stood next to a female figure sitting in a chair. Chains wrapped around her wrists and ankles, binding her to the metal seat. Her dark hair hung forward, obscuring her face, but I would know the butterfly tattoo on her shoulder anywhere. It was the same one I'd held her hand through when she got it on her eighteenth birthday. I knew the silver ring on her right hand, too: Louis had given it to her when she had graduated high school.

"No," I whispered. "Please, no."

Balthazar reached down, fingers tangling in her hair. He pulled her head back with deliberate slowness. I saw the wounds first—the right eye swollen shut, the lip split and crusted with dried blood, the left cheek a violent purple. But it was still unmistakably Joy's face. My best friend. My sister in every way but blood.

My hands trembled but my rage came fast, burning away the horror. "I'll kill you for this."

"Me?" Balthazar released her hair, letting her head fall forward again. His smile was almost gentle. "Oh, I'm not the artist responsible for this work." He lifted his hand and snapped his fingers. "He is."

Detective Louis DuPont emerged from the shadows like he'd been part of them. The man who'd treated me like a second daughter, who'd let me stay with them so I could escape from Freakie Freddie, the man who had kept me safe all these years. He was the only father figure I'd ever known. He was my real father in every way that mattered. His badge still gleamed on his belt, a mockery of everything it stood for. The sleeves of his dress shirt were rolled up, spattered with what could only be his daughter's blood. His usual methodical stride had changed to something... wrong. Like he'd forgotten how legs were supposed to work.

Then I saw his eyes. Solid black, like two holes punched in reality. Something shifted beneath the skin of his face, a ripple that shouldn't be physically possible, and every instinct I had screamed at me to run. But what hit me hardest was seeing the man who'd promised always to protect us both standing there with his daughter's blood on his hands.

I took a shaky step forward. "What's wrong with him?"

Balthazar prowled behind Louis, placing his hands on his shoulders. "He works for me now."

Tears blurred my eyes, hot and angry. "You bastard."

Balthazar moved away from Louis, his shoes clicking against the floor as he walked. "But you can heal him, Serenity." His voice dropped lower. "Come to St. Christopher's Church." His lips curved into a cruel smile. "If you don't, dear Louis will finish what he started, and you'll lose your best friend."

• • •

I woke with a start. My mind swam, thoughts scattered like broken glass. This room... I recognized it. It was the same room where Angelo had first held me captive. The memory of those early days hit me—the fear, the shock, not knowing if I'd live or die.

Drool had dried on my pillow, and my neck ached from sleeping in an awkward position. I felt awful. My mind was strangely blurry, and a slick sweat made my blue silk robe cling to me like a second skin. The sheets beside me were rumpled but empty.

Where was Angelo?

My temples throbbed like someone was driving railroad spikes into my skull. Every heartbeat sent fresh pulses of pain ricocheting through my head. I squinted at the clock through a fog of agony—three-thirty. It was pitch black in my bedroom, so it had to be three-thirty in the morning.

My heart quickened as the dream came flooding back. Joy's bruised face. Those things moving under Louis' skin. Balthazar's ultimatum.

How was Balthazar able to contact me again? Angelo had said that I was powerful enough to keep him out of my mind. He'd also strategically placed those ancient coins that were supposed to keep him out. Obviously, they hadn't worked. And if Balthazar could break through Angelo's magic...

I had to tell Angelo. Now.

The door was out—Luigi would never let me pass. But

the window was a possibility.

I stumbled out of bed, steadying myself on the table when my legs threatened to give out. The room spun, but I forced myself toward the window. Only three stories. Not too high, and there was the thick ivy growing up the side of the mansion. If I could just—

My hands banged against iron as I reached for the heavy curtains. I yanked the fabric aside. Thick bars crisscrossed the entire window frame, the metal thrumming with protective magic. Angelo hadn't just posted a guard —he'd turned the entire room into a cage.

I stumbled away from the window, already forming a new plan. If I could convince Luigi that Angelo was in danger, maybe he would let me out. The room spun viciously, the aftereffects of Balthazar's dream-walking still clouding my head.

"Luigi. Luigi!" I pounded on the door desperately.

He opened it, his broad shoulders blocking the hallway. He gave me that familiar scowl, the one that always made his scar twist across his cheek.

"Where's Angelo? He's in danger." I moved away from the bed, still unstable, my sweaty palm sliding across the slick comforter. The overhead light was too bright after my nightmare. "Please, Balthazar's going to—"

"No." He crossed his arms and planted himself in the doorway, muscles bulging under his black shirt as if I were some dangerous prisoner trying to escape. A cold smile touched his lips. "The *capo* warned me you might pull something like this. Said you'd probably try to convince me he was in danger." He scoffed, and his dark eyes hardened. "The *capo* is too powerful for a demon to take down. Besides, he's got Enzo and Dimitri with him." He shifted his weight, blocking even more of the doorway.

My stomach dropped. Of course Angelo had thought of this—had predicted exactly how I'd try to escape. He didn't just plan for threats; he anticipated every possible move I might make. I wasn't just trapped by the bars and the guard; I was trapped by Angelo's ability to think ten steps ahead of me. God, he probably had contingencies for his contingencies.

"Where did he..." Another sharp pain shot through my skull. Then the pieces clicked together despite my pounding head, and fury cut through the pain. "Did Angelo have you drug me?" My legs felt weak as realization hit—he'd planned this, all to keep me trapped in this house.

The fuzzy feeling, the weakness, the way the room spun—memories crashed through me. Being drugged before, waking up in that auction house. The same helpless feeling, the same violation. And now Angelo, who'd sworn to protect me, who'd helped save me from that nightmare, was using the same tactics. Different purpose, same method. Different cage, same loss of control.

The room spun, but I couldn't tell anymore if it was from the drugs or the rage. Had this been his plan all along? How many other "contingencies" did he have ready? How many other ways was he prepared to control me while calling it protection?

Luigi's face paled, guilt flashing across his features briefly before he schooled them back to enforcer-blank. "No."

My fingers curled into fists at my sides as I stared at Luigi's immovable form in the doorway. Angelo needed me whether he wanted to admit it or not. So did Joy and Louis. I could save them—I was probably the only one who could. Fury pulsed inside me, and with it came my power stirring like a wild thing beneath my skin. I crossed the room, going nose-to-nose with him. The spicy scent of his cologne couldn't quite mask the metallic smell of blood that clung to him. 'You need to take me to him.'"

"No." He crossed his arms and spread his legs apart, using every inch of his height advantage to loom over me. He was ready for a fight.

"Let me pass." I tried to slip past him, feinting left, but he moved surprisingly quickly for someone his size. His hand shot out and grabbed my wrist, iron fingers pressing into my delicate bones.

"You're not going anywhere." Luigi stepped in front of me, his stance unyielding but careful not to touch me. His dark eyes were apologetic but firm as he gestured toward the bed. "Please return to bed, Miss Serenity. The *capo* was explicit about keeping you safe." When I hesitated, he sighed. "I understand you're restless, but you know how Angelo is about your safety. He would have my head if anything happened." He picked up the comforter and held it out. "Please. Rest. He'll return soon."

"You can't keep me here, Luigi." I rolled to the other side of the bed, but he was there in an instant, his supernatural speed making my attempt at escape look painfully slow.

"I can and I will. I will not disappoint the capo again." I wasn't sure, but I thought I heard fear in his tone. I remembered the rumors about what happened to guards who failed Angelo. The ones who...disappeared.

I glared up at him, my heart pounding against my ribs. "You don't understand. If I don't go, Balthazar will kill Joy." The image of her bruised face was still fresh in my mind.

He shrugged but wouldn't meet my eyes. "The *capo* made it clear that you're the only one that matters. He's not concerned about anyone else." The words sounded rehearsed, as if he'd been practicing them.

I wanted to scream at him. To make him understand that Joy wasn't just anyone—she was family. That Louis was more than just another victim.

Behind him, a shadow moved. Not the natural shift of light and dark, but something alive, something wrong. I scrambled backward across the bed, my heart battering my ribs like it might shatter them. The drugs made everything blur, shadows dancing and shifting. Was that Gage's silhouette? My mind spun with memories of the plantation, of being trapped, helpless. Terror exploded through me, turning my blood to ice water as the shadow loomed larger behind Luigi's shoulders.

Crapcrapcrapcrap

Gage. It had to be Gage.

He'd found a way in. Past the guards, past the security, past everything Angelo had done to keep me safe. My hands shook so badly I could barely grip the sheets, cold sweat soaking through my silk robe.

My guard, with all his muscle and loyalty, had no idea he'd just trapped me in here with a wolf enforcer. And I was still too weak from the drugs, my powers feeling distant and sluggish when I needed them most.

There was a whistle of movement behind Luigi. A vase smashed into his head, and he crumpled to the floor with a groan. Blood matted his dark hair as he tried to push himself up. Gianna dropped the bookend with a dull thud, then lunged at Luigi, moving faster than my eyes could track. She sank her fangs into his neck. Luigi's legs and body convulsed, his fingers clawing at the carpet, then he went limp.

Something was wrong. Gianna's movements were too jerky, too violent—even for a vampire. The way she'd struck Luigi... This wasn't just about freeing me. My stomach lurched as I studied her face. Her eyes weren't black like Steve's had been, but that didn't mean anything. The demon prince was clever. Perhaps he had found another way to control her. What if—oh God—this wasn't really Gianna anymore?

"What's wrong?" I almost laughed at the question. What *wasn't* wrong? First Joy and Louis, now this.

"Dimitri." Her shoulders curved inward, grief etched in every line of her body. "He's nearly lost his mind. He's sure Balthazar has his brother. Angelo had him chained up in the interrogation room until he calmed down." Her voice cracked. "But then he talked one of the guards into undoing the chains, then he overpowered him. I've never seen him like this—not even when we were fighting the wolves." Her fingers tightened around mine with desperate strength. "I know my husband. He'll sacrifice himself to save Valentin. He doesn't care if he lives or dies, as long as his brother survives. We have to help him, Serenity. We have to save him from himself."

I gave her a doubtful look, glancing at Luigi's unconscious form. "Can you get us out of here?" Angelo's compound was like a fortress, with guards at every exit. Even with one down, there had to be dozens more. I could already picture Carmine at the front gate, Nicola patrolling the east wing and who knew who all else, all of them ready to drag me back to this bedroom.

She gave me a mischievous smile. Blood still stained the corner of her mouth. "Yup. Thanks to Elena. She drugged Angelo's men's tea." A soft laugh escaped her. "Who would suspect the sweet little witch who makes their espresso every morning?" She nudged Luigi's boot with her toe. "They'll wake up with nasty headaches, but they'll live."

I nodded. "Take me to Angelo." If Balthazar was powerful enough to break through all the wards, powerful enough to invade my dreams despite everything... My stomach knotted, imagining finding Angelo too late, finding him facing that demon prince alone. Yes, he'd be furious when he saw me—I could already picture that look, that mix of fury and fear that meant he'd been trying to protect me. Again. But I'd rather face his anger than his funeral.

And it wasn't just Angelo I could lose tonight. Joy's bruised face flashed through my mind—my best friend, my sister in every way that mattered. Plus those things writhing under Louis' skin... Balthazar had already hurt so many people I loved. The demon prince would keep taking and taking until there was nothing left.

No more playing it safe, no more being the one left behind to be protected. I couldn't stand in this gilded cage while Angelo faced a demon prince, while Joy suffered God knows what tortures. My hands trembled, but not from fear—from the thought of losing either of them. Let Angelo rage. Let him punish me later. Some things were worth his fury, and this—saving the two people I loved most in this world—this was one of them.

THIRTY-THREE

I PEERED AT ST. Christopher's Church from the shadows, Trystan and Keir flanking me. Three kings standing in the darkness together—if someone had told me a century ago I'd be working with a wolf and an Unseelie I'd have drained them dry for the insult. But here we were: Trystan, the wolf king of the French Quarter, his custom-made suit barely containing the beast that lurked beneath the polished exterior, and Keir, that dangerous bastard who ruled the Garden District with Unseelie tricks and ancient debts, toying with a gold coin like we were at one of his favorite gambling dens instead of facing war.

Every stained-glass window had been smashed out, leaving jagged teeth of colored glass in rotting wooden frames. Moss and vines crept up the gray stones like grasping fingers. It had been a beautiful church before Katrina, a place where the old families had made their deals and sworn their loyalties. I'd sealed more than a few blood oaths within its walls myself. Now it lay in ruins, just another fallen piece of our city.

The faces of the stone angels that guarded the entrance were eroded by the elements into hollow-eyed masks. A crow perched on one's shoulder—not one of my spies. It made my fangs itch. The heavy wooden doors hung askew on rusted hinges, creaking softly in the night breeze.

Red light pulsed from within the building, seeping through the broken windows like fresh blood. Evil emanated from it like a beacon, an ancient darkness that made even my undead flesh crawl. Something was waiting inside those walls, something so evil that it had forced three kings to set aside years of blood feuds and territory wars.

A blur of motion caught my eye. Dimitri materialized at the crypt entrance, rage and bourbon rolling off him in waves. "Anybody order a slightly pissed-off vampire with a rescue plan? No? Just me then?"

"How did you get out?" Ice filled my voice. No one had ever escaped my interrogation room.

"Funny story, that." Dimitri brushed imaginary dirt

from his sleeve. "Turns out your guard thought I had calmed down and would be a good boy. Shame he's really bad at holding his liquor. And his keys. And his consciousness."

Fury exploded through me. In less than a heartbeat, I had him pinned against the crypt wall, my hand crushing his throat. The stone cracked behind him from the force. Decades of iron control threatened to shatter. Someone had betrayed me. Someone had failed in their duty. "Which. Guard." Each word dripped with promised violence. The fool who had compromised my security would pray for death long before I granted it.

"What, and ruin the mystery?" Blood darkened the veins under his eyes. "Besides, we have more pressing matters. Like my brother being tortured while we stand around discussing your staff retention issues."

I dragged him over to Enzo's post at the Nightshade family crypt.

"Enzo." I tightened my grip on Dimitri's throat. "Chain him if he moves from this spot. And when we're done here, I want to find out who helped him escape."

Drawing on my vampire speed, I returned to where Trystan and Keir waited for me.

Trystan cocked an eyebrow. "Problems?"

"Nothing urgent." The lie tasted bitter. Three enemies moving against me at once, and now Dimitri losing control... I needed to end this quickly, before the situation with Serenity's guard became another weak point Balthazar could exploit.

The door opened with a groan of rusty hinges. Louis DuPont stepped out holding onto a blond woman's arm, his movements still unnatural and puppet-like. I detected the evil rotting inside him, and even from here, I could see the things moving beneath his skin. What once had been an honest cop now housed something ancient and dark. The man was gone—hopefully to a better place.

The woman's hands were bound behind her back with what looked like spelled rope. Another one of Balthazar's victims? When the fading moon caught the side of her face, my undead heart actually skipped. I recognized her. Rose Dragan—Dimitri's sister-in-law. Part vampire, part witch, and heir to one of the most dangerous magical legacies in New Orleans. She was from the Nightshade family, and I knew exactly where she was being taken: to the crypt that held centuries of dark artifacts her ancestors had collected.

Valentin had to be inside. The thought of what they might be doing to Rose's mate made my fangs itch. A witch-vampire hybrid was powerful, but with the right leverage, even the strongest supernatural could break.

Gage emerged from the church's shadow with two men I didn't recognize. Their movements were definitely not human, but they didn't carry the signature tell of any supernatural race I knew. More of Balthazar's black-eyed puppets, perhaps.

Beside me, Trystan released a low growl, the sound carrying centuries of wolf-king authority, but didn't move, even though the moon had not set and it was still his time of power. Good. We couldn't afford to act too soon, not with what was at stake.

Two harpies glided down from the dark sky and landed on a nearby oak tree, their razor-sharp talons digging into the branches. Spanish moss swayed around them like funeral shrouds. I glanced at Keir. His Unseelie spies had positioned themselves perfectly—another advantage Balthazar didn't know we had. The Garden District king's intelligence network was unmatched, even by my own.

Enzo had the strength and experience to handle Dimitri if he snapped. More importantly, he knew how family could make even the most controlled vampires dangerous. He'd follow my orders without hesitation—even if that meant putting Dimitri down temporarily.

Their assignment was simple: extract information from anyone approaching the crypt. Balthazar hadn't chosen this location by chance. Something in that crypt was valuable enough to draw a demon prince to risk war with three supernatural crime families. Whatever secrets the Nightshade family had buried there, I needed to find them out before Balthazar did.

Keir glanced at Trystan. "Bring your wolves in closer. They need to sniff out more of the rebel wolves." The

Unseelie's king's golden coin disappeared into his pocket —when he got serious, the games stopped.

"They need me to lead them," Trystan mumbled as he tore off his suit. His eyes were locked on Gage who stood on the steps, his hatred for the traitor wolf evident. "We won't attack until we get the signal."

Keir put his hand on my shoulder. "Time for you to find out what's happening inside that church."

My transformation into a bat was almost instantaneous, a fluid change of form perfected over the centuries. I soared through the night air, wings cutting silently through the cool breeze. Yet even before the silhouette of the church appeared, a disturbing wave of evil brushed against my senses, cold and foreboding.

A malign presence emanated from the church, invisible yet powerful, intensifying as I drew closer. The once-sacred grounds now radiated dark energy so potent as to be almost visible in the moonlight, a shimmering haze of malevolence that writhed like serpents in the air. The gargoyles, ancient guardians meant to ward off creatures like me, sat silent and powerless, their stone faces twisted in eternal grimaces.

I hovered outside the window with its saints and demons captured in broken stained glass. The fractured imagery mirrored the disturbed aura I felt—saints disrupted, demons intact, foreshadowing the corruption within. Through the shattered panes, moonlight split into prismatic shards, casting blood-red and midnight-blue shadows across the nave below. The air itself pulsed with unholy energy, each wave making my heightened senses recoil.

Tension curled within me, every instinct honed from uncounted past battles readying for what lay ahead. My unnaturally sharp senses dissected the layers of darkness emanating from within: the acrid smell of burnt offerings, the metallic tang of spilled blood, whispered echoes of forbidden incantations that still lingered. As I perched on the edge of the window's jagged frame, preparing to enter, I drew in the night air, thick with the stench of evil. It fortified me, fueling the ancient power that coursed through my veins that had seen me through centuries of confronting such abominations.

The cross above the altar hung upside down, its sacred power perverted into a beacon for the darkness. Below it, shadows danced and twisted in unnatural ways, suggesting movement where there should be none. Something was waiting in that darkness, something that had corrupted this holy place for its own nefarious purposes.

I embraced the shadows, letting them envelop me as my ally in the impending battle. I had walked on the edge of the line between light and darkness for centuries— neither fully of the night nor welcomed by the day. Tonight, that unique position would serve me well as I cleansed this desecrated ground.

Inside, the red glow pulsed stronger. It came from bowls placed in a five-point star pattern around the altar, each filled with something that moved and writhed. The glow painted everything in shades of crimson, making the church look like a butcher's chapel. The air itself felt thick, tasting of copper and decay.

Balthazar and Petar stood near the altar, their shadows twisting on the walls, but it was the third, hooded figure that drew my attention. His presence carried an ancient weight that made even my blood run cold. His hands were marked with symbols that appeared to crawl across his skin like living things, disappearing under his sleeves only to emerge again at his neck—old, old magic that predated my own turning. Something about his movements felt familiar, though I couldn't place why. Each gesture was controlled, perfect, like a teacher demonstrating proper form.

It was just as a well I had left Dimitri at the crypt with Enzo. Valentin was stretched out on the altar, his arms and legs spread wide and bound with chains that glowed with spelled metal. If Dimitri saw his brother like this, displayed like a sacrificial lamb on a slab, he'd lose his mind.

Blood already stained Valentin's shirt, and symbols had been carved into his chest, still wet and gleaming. He wasn't just a hostage anymore. From the positioning of the altar in relation to those three crypts outside, I could tell this wasn't just about accessing the Nightshade vault. This was bigger. They were going to use whatever was in that crypt here and now, using Valentin's blood and Rose's power as the keys.

Then I felt it. A presence that shouldn't be here, one that made my entire body go rigid. No. Impossible. She was supposed to be safe in a guest bedroom, surrounded by my wards, with Luigi…

But pain slammed in my skull.

Serenity.

Her thoughts hammered in my head like gunfire, each word laced with panic and determination.

Angelo, I'm coming. Please don't be angry. Gianna's bringing me to the Nightshade crypt. I can't let you die.

She was moving through the shadows straight into whatever trap Balthazar had set. All my carefully laid plans, all my precautions—shattered. Fear clawed through my chest, followed by a rage so intense it nearly made me shift back to human form mid-flight. Damn Luigi. He'd had one job. *One!*

Gianna's involvement was something else entirely. She wasn't betraying me—she was protecting her mate. Dimitri's control was already fracturing over worry for his brother. Of course she'd come. And of course she'd bring Serenity, who never could stand idly by when someone she loved was in danger.

Focus. I forced the fury down, cold logic taking over. I couldn't maintain surveillance now—not with Serenity walking into the middle of this power play. But charging in would alert Balthazar to her presence. If he didn't already know. And that hooded figure… Something about his presence set off ancient warnings in my blood. The way he moved, the symbols on his arms that spoke of power older than my own—he was the wild card I couldn't predict.

I banked left, keeping to the shadows cast by the broken spire. We had three minutes, tops, before chaos erupted. Our original plan now lay in tatters. With Keir's harpies tasked to surveil the church, it was up to me to intercept Serenity. I signaled Keir with two quick flaps of my right wing, a pre-arranged signal for heightened vigilance.

Time was critical. I needed to reach Serenity before she approached the crypt and Dimitri saw her. Even with Gianna there to calm him, Serenity's appearance risked driving him to the brink. He would see Serenity as a means to an end—namely, finding his brother. His instinct to protect Valentin would kick in, blinding him to all else, jeopardizing our chance to uncover what Balthazar truly sought from the crypt.

Above all else we couldn't disrupt the ritual circle they'd carved into the floor. Whatever they were planning to pull through that gateway, containing it would be impossible once it emerged. The symbols were too perfect, too carefully placed. This wasn't just about power—it was about punishment. About teaching someone a lesson.

No way would Serenity become part of his curriculum.

THIRTY-FOUR

*S*erenity

GIANNA DRAGGED me across a creepy graveyard that could have been straight out of a Stephen King movie. Tombs and mausoleums—no one was buried underground in New Orleans, not with the water table so high—crowded together like a city of the dead. The crypts loomed over us, their whitewashed walls stained with black mold and age, their copper and iron fixtures oxidized to a green patina. Spanish moss hung over everything like ghostly veils, and the moonlight cast shadows that I could swear moved the second I wasn't looking directly at them. I kept waiting for the crypts to open and the dead to emerge.

The narrow aisles between the tombs felt like the streets in the French Quarter, only instead of tourists and music, there was silence and centuries of decay. Some of the older tombs bore names I recognized from Angelo's history lessons about New Orleans' oldest supernatural families—Villere, Laveau, DuBois. Their carved facades were elaborate even in decay, stone angels standing sentinel with empty eyes. My heart clenched thinking about Dimitri waiting at the Nightshade crypt, ready to tear apart anyone who got between him and his brother.

And Angelo. My chest tightened even more. He would face Balthazar head-on, too proud and too powerful to back down. The demon had already taken so much from him, had violated his territory and threatened his people. What if this was exactly what Balthazar wanted? What if the crypt was just another trap, designed to destroy my vampire king and everyone loyal to him in one brutal stroke?

The night air felt thick, heavy with decay and that copper-penny scent of old magic. Or maybe that was just the fear coating my tongue. Every click of our shoes against the brick pathways was so loud as to be heart-stopping, and I was sure I felt eyes watching us from the shadows between the tombs.

I scanned the graveyard and then the church, my heart hammering against my ribs as I searched for Angelo. Where was he? The shadows between the tombs seemed to breathe, to pulse with wrongness, and my chest tightened with each unnatural movement. These weren't the familiar shadows I'd learned to read in my months of training. They writhed like living things, carrying whispers that made my skin crawl.

They didn't contain Angelo. They couldn't. I'd know his presence anywhere—that familiar cool pressure in my mind, like midnight frost on windowpanes. Now, where his telepathic touch should be, there was only a void that made my teeth ache. Something ancient, dark and evil had severed our connection, replacing it with a crawling unease that slithered up my spine.

Red light seeped from the church's broken windows, pulsing like an infected wound. Each throb pierced my psychic shields, the ones Angelo had so carefully helped me build. They were crumbling now, leaving me exposed to whatever malevolent force had taken root in the sacred space. If it could do this to me, what was it doing to him?

The thought of Angelo facing this alone made my heart clench. He was powerful, yes, but this... This was the kind of darkness that devoured evil itself. And somewhere in there, he was fighting it without me.

Gianna squeezed my arm reassuringly, but I barely felt it through the numbing fear. We had to get to him and help him. The alternative—losing him to whatever waited in that church—wasn't something I was prepared to consider.

Near the church, two winged creatures with red eyes perched on a branch. Were they vampires? They didn't look like any vampires I'd ever seen. Some sort of creature from hell? More demons? After what I'd seen crawling beneath Louis' skin, anything was possible.

Balthazar had lied to me. Every word, every gesture had been carefully calculated deception. While he presented himself as forthright like Angelo, the truth was far darker. He didn't share his violent nature out of honesty—he wielded it like a weapon. Each demonstration was a performance: Joy's torture, Louis displayed as his marionette, Shannon's throat torn open. The brutality wasn't random; it was orchestrated. He wanted me to witness his capabilities, to understand the extent of his power. Each victim brought the horror closer to home: Shannon's savage attack, Joy's methodical torture, Louis' complete possession. A deliberate progression, each act more intimate than the last, showing me exactly what awaited those I held dear.

I hadn't had any nightmares about Shannon. That had to mean she was safe, or at least safer than Joy. He always made sure I saw the worst moments, the darkest possibilities—like he enjoyed watching me wake up screaming, drenched in the terror of what might happen. The visions I'd had of Joy... My chest tightened at the thought of what Louis might be doing to her. No, not Louis anymore—whatever dark thing now wore his skin like an ill-fitting suit.

My resolve hardened, pushing back against the memory of those nightmare visions. I just needed to get close enough to touch Joy, even for a moment. One brush of skin against skin, and I could pull her into the shadows with me and away from whatever they had planned. Angelo had said my angelic blood could sense evil. If I could pick up Louis' essence—that corruption that clung to him now like a disease—it would lead me straight to Joy. I was sure of it.

I pushed down the fear that threatened to choke me. The memory of the horrible blood messages appearing in our bedroom still haunted me. I couldn't afford to fail— not with Joy's life hanging by a thread. Not after seeing her chained up in that chair. Whatever dark force had taken over Louis' mind and spirit, whatever they planned to do with the Nightshade crypt, Joy wouldn't be their sacrifice.

Not tonight.

Not ever.

Gianna stopped so suddenly I almost ran into her. "I see him." She pointed toward a crypt, but I couldn't make out anything in the darkness between the tombs. My eyes strained against the shadows, trying to separate movement from moonlight.

I hoped she was talking about Dimitri and not something else in Balthazar's arsenal. After what happened to Louis in my dream, I wasn't sure I wanted to know what other horrors Balthazar had tucked away in the shadows.

Gianna wrapped her arm around my waist, lifted me up off the ground, then poured on her vampire speed. The world spun past me the same as it did when Angelo carried me—blurry moonlight, shadows, and weathered stone tombs all melting together. My stomach lurched when we stopped. She released me abruptly and I staggered, grabbing a nearby crypt to steady myself as the world gradually stopped spinning.

Dimitri stepped out of the shadows, his smirk not quite hiding the murder in his eyes. "Well, well, well. Gianna, what are you doing here? Come to join the party?"

"Not letting you do anything stupid is what I'm doing." The color drained from her face more with each word, her composure crumbling.

"Stupid?" Dimitri twirled Valentin's bloodied medallion between his fingers, his smile all sharp edges and barely contained violence. "Let me spell this out for you, since you're clearly having trouble with basic comprehension: My baby brother is being tortured by psychopaths while we're standing around having strategy meetings."

He spat the last words like poison, his eyes darkening with murderous intent. "What am I supposed to do—stand around playing Angelo's good little soldier?" A dangerous laugh escaped him, one that promised blood and carnage. "Here's my own strategy—I'm going to rip out some hearts, save my brother, and if anyone has a problem with that"—he spread his arms wide, smirk turning lethal—"feel free to try and stop me. Come on. It'll be fun."

He closed his fist around the medallion, Valentin's

blood smearing across his palm. "I won't let my brother die. And, spoiler, anyone who gets in my way risks being collateral damage."

"No. I won't let you sacrifice yourself." Gianna moved to him with vampire swiftness, gripped his shirt in her fists and pressed her forehead against his chest. Her voice came out raw, desperate. "You're my mate, Dimitri. You're my husband."

Someone grabbed my arm and fear exploded through me like ice water in my veins. The fingers locked around my bicep like iron bands, brutal enough to make me gasp. I couldn't move. Couldn't breathe.

"The boss won't be pleased."

Enzo.

My muscles seized up, torn between the urge to struggle and the knowledge that fighting Enzo would be like trying to get out of a steel trap. He wasn't just any vampire—he was old, as dangerous as Angelo. He was the kind of vampire that made other vampires nervous. He was fiercely loyal to Angelo and would carry out his bidding without question—and right now, I was exactly the kind of problem he was trained to handle.

Soft footsteps approached, the slow, deliberate tread of a hunter. Each step against the brick path echoed off the tombs with a steady rhythm that made my skin crawl. Not human footsteps—too smooth, too measured.

Enzo put his hand over my mouth and pressed me against the wall of the tomb, his body rigid with tension.

His cold skin smelled of copper and earth, and that particular metallic scent that clung to vampires who'd recently fed. "Don't say a word." His low murmur was so quiet I barely heard it, though he was pressed right against me. Every muscle in his body had gone predator-still.

My heart thundered in my chest. I felt each beat would give us away, a drum announcing our location. The rough stone of the tomb scraped my back through my thin shirt, and my legs trembled with the effort of staying still. Sweat trickled down my spine despite the cold.

Please don't be Balthazar Please don't be Balthazar Please don't be Balthazar

Dimitri and Gianna pressed themselves against the tomb, blending into the shadows. Her hand gripped his arm, white-knuckled, trying to anchor him in place. I could see the conflict warring in Dimitri's eyes—the need to protect his mate wrestling with the urge to hunt whatever was coming. Gianna's other hand pressed on his chest, right over his heart, a silent plea to stay put. The footsteps were getting closer, echoing off the stone walls of the crypts. The measured pace suggested that whoever —or whatever—was out there knew exactly where they were going.

"Open the door," a male voice said.

My thundering heart stopped. I knew that voice. Louis. But it sounded more gravel than human. Like something was scraping the words across broken glass before releasing them, and whatever was wearing his skin hadn't quite figured out how human voices were supposed to sound. The memory of the things moving under his skin made me want to gag. This creature wearing Louis' face, using his voice—it was obscene.

Suddenly, some wolves stepped out of the darkness, and my heart nearly burst. They weren't normal wolves—they were massive, their shoulders coming up to my chest, with eyes that gleamed with human intelligence. My legs trembled with the urge to run, but I forced myself to remain still.

As they drew closer, they growled and their eyes reflected red in the moonlight like burning coals. These weren't Trystan's wolves—their fur was matted with something dark that might have been blood, and they moved as if their joints had been put together backwards, bones cracking with each step. They smelled like wet dog mixed with something rotten, like meat left too long in the sun. Their teeth were too many and too sharp as they gleamed wetly in the darkness. Their red eyes fixed on me with hungry intelligence. These weren't just corrupted wolves—they were wolves that had forgotten how to be wolves, or perhaps had never known. With each movement, their skin rippled and shifted, as if what was inside didn't quite fit the shape it was wearing.

Shit, maybe they weren't wolves at all. Maybe they were hellhounds. I remembered reading about those in one of Angelo's books—creatures that hunted damned souls, that could smell fear and sin and weakness. The kind of monsters that even demons kept on chains. The way they moved reminded me of the things crawling under Louis' skin, like something dark and ancient playing at being normal and failing.

The wolves' growls grew louder, a sound that vibrated in my chest and set my teeth on edge.

A woman suddenly cried out and fell to the ground quite close to me, the impact sending gravel skittering across the cemetery path. My heart lurched in my throat—Joy? No: this woman had blonde hair that gleamed pale in the moonlight. She groaned in pain, and the sound brought tears to my eyes. My hands trembled as I covered my mouth, fighting back the urge to scream.

She whimpered, the sound cutting straight through me, and my body moved before my brain could catch up. I couldn't leave her here, couldn't watch yet another person suffer. This woman might not be Joy, but her pain was equally real. And I could actually do something about it.

Enzo stepped in front of me gracefully, the movement liquid smooth, every muscle poised for attack. "Stay behind me." His voice was a tomb door creaking open, promising darkness to anyone foolish enough to enter. I'd seen what he was capable of when he and Angelo had rescued me from Balthazar. He was just as dangerous as Angelo, perhaps even more because he hid it better. Where Angelo wore his power proudly like armor, Enzo kept his contained, like a serpent waiting to strike.

Louis stepped from around the crypt, and in the

moonlight, I could see those things still moving under his skin, like snakes writhing beneath his flesh. My stomach lurched.

Enzo shifted almost imperceptibly beside me, and something in his demeanor made my blood run cold. Gone was the quiet enforcer I knew from Crescent Manor. "Let me make one thing perfectly clear. The lady isn't going anywhere. And you..." His lips curved into a smile that spelled death. "You're about to have a very unfortunate accident."

I remembered what Balthazar said in the dream. He'd said I could heal Louis. I couldn't let Enzo kill him. At least not yet. Not if I could heal him.

Angelo had said that some possessions ran too deep, changed their victims too much. But watching Louis - the man who'd let me stay at his house when I had nowhere else to go, who'd protected me from Freakie Freddie, who'd always bought me a birthday present when no one else did - standing there with those things moving under his skin... It was like watching something sacred being corrupted, those small acts of kindness twisted by whatever was puppeting his body.

Maybe Angelo was wrong. The thought crept in like hope, dangerous and tempting. My heart thundered, sending blood pumping through my veins. My power stirred underneath my skin, that familiar tingling warmth spreading through my chest, down my arms. Blue light formed around me, lighting me up like a Christmas tree in the darkness, but concealment didn't matter now. I had to save him.

This was Louis. My Louis. The man who'd broken down a door to save me, who'd been there when I needed him most.

I had to try. Not just for me, but for Joy. I would never forgive myself or be able to face her if I did nothing. I couldn't lose him to whatever darkness Balthazar had stuffed inside his skin. My power pulsed stronger, light gathering in my palms. If there was even a chance I could burn out whatever was wearing him like a suit... I had to take it. Even if I failed, at least Joy would know I tried to save the father she loved.

THIRTY-FIVE

*S*erenity

I TOOK A STEP TOWARD LOUIS, but a loud, unnatural howl stopped me in my tracks.

The wolflike and yet not wolflike creatures lunged at Enzo, Dimitri, and Gianna in a blur of matted fur and twisted limbs. Enzo met the first one mid-leap, his hands sinking into its throat. Dimitri and Gianna moved in perfect sync, back-to-back, as two more of the hell-creatures circled them. The fourth one went straight for the fallen girl, its jaws opening impossibly wide.

I lunged for her arm, sweat-slicked fingers scrabbling against her leather jacket. The wolf's teeth gleamed too close, blinding white in the darkness. My heart slammed so hard I could barely breathe, barely think. I grabbed again, fingers trembling so badly I could hardly keep my grip. The jacket slipped through my hands like water as massive jaws snapped inches from her leg.

Then Louis was there. Not the Louis I knew, the thing wearing his face. His hands tangled in my hair and the woman's blonde strands, yanking us both back with inhuman strength. He slammed us against the crypt wall so hard my teeth rattled. Stars exploded behind my eyes, and the taste of copper flooded my mouth.

Rough stone scraped against my back as he held us pinned, its cold bite nothing compared to the ice in his eyes. Those weren't Louis' eyes anymore—the warm brown that had danced when he teased Joy and me was gone, replaced by something dark and ancient that looked at us like we were insects to be crushed. My chest seized with each desperate attempt to breathe, ribs screaming in protest where they'd hit the wall. Fear clawed up my throat, and beneath it surged something even worse— grief for the man who'd been Joy's and my protector, now twisted into this monster.

Behind us, I heard the sounds of battle: snarls and growls mixing with the impact of bodies, the wet tearing of flesh, the crack of stone as someone or something hit the tomb walls. But I couldn't turn to look. Louis held us immobile, the things under his skin writhing faster, like they were feeding off the violence around us.

I tried to summon my power. Healing light flickered in my chest, wanting to help, wanting to burn out whatever was inside him even though Angelo said it was impossible.

You can't heal me," he whispered in my ear, his breath cold where it should have been warm. The voice was Louis' but fractured, multiple voices trying to speak through one throat. "Louis isn't here. We are many."

I stuck out my chin in utter defiance. "I can heal you. I know I can." I struggled against his grip, trying to turn to face him so I could look into those eyes and find some trace of the man I knew and loved. "Louis, please. I know you're in there. Fight them."

His grip tightened, fingers digging into my scalp. "The crypt," he hissed, but this time his voice was different. Strained. Fighting. "Get...the dybbuk box...before..." The things under his skin twisted violently, and his next words came out in that horrible splintered voice again. "Foolish girl. He's trying so hard to reach you. It's almost... amusing."

Tears streamed down my face. The thing wrapped Louis' fingers tighter in my hair, using me like a shield as he turned on the other girl. "Now, bitch, if you want your little vampire to live, you'll get the dybbuk box." His voice had that horrible multi-toned sound again, like a choir of the damned singing through Louis' throat.

"Please don't kill him," she pleaded. Raw anguish

broke through her careful control, and I realized this must be Rose—the one Gianna had mentioned. Valentin's wife.

He shoved her and she fell onto one knee, catching herself against the crypt wall. "Get the dybbuk box or we bleed him out." The things under Louis' skin writhed faster, excited by her pain. "Slowly. While you are forced to watch."

I didn't even know what a dybbuk box was, but from the way Rose's face had gone white, it was something that should stay locked away in that crypt.

She gritted her teeth, blood trickling from the corner of her mouth where he'd slammed her into the wall. "I can't get the box if my wrists are tied."

Louis slapped her across the face so hard her head snapped to the side. The crack of palm against flesh echoed off the tombs. "Shut up."

"But she's right. She can't pick up the box with her hands like that." My voice shook, but I had to try to reason with the thing inside him.

He looked at me and red flames ignited in his black eyes, like someone had lit hellfire behind them. It stole my breath away, turned my lungs to ice. He held out his hand, and I watched in horror as his fingernails lengthened, curved, turned into razor-sharp claws that gleamed in the moonlight. Each finger elongated with a wet, cracking sound, like joints and bones breaking and reforming.

Then his claws swiped through Rose's bindings with

surgical precision, cutting her loose but leaving thin red lines on her wrists where they'd grazed her skin.

"Get the box," the thing inside Louis growled, "or your vampire will die a slow, agonizing death." Those claws flexed, dripping something dark that sizzled when it hit the ground. "Perhaps we'll start with…yes…his eyes."

She glanced at me, and in that moment I understood. Once she gave him that box, she was dead. We both were. Some things were meant to stay buried in those crypts.

"Rose, don't give it to him!" Dimitri cried out from the fray. He ripped into another wolf's throat, blood spraying across his expensive shirt. "Seriously? I just bought this shirt. And honey, if you open that door, we're going to have a very long conversation about poor life choices!"

He was fighting wolf after wolf, trying to reach us, each movement a deadly dance. Every time one fell, another materialized from the shadows in an endless game of whack-a-mole. Dimitri and Gianna fought back-to-back, their movements lethal and precise, but they were getting nowhere. Blood and fur matted the ground around them.

Gianna cried out, her voice strained with desperation, "Serenity, use your shield to protect us!" She ducked under snapping jaws, only narrowly avoiding teeth that could tear through her vampire flesh. Blood matted her usually perfect hair.

"You'll never do it in time," Louis taunted, the claws of one hand pressing into my scalp. His other hand shot out, his razor-sharp claws hovering over Rose's chest, right above her heart. "Use your power to protect them, and I'll rip Rose's heart out and eat it."

He leaned closer, his breath cold in my ear, and my entire body went rigid as the memory of Joy's slumped body flooded back. Her blood on the floor, her face so swollen I barely recognized her. Bile rose in my throat as those same hands that had beaten Joy pressed against my skin. "And I'll make you watch. Just like I made you watch what I did to Joy."

I wanted to scream, to fight, to do something—anything—but the memory of Joy's battered body paralyzed me. Because I knew with sickening certainty that he'd do worse to Rose. And he'd enjoy every second of making me watch.

Rose put her hand on the door and it slid open as if by magic, ancient symbols lighting up under her touch.

"No," I whispered, the word catching in my throat. A vision slammed into me—Rose and I lying broken on the stone floor, our blood pooling together, Louis standing over us with that terrible smile. The same smile he'd had after torturing Joy.

My mouth opened in a silent scream, but terror froze the warning before it could escape. The scrape of metal against stone as she pulled the door open was the sound of a coffin lid closing. Because that's what this crypt was about to become—our tomb.

My legs shook so badly I nearly collapsed. We were

going to die. Rose was going to die. And there wasn't a damn thing I could do to stop it.

The darkness beyond seemed to breathe. I wanted to race in there and get out of the terror around me, but something told me the real horror was waiting inside that crypt.

It was as if the thing could read my mind. "You'll never make it," Louis said as he lifted a strand of my hair with his claw, the sharp point grazing my scalp. "Though watching you try might be...*fascinating*."

I placed my hands on his face. "Louis, fight it, come back." Something slithered underneath my palms, like snakes writhing beneath his skin. I fought back the urge to recoil.

Power flooded through me, the familiar warmth turning into a burning river. I poured it all toward him, trying to bring back my father, trying to burn out whatever darkness had nested inside him. Light blazed from my hands, illuminating the tombstones around us.

Anger and hate flashed in the creature's red eyes, turning them into pools of blood. The things under its skin moved faster, agitated by my power, and its face contorted into something that had lost all humanity.

Every ounce of power poured through me, light burning beneath my skin until I thought I'd burst. I searched harder, looking for any trace of the real Louis beneath the corruption. There had to be something left— some ember of the detective who'd protected Joy, who'd always risked everything to keep her safe. My power probed deeper, my fingers clawing through ashes for a spark.

But instead of finding the true Louis, I only ignited the anger of the darkness inside him. It writhed against my light, slipping away like oil on water. Where my power should have cleansed, it just made the evil more obvious —the way his soul had been hollowed out, only to be stuffed full of something ancient and cruel. Angelo's warning echoed in my head: once Balthazar corrupted someone this deeply, there was no coming back.

I kept searching, desperate for even a flicker of the man who'd been Joy's protector. But each pulse of power only revealed more emptiness, more proof that Angelo had been right. The thing wearing Louis's face wasn't him anymore. It hadn't been for a long time.

He stuck out a hand and grabbed my neck, his claws digging into my flesh like ice-cold needles, squeezing tighter and tighter around my throat. I choked and beat on his wrists, my lungs screaming for air. My fingers scraped against his skin, my stomach heaving when I felt those things squirming underneath it. Tears filled my eyes, and I kicked at him, but my movements grew weaker with each passing second. Black spots danced at the edges of my vision, and a high-pitched ringing filled my ears.

He only chuckled and opened his mouth, revealing rows of sharp teeth where Louis' warm smile should have been. The teeth kept growing, multiplying, his jaw unhinging like a snake's. "You shouldn't have tried to heal us. Balthazar will lose his prize now. He will be most displeased." His breath smelled like rancid meat and sulfur.

A loud snarl rippled through the night, something from humanity's oldest nightmares that vibrated in my chest and made my heart stutter. Louis turned, and a massive black wolf plowed into him with the force of a freight train, forcing him to loosen his grip. His claws raked across my neck as he released me. I collapsed onto the ground, desperately sucking in air.

The black wolf and Louis battled each other, a dizzying blur of fur and flesh and spraying blood. When the wolf's teeth tore chunks from Louis' body, black smoke leaked out instead of blood, curling into the air like living shadows.

Louis' eyes filled with fear as he backed away—the first real emotion I'd seen in those hellfire eyes. For one horrible moment, I saw my Louis there, the man who'd protected me and Joy, trapped inside his own body as it was torn apart. But then that writhing darkness poured from his wounds, and I knew the real Louis was long gone. The wolf's jaws clamped down on his throat and ripped it open. Blood gushed out like a crimson waterfall, but it was dark, thick, moving like oil.

I pressed my hand against my mouth, caught between relief and horror. Relief that the thing wearing Louis' face was dying, horror at watching the death of the good man he'd once been. Bile burned in my throat as twisted darkness poured from his ruined neck, taking with it the last traces of Detective Louis DuPont.

The wolf shifted into Angelo, the transformation fluid and violent all at once, bones cracking and reforming in the space of a heartbeat. He'd found me like he always did, appeared exactly when I needed him most. But he wasn't—he couldn't be—he was powerful like no other vampire, but this? My breath caught as I watched him straighten up, deadly grace in every movement, Louis's blood still staining his mouth crimson. Everything I thought I knew about him changed in a heartbeat, but one thing remained constant—he'd come for me. He always came for me.

In one brutal motion, Angelo plunged his hand into Louis' chest and ripped out his heart. The sound was wet, horrible—one I'd hear in my nightmares forever. The heart in Angelo's hand was black and pulsing, covered in runes and symbols that moved like living things.

He crushed it in his hand, and black ooze burst through his fingers.

Louis screamed, but it wasn't his voice. It was that choir of the damned again, shrieking in collective agony, the hellish sound shattering the stained glass in nearby tomb windows. Black smoke poured out of him like living darkness, then spun out of control, hurtling toward the church, back to Balthazar. It left Louis an empty, discarded husk that crumpled to the ground, face frozen in its last moment of fear.

"I'm sorry, Louis! I'm sorry, Louis." The scream tore from my raw throat, tasting of blood and salt. My vision blurred with tears as I stared at his body lying there like garbage, destroyed by evil.

Angelo grabbed me, his grip iron-strong but gentle, careful to avoid the claw marks on my neck. Bloody scrapes ran down his face and his usually immaculate suit was shredded, soaked in blood that wasn't his own. Long cuts across his chest were still healing, the flesh knitting together only slowly—whatever he'd fought to get to us had been profoundly powerful.

"I told you not to come." His voice was harsh, but his eyes held ancient sadness. He'd seen this before, I realized. How many times had he seen people lose the ones they loved to darkness? "You couldn't have healed him. Louis was gone. Only the demons inhabiting his body remained." He pulled me against his chest, trying to shield me from the reality of what I'd lost. "He was gone the moment they took him. What you saw wasn't him anymore."

I tangled my fists in his bloodied shirt. "I should have listened to you. It's my fault he's dead." Grief and rage and guilt crashed through me like a tidal wave and my voice broke as I sagged against Angelo while the sounds of battle continued around us.

THIRTY-SIX

A*ngelo*

SERENITY CLUNG TO ME, heartbroken, sobs wracking her small frame. I wrapped my arms around her, wanting to shield her from the horrors around us. The marks Legion's claws had left on her throat made my ancient blood burn. I'd dealt with Legion before, back in Italy in 1742. That time, they'd possessed a cardinal. I'd handled it the same way: quick, clean, final.

Luigi would wish he was dead when I got through with him. He had one fucking job: keep Serenity locked up in the bedroom. His failure nearly cost me something irreplaceable. The moment this was over, he and I would have a long, painful conversation.

Louis' twisted body lay broken and gory on the ground. Legion's tainted blood pooled black and thick around him, moving like oil even after death. The stench of the corruption—bitter, like sour vinegar—made my stomach churn. I didn't hesitate when I saw those claws at Serenity's throat. You don't, not with Legion. You don't even try to exorcise them. You just end it. Quick. Clean. Final.

I kissed the top of Serenity's head. "I'm sorry you had to see that." The words came out gentler than I expected. Even after centuries, some vestiges of humanity lingered.

Serenity looked up at me, tears cutting tracks through the blood and dirt on her face. "He wasn't Louis anymore. He was a monster."

"Anyone who harms you is dead." It was a simple statement of fact, the same way I might say the sun would rise. "No one will ever hurt you. That I promise you." In my world, promises weren't just words—they were blood oaths, carved in bone and sealed in violence.

"Balthazar lied. Why would you believe him over me?" Legion had been my enemy for centuries. I knew their corruption, their irreversible hold. Balthazar played games with truth—I dealt in absolutes.

She twisted her fists in my shirt. "He was my father." She trembled as another hellhound's howl split the night. "You don't know what it was like having Freddie as stepfather after my mom died. Louis was the one that tried to protect me. The whole DuPont family did. I hate Balthazar for turning him into that thing." Each word carried old wounds, memories of bruises that had nothing to do with supernatural battles. Behind us, I heard Dimitri snarl, followed by the wet sound of flesh tearing.

Like Louis, Freddie had paid for hurting her. One by choice, one by circumstance—both men who'd marked her life. Another hellhound lunged past us, Enzo meeting it mid-air with deadly perfection.

"I know. I'm sorry." Words I rarely spoke, but the real Louis had earned them. He'd protected what was mine before she was mine to protect. That debt wouldn't be forgotten, even if circumstances had forced my hand tonight.

She looked up at me with her tear-streaked face. "You had to do it, Angelo. I didn't want Louis to have that thing...things...living inside him. And... He's at peace now, isn't he?"

I kissed her trembling lips. "Yes, he is." The lie tasted bitter on my tongue, but I couldn't bear to tell her the truth—that once possessed, souls hung in an eternal limbo between Heaven and Hell. Let her believe Louis had found rest. She'd seen enough horror for one night. The taste of her tears against my lips made something ancient and protective stir in my chest. I'd tear apart anyone who tried to put that look in her eyes again.

The scene had changed. Hellhounds multiplied around

us, Legion's blood staining the ground at our feet. I needed to get her out of here.

Just then, a creak of ancient hinges cut through the sounds of battle. Rose emerged from the Nightshade crypt, carrying a locked wooden dybbuk box. There were carvings on it designed to keep whatever evil was in there firmly within. My stomach recoiled and I moved Serenity slightly behind me, not wanting her to get near it. Even from here, I could feel the malevolence emanating from that box, centuries of contained evil pulsing against its bonds.

I grabbed her wrist. "Where are you going with that?"

Rose jerked her chin up, determination flashing across her tear-stained face. "Balthazar—"

"You're not giving that to him," I growled, watching another pawn getting caught in Balthazar's web of threats.

Serenity clung to me, still reeling from Louis' death. "But if she doesn't, he'll kill Valentin."

My jaw clenched. The pattern was clear—first threats, then hostages, then corruption that forced loved ones to become killers. Just as he'd manipulated Serenity with Joy, just as he'd twisted Louis into a weapon. All leading to choices no one should have to make. "He'll kill him anyway," I said, my voice tight with barely controlled fury. "Three centuries of dealing with demons has taught me that."

"No," Dimitri roared. He sped toward us, eyes crazy

with grief. Blood still dripped from his fangs, and hell-hound gore matted his expensive suit.

Something was coming out of the darkness. The air grew heavy, thick with a corruption that made my fangs ache. Evil couldn't penetrate the Nightshade crypt—generations of blood magic and wards had seen to that. I shoved Serenity inside, feeling the ancient protections buzzing on my skin as we crossed the threshold.

She gasped. "What are you doing?"

"Stay here." The words were an order, not a request. I turned around to face whatever was coming, positioning myself in the doorway. The shadows between the tombs were moving strangely, flowing against the wind like liquid darkness. Whatever Balthazar had unleashed was worse than Legion, worse than the hellhounds. The very air felt like it was rotting away.

Gage drifted out of the darkness. I could smell something on him as if he had rolled in it like a dog. The iridescent black blood of the Unseelie coated his clothes and skin, shifting like oil on water even after leaving its host. The scent of winter frost and dark magic clung to him.

"Open the box, bitch," he snarled.

He had black blood on him—too much of it. Fighting Keir's Unseelie warriors was no easy task, even for a wolf like Gage. Where the hell were Keir and his beloved harpies? The Unseelie were elite fighters, trained in the Dark Court's brutal ways. For Gage to be standing here, covered in their blood...no. Something was off.

I stepped in front of Serenity, then snatched the box from Rose. "Fuck you, Gage. It's not happening."

Gage's laugh came out unusually deep, as if something unholy was already inside him. His eyes glowed with an unnatural amber light. "Oh, Angelo. This was never about the box. It's about what's inside it." He rolled his shoulders, bones cracking and joints popping as if something was trying to reshape him from the inside. "Balthazar promised us power. Real power. Power enough to tear down your precious kingdoms."

Behind him, Petar emerged from the shadows, his usual cold smile now twisted into something hungrier. The box in my hands pulsed, as if whatever was inside recognized its purpose. Two traitors, thinking they could take down three kings in my territory. The sheer fucking audacity.

Petar ran his eyes over me as if I was just another body waiting to be buried in the bayou. A deadly mistake. One the world had learned generations ago: you don't disrespect Angelo Santi and live to brag about it.

Arctic, lethal rage swept through me. Valentin, Dimitri's brother, tortured on my territory, used like some ritual sacrifice. Most likely, he was already dead. The debt ledger in my mind filled with red. Gage's wolves...these wannabe hellhounds...Balthazar—they'd learn why even demons respected boundaries in New Orleans. No one conducted blood rituals in my city without paying the price.

The fool talked about power like a teenage street thug bragging about his first gun. He had no idea what real power was—the kind earned through rivers of blood, through deals sealed with iron-clad promises and enforced with finality. The kind that made even immortals remember why they feared the dark.

He stretched out his hand. "Give me the dybbuk box and your sweet little Nephilim might live."

Rage turned my blood to acid. My fangs descended, not with their usual slow slide, but with a savage snap that filled my mouth with the copper taste of my own blood.

"You touch her, and I'll make what happened to Freddie Evans look like mercy." Each word hinted at torture techniques perfected in the dark corners of history. "They never found all the pieces, did they? Your father was there that night. Ask him what happens to those who think they can threaten Angelo Santi's family."

A howl echoed across the graveyard. Trystan had shifted into his wolf form—three hundred pounds of white fur and French Quarter vengeance—as he slammed into Gage, hurling the traitor toward snarling vampires and hellhounds. He might be a pain in my ass most nights, but he understood territory. Understood loyalty. Understood what happened to dogs who bit the hands that fed them.

Gage whirled around and tore through his clothes. Muscles and bones cracking, but not in the usual way of a wolf's shift. His skin rippled and bulged as if something was trying to claw its way out. Bones snapped and reformed, longer than they should be, joints twisting in impossible directions. The same red glow from the church started to pulse beneath his stretching skin.

The fur that burst through wasn't the natural brown and white of his wolf form—it was darker, matted with something that looked like sludge. His muzzle elongated, teeth multiplying in rows like a shark's mouth. When the transformation finished, he was massive—larger than any wolf should be, with muscles writhing under his fur like live things.

Enzo swiped at him, his nails extended, his eyes red, fangs bared, but Gage knocked him away like he was swatting a fly. He hit a tomb wall hard enough to crack the stone. What the hell? I had never seen that happen to Enzo. I was the one that turned him and he was almost as powerful as me. No wolf should have that kind of power.

Enzo recovered quickly, took out the Void Chain and twisted it around his knuckles. One cut with it, and Gage would be dead.

At least, I hoped so.

Petar stepped back when he saw the Void Chain. Trystan snapped at Enzo as if to say *Gage is mine.*

The red glow from St. Christopher's Church was pulsing stronger now, in sync with Gage's movements. Whatever ritual Balthazar had started in there, whatever darkness he'd tapped into, it was feeding power to his pet traitor. And if this was what Gage could do with just the residual energy…

Gage lunged at Trystan, jaws clamping around his throat with a sickening crunch. Blood sprayed in a wide arc as he savaged Trystan's neck, turning his fur crimson. The wolf king went down hard, his massive body slamming against the cemetery dirt.

Gage was foolish if he thought Trystan was so easily killed. Even with his throat torn open, even with blood turning the ground to crimson mud beneath him, Trystan's eyes still blazed with centuries of alpha power. He twisted with impossible speed, muscles bunching under his gore-matted fur. His massive paws caught Gage's shoulders, claws sinking deep into meat and bone. The sound of Gage's ribs cracking under Trystan's weight echoed like gunshots through the graveyard.

Trystan's jaws found Gage's soft belly and ripped upward. The traitorous wolf's howl of agony cut off in a wet gurgle as Trystan tore him open from sternum to throat, painting the cemetery stones with pieces of his former packmate's flesh. Gage's enhanced blood splattered across the tombs, steaming in the night air—all that extra power meaning nothing in the end when faced with a true wolf king's fury.

A choked sound escaped Serenity's throat—not quite a scream, not quite a sob. The dybbuk box burned cold in my hands as I turned to see her doubled over, one hand pressed to her mouth and the other clutching her stomach as she fought not to be sick. The squelching sounds of Trystan tearing Gage apart filled the air, and she flinched with each crack of bone, each spray of blood.

I shifted the dybbuk box to one arm, ignoring its icy bite as I pulled Serenity against my side with the other, trying to shield her from the carnage. Her whole body trembled against me. This was exactly what I'd wanted to protect her from—the raw brutality of our world, where old powers settled scores in blood and bone. She'd already seen too much death tonight. She didn't need to watch a wolf king reduce his enemy to scattered pieces across sacred ground.

The dybbuk box felt heavier underneath my arm. This wasn't just about territory anymore. This was about power that could upset three centuries of carefully maintained order. The kind of power that could rewrite the rules of New Orleans itself.

Dimitri's snarl came a split second before he lunged, hands reaching for it like a junkie desperate for a fix. I released Serenity and caught him by the throat, slamming him against the stone wall hard enough to crack the ancient marble. "Calm down, you fool."

"Oh, I'm sorry, am I interrupting your perfect little power play here?" His voice was laden with his signature sarcasm, but his eyes were wild with barely contained panic. "You heard what Louis said... My brother's in there being carved up like a lab rat, and you want me to what— stand here and strategize?" He kicked and flailed his arms.

"His very life is at stake. Family first—or did you forget that in your centuries of playing king?"

Petar lunged forward, his fingers like claws as he snatched the box from my grip. Before I could react, he swung it in a vicious arc, connecting with my temple. Stars exploded behind my eyes as my knees buckled. I hit the ground hard, tasting copper and dirt. Ancient rage surged through my veins like molten steel—how dare this pathetic creature strike me?

Through my swimming vision, I saw Serenity stumble, her arms pinwheeling as she fell backward into the dark maw of the crypt. Warm blood trickled down my face, its metallic scent filling my nostrils as Petar's form twisted and contorted. His body shrank and darkened, bones cracking and reforming until a bat lifted into the air, wings beating frantically as it fled toward the looming shadow of the church. Dimitri lunged, fingers grasping at empty air, then immediately shifted into a bat and flew after him.

Still dazed, I shook my head. "Dimitri, no."

Serenity got off the floor and stood in the crypt doorway—protected, but alone. I had two options. The smart choice was staying with Serenity. The necessary move was stopping that box from reaching whatever hell Balthazar had cooked up in that church.

Gianna's scream pierced the night. Three massive wolves circled her, their bodies forming a wall of fur and muscle that cut off any escape. Blood already soaked her clothes, and their fangs gleamed pink in the moonlight—a preview of the fate they had planned for her.

"No!" Serenity burst from the protection of the crypt, power blazing around her until she glowed like a shooting star. Her hands shot up, and pure celestial energy exploded from her palms. The blast caught the wolves like a divine hammer, sending their massive bodies flying like broken dolls.

I leapt off the slab, running toward her, my mind still struggling to process the raw power I'd just seen this impossible girl unleash—the girl who kept shattering everything I thought I knew about her limits.

Then came the sound—like leather being torn by giant hands, like a thousand wings beating in hellish unison. The air itself seemed to thicken with dread.

Serenity's face contorted in horror. "Angelo, look out!"

I spun just as razor-sharp talons sank into my shoulders. The harpy's grip was iron, its touch cold as it ripped me from the ground. Through the red fog of pain, I saw another one snatch up Trystan, his wolf form thrashing helplessly in its grasp.

"Let go of me!" I slammed my fists against its scaled legs, but the creature only shrieked—a sound like metal scraping bone. Each beat of its wings carried me further from Serenity, and her desperate cries faded behind me as the harpy bore me toward St. Christopher's Church. Toward whatever horrors awaited in that corrupted sanctuary.

THIRTY-SEVEN

*S*erenity

THE SAME RED-EYED creatures I had seen lurking in the trees now had Angelo and Trystan in their twisted claws. Their wings blotted out the moon as they wheeled overhead, and something primal in my chest seized up at the sight of Angelo—my powerful, unstoppable Angelo—dangling helpless in their grip.

"Angelo! Angelo!" My screams tore my throat raw, but he couldn't break free no matter how hard he fought. Each desperate blow he landed seemed to bounce off the crea-ture's scaled legs like it was made of stone. How was this possible? Nothing could overpower Angelo. Nothing.

The possessed wolves suddenly turned as one, racing toward the church like they were being pulled by an invisible leash. The synchronicity of their movement sent chills down my spine—something was controlling them, calling them back.

I had to help him. My hands still tingled with the power I'd used against the wolves, but it wasn't enough. It would never be enough. Everything must be happening in that church. Maybe Joy was in there too. The thought of both of them trapped in that corrupted place made my chest tight with panic, but I couldn't fall apart.

Not now.

Not when they needed me.

Enzo came up alongside me and grabbed my arm. He looked like he had gone through a meat grinder, blood matting his hair, deep gashes across his chest still weeping red. "You need to stay here in the crypt."

"No." I gritted my teeth, fury giving my voice an edged tone I'd never used with him before. "I'm not going to let him die."

Rose and Gianna joined us, their clothes shredded and bloody, looking like survivors of a war zone. Gianna was one of the strongest women I knew, but right now she could barely stand, blood seeping from ugly claw marks across her ribs. Rose's face was swollen where Gage had hit her, one eye nearly sealed shut and already darkening to purple, dried blood caking the corner of her mouth. Seeing them like this, broken but still standing, made my stomach turn. If they'd done this to Gianna and Rose, what might they be doing to Angelo?

Gianna put her hand on Enzo's shoulder, leaving a bloody handprint on his torn dress shirt, his suit jacket long discarded. "She's right, Enzo. As much as you don't want to admit it, she can help us. She just saved my life."

Enzo examined me with eyes that had seen too many people he cared about die. "How are you feeling?"

Usually I felt spent after my power came over me, but right now adrenaline rushed through me like a bulldozer, making my hands shake with the need to act, to fight, to save them.

I met his concerned gaze, letting him see the steel beneath my fear. "I'm fine, Enzo. We can't stay here wasting time. Everyone we love is in that church about to be tortured or killed. Do you really want to fight me on going?"

I held my breath, waiting for his answer. There was no way I was going to stay stuck in the crypt like some helpless princess needing protection. Power swelled inside me, humming through my veins like electricity, and my skin still held that faint blue tinge—evidence of the storm brewing beneath my surface. Something had changed tonight. The girl who needed constant protection was gone, replaced by someone who had knocked down demon-possessed wolves like bowling pins. A tigress had been unleashed, and I was ready to bite, kick, and punch any demon that threatened Angelo, Joy, and everyone else I loved in that church.

Enzo wiped the sweat and blood off his brow with his other arm. "Angelo's going to have my balls for breakfast for this. If you come with us, you have to do exactly as I say. Got it?"

"Got it." I turned to run to the church.

Something flapped behind me and my heart tried to punch through my ribs. The sound—beating wings—oh god, not again. I whirled around, expecting to see the red-eyed horrors that had stolen Angelo, but instead I found myself staring at a massive bat. Before I could scream, clawed hands gripped my shoulders and the ground fell away beneath my feet.

I thrashed in panic until two more bats swooped alongside us, and recognition hit me like a slap. It was Enzo gripping my shoulders, firmly but carefully, and Rose and Gianna were flying beside us, dark shapes against the darker sky. My hysteria dissolved into wild laughter—of course they could turn into bats. They were vampires. Why was I even surprised anymore?

Below us, possessed wolves circled the church like sharks sensing blood in the water. Their red eyes tracked our flight, but we were well beyond their reach as Enzo lowered me onto the roof near a broken window. From up here, I could see just how many wolves surrounded the church— an army of corruption waiting to tear us apart if we fell.

Below I could see what looked like men that had been ripped apart, but instead of red blood, theirs was black—thick and slick like tar. My throat seized up as I watched the wolves tearing at the flesh and eating it, smacking their lips with obscene pleasure. The wet sounds of their feasting carried up to us, and I swallowed hard against the bile rising in my throat.

Gianna shifted and followed my gaze. "Those are Unseelie that Gage's wolves are feasting on. The Unseelie are magical, and I suspect no matter what spell possesses those wolves, eating Unseelie flesh would strengthen it and make them even more powerful."

My stomach clenched so hard I doubled over, pressing my fist against my mouth to keep from being sick. The wolves below kept gorging themselves, black blood dripping from their muzzles, and all I could think was: this was what Joy might have seen. This was what Louis might have done. The sounds of tearing flesh and crunching bone echoed in my ears, and the world tilted sideways. I'd seen death tonight, seen Louis torn apart, but this—this was something else. This was monsters making themselves stronger by eating other monsters.

Balthazar stood with a hooded figure and Petar, but they weren't the ones that made my stomach heave. A dark-haired man lay stretched across the altar like a sacrifice, his bare chest a canvas of carved symbols that seemed to writhe in the red light. Each symbol looked wrong, like something that shouldn't exist in our world—and looking at them directly hurt my eyes.

Blood—his blood—didn't just drip from the altar, it moved with terrible purpose, snaking through the grooves of a pentagram like it was alive. The symbols pulsed with each beat of his heart, as if they were feeding on his life force, and with each pulse, the shadows in the church grew deeper, hungrier. Something ancient and evil was awakening beneath those carved runes, and I could feel its cold touch even from here.

Two men held Dimitri, who thrashed against their grip, a gag in his mouth. His eyes were fixed on the man on the altar—his brother, I realized with horror. That was Valentin. The one whose blood they were using for...whatever unholy ritual was taking place below.

Everything about the scene felt evil—the way the blood moved, the shadows that seemed to reach for Valentin's body, the air itself that rippled like heat waves above the pentagram. Even from here, I could feel the malevolence pressing against my skin like oily fingers.

But where were Angelo and Trystan and those winged creatures?

Enzo put a finger to his lips and pointed.

Deep in the shadows of the church, I spotted Angelo, Trystan, and Keir. Or at least I thought it was the Unseelie king—something about his presence made the air shimmer, like a heat mirage. What were they doing? We didn't have enough men. This wasn't going to work. Evil radiated from below like heat from an open furnace, making my skin crawl and my power curl in on itself.

Angelo, what are you doing? I'm here.

He heard my mental call, his head snapping up to meet my gaze, and my heart stuttered. His eyes weren't just murderous—they blazed with a fury I'd never seen before, ancient and lethal, that made even Enzo suck in a sharp breath beside me.

Balthazar strutted around the church like he was on stage at a rock concert, all arrogance and raw power. His bare chest gleamed with sweat in the candlelight, black leather pants clinging to him like a second skin. Every movement screamed predator, but not like Angelo's controlled danger—this was chaos barely contained in human form.

He glanced up at our hiding spot and I jerked back so hard I nearly fell, my heart trying to hammer its way out of my chest. I squeezed my eyes shut, but I could still feel his gaze burning through me. Beside me, Enzo's body went rigid, his hand already reaching for the weapon at his hip. The gesture told me everything—a man like him didn't survive this long by ignoring his instincts. We'd been made. Balthazar had been playing us this whole time.

His chuckle echoed through the church as he took the dybbuk box from Petar, the sound crawling down my spine like ice.

"Open it," Petar urged, his eyes darting to the dark

corner where Keir, Trystan, and Angelo lurked like gathering storm clouds. "They're all here."

Balthazar's grin spread slow and terrible across his face. "Oh, yes. I know they are."

The double doors of the church burst open with a thunderous crack, and those red-eyed horrors swept in on leather wings. Balthazar didn't even blink. He mumbled something in a language that hurt my ears and the dybbuk box opened. Black smoke burst from within—not like regular smoke, but something alive and hungry. It slammed into the creatures with the force of a runaway train, and they dropped from the air like dead birds, their bodies hitting the stone floor with wet splatters.

The black smoke twisted toward us like a living nightmare, moving with horrible, deliberate purpose. Enzo yanked me back from the window, but the smoke followed —hungry, searching. It swirled around us, and then... The voices started. Not multiple voices like Louis. These were ancient, speaking in a language that made my ears bleed and my soul try to crawl out of my skin. They whispered promises of pain, of eternal darkness, of things worse than death. My blood felt like it was trying to escape my body, every cell screaming in protest at the unspeakable evil surrounding us.

Razor-sharp claws dug into my flesh, and the world blurred into a tornado of black smoke and screaming voices. My stomach lurched as I was ripped through the air, then slammed down onto the altar. The carved symbols burned into my back like branding irons, and I could feel Valentin's blood, still warm, soaking into my clothes.

Angelo's roar shook the church foundations as he burst from the shadows, a blur racing toward me. The moment he crossed the pentagram's edge, he froze mid-stride. It was as if he'd hit a wall. Horror replaced rage on his face—Angelo, my unstoppable Angelo, trapped like a fly in amber.

"Balthazar, you will release me." His voice carried death, but there was something else there too—fear. If Angelo was afraid...

Balthazar's eyes had gone completely black, and something moved beneath his skin, pressing against it from the inside, trying to break free. His laugh spread across my skin like poisoned honey. "Oh, no. The fun is just about to begin."

THIRTY-EIGHT

MY FEET MIGHT AS WELL HAVE BEEN encased in concrete—I couldn't move, couldn't even twitch my toes against the filthy church floor. The pentagram blazed around me like living fire, its light pulsing in time with Valentin's heartbeat. Stupid, stupid, stupid. We'd walked right into his trap.

Serenity was sprawled across Valentin until Balthazar dragged her off, throwing her down within the pentagram. She landed hard on her hands and knees ten feet away from me, her eyes wide with fear as the symbols pulsed beneath her. Every instinct screamed at me to reach her, to tear apart anything between us, but I couldn't move. I, the vampire king of New Orleans, couldn't even cross this corrupted ground to protect what was mine.

My gaze swept to where Rose, Gianna, and Enzo were pinned against the wall like insects in a collection, held by invisible chains that reeked of dark magic. Enzo met my eyes with a look that carried years of shared violence. He knew what would happen when I got free. We both did. The last time someone had dared chain my people like this, I'd spent a month teaching New Orleans exactly why you didn't cross Angelo Santi.

But this time was different. This time they had Serenity. And the rage that filled me wasn't just the cold fury of a mafia king—it was something ancient and terrible that made even the shadows around me grow darker.

The black smoke writhed overhead like a nest of serpents, and my stomach lurched as understanding hit me. Our plan had been so simple: grab the dybbuk box, rescue Valentin, break Balthazar's power. Keir had been certain that Valentin's blood was the key—the catalyst that made the whole spell work. In a flash, I understood why.

Balthazar's eyes gleamed with triumph as he looked toward where Keir and Trystan were hiding. Of course he'd want Valentin's blood—he was part Dark Demon, something that made him rare and lethal even among vampires. His blood was unique—an accelerant that could amplify Balthazar's darkest spells. Valentin's father had been one of the deadliest Dark Demons in existence, a creature that could shift into any form and whose very blood was pure poison.

That's what Balthazar was really after—that inherited venom running through Valentin's veins. Keir had figured it out too late: break the pentagram, stop Valentin's blood from feeding the spell, and Balthazar's whole plan would crumble.

But now we were trapped, and that toxic demon blood was about to give Balthazar exactly what he wanted. The black smoke—writhing with faces of the damned, their silent screams visible in its churning depths—raced over my head and shot toward Keir and Trystan's hiding place like a heat-seeking missile of pure malevolence.

Release me," Keir demanded, his voice carrying all the authority of the Unseelie throne. "Or I'll show you what true power—" But before he could finish, the smoke wrapped around his throat. His jaw snapped shut as if gripped by an invisible hand, and he thrashed his head back and forth, fighting for words that wouldn't come.

Trystan, still in his massive wolf form, snarled and lunged—but the smoke was faster. It seized him like a living chain, slamming him against the wall and holding him there like a muzzled beast. His claws scraped uselessly against stone as he fought the bindings.

The smoke wasn't done. It coiled around them both with terrible purpose, crushing them against the wall.

Bones cracked as the dark force pinned them in place beside Enzo, Rose, and Gianna. They all hung there together, faces twisted in silent agony as the supernatural chains slowly tightened, promising a long and agonizing death.

The evil in the church twisted around me, making it hard to breathe, to think. The very air felt tainted by whatever ancient horror the Nightshade witches had locked away in that dybbuk box. No wonder they'd bound it—this wasn't just dark magic, this was something older, something that had existed before light itself.

Balthazar stalked toward Serenity, and the shadows crawled after him like eager pets. "I told you I'd get you back." His voice echoed with something ancient and evil, like fingernails scraping against my soul.

"Stay away from her, Balthazar," I growled, but even my rage felt small against the primal, perfect darkness filling the church.

His laugh was the sound of cemetery dirt hitting a coffin. "Or what? You're in no position to do anything." He reached for Serenity's face with fingers that were too long, too sharp, like they were struggling to maintain human form.

"I'll send you back to Hell in a matchbox," I growled, my voice rough with suppressed rage. My fangs ached with the need to tear his throat out, to make him suffer for every second he kept us trapped here.

"I think not." His smile made my blood recoil in ancient horror.

"Balthazar, don't hurt them." Serenity's voice cracked as she looked around the church frantically, taking in each imprisoned face. Her eyes lingered on Enzo's twisted form, on Rose's silent scream. "Please." The single word held all her desperation, all her fear.

"That depends on you." He lifted her chin with fingers that left frost on her skin. The sight of him touching her made my vision bleed red.

Hatred and anger swirled in me like a hurricane of razors, each second of helplessness adding to the storm. When I got free, there wouldn't be enough left of him to fill a thimble.

"Don't listen to him, Serenity!" My voice echoed off the corrupted church walls, carrying all the authority of New Orleans' king.

Balthazar's lips curved into a serpentine smile as he looked from me to the hooded figure. "Time to meet our mystery guest."

The figure reached up with trembling hands and lowered his hood. Recognition slammed into me as he lowered his trembling hands. Costin Tarus, headmaster of Red Rose Academy, here in this unholy circle.

Rose stood there, frozen in place, her eyes the only thing that could move—wide with betrayal as they fixed on the man she'd trusted for so many years.

"I had no choice." His words were those of a man who had lost everything. "He has Julienne."

"Remove your glamour, *Headmaster*," Balthazar purred, drawing out the title like poison. The air around me grew heavy with anticipation.

Costin's shoulders slumped in defeat. He began to chant in an ancient language that made my ears ring and my teeth ache—words that seemed to suspend through the chamber like venomous spiders on invisible threads. "*Velamen cado, forma vera emergo, essentia mea revelatur.*"

The air around him rippled like heat waves, and his human form began to dissolve. The glamour that had hidden his true nature for so long peeled away like scorching paper, revealing what had lurked beneath that carefully maintained mask of humanity.

Oh, fuck.

He was Vlad Tepes—Dracula. My maker. My hand twitched at my side as the blood drained from my face. The vampire who'd spent centuries trying to end me for daring to defy his new vision of what our kind should be.

Love had changed him—Julienne, as he called her, had changed him. I knew her true name, knew how her kindness and wisdom had transformed the most brutal vampire in history into someone who vowed to protect rather than destroy.

No wonder she taught at Red Rose Academy—she'd always had a gift for guiding young supernatural beings. But she too kept her true identity hidden behind glamour and a borrowed name, and for good reason. There were those who would do anything to find her, to use her power for their own ends.

Like Balthazar.

Vlad had transformed from the most brutal vampire in history to preaching that vampires shouldn't drain and kill humans. According to him, it made vampires too powerful. He wanted us to have willing victims or drink from blood banks.

But that's exactly how I'd built my empire—by taking power from those too weak to keep it. And I wasn't ready to give it up just because my maker had found his mate. Only the Aeternum Stone had prevented him from tearing apart everything I'd built in New Orleans. And now he was standing before me.

Serenity gave me a questioning look. I could read her mind, but she couldn't read mine. I didn't even want to utter his name.

Balthazar looked between us. "Ah, let me do the introductions. Serenity, I take it you two haven't met." He gestured toward Vlad. "This is Vlad Tepes. Or in your cultural vernacular...Dracula."

Terror flared in Serenity's eyes as she gasped, and my chest tightened. She knew exactly who Vlad was—knew that he wanted to kill me, knew that the Aeternum Stone was all that kept him at bay. But to find out now he'd been here in New Orleans this whole time, running that damn school, watching me, biding his time... Rage burned through me, cold and lethal. If I got free of this pentagram, I'd tear him apart for daring to terrify her like this.

Balthazar raised his arms, and the temperature in the church plummeted. When he spoke, his voice echoed with other voices, ancient and terrible, the words crawling through the air like venomous spiders: "*Tenebris antiquis, potentia daemonum, animae damnatae, mergemus in carne mortali.*"

The black smoke writhed and split into two serpentine streams, each pulsing with faces of the damned as they shot toward Vlad and Petar. Unlike Keir and Trystan, they didn't resist—they opened their mouths in perfect sync, eagerly letting the smoke pour into them.

Their bodies contorted, backs arching at impossible angles as the smoke disappeared into them. Their eyes turned completely black, then blazed red like fresh blood. Power rolled off them in waves that made my skin crawl, each pulse stronger than the last. Whatever Balthazar had just done, he hadn't just made them stronger—he'd turned them into vessels for something ancient and unspeakable.

Balthazar rubbed his hands together, power crackling between his fingers like black lightning. "My plan is finally coming together."

I glared, tasting copper as Valentin's blood-magic pressed down on us. "Your plan? What plan?"

"The one to tear down Serenity's father." His smile split wider, showing too many teeth. "He's the one that corrupted Dracula's deal. Not something I will forget. His punishment will be his daughter hunting him down."

"I'd never do that." Serenity's voice shook, but she squared her shoulders, trying to look braver than we both knew she felt.

"Ah, but you will." Balthazar's eyes gleamed with ancient malice. "Vlad, my friend...you may proceed."

Vlad moved with terrible purpose, his eyes blazing blood-red as he approached. When his mouth opened, his fangs weren't just extended—they dripped with something black that smoked where it hit the floor. His hand locked around my throat like a steel trap, and when those corrupted fangs sank into my flesh, agony exploded through every nerve. This wasn't just feeding—he was pumping something toxic into my veins. I fought against his grip, but whatever dark power Balthazar had given him made him impossible to budge.

"No!" Serenity's desperate scream shattered the air in the church. "Stop!"

The world crystallized. The pain vanished, but so did everything else. I couldn't move, couldn't speak. But I could hear. I could see. I would witness everything that was about to happen, helpless to stop it.

Even Vlad was frozen in place. His chin dripping with my blood and his red eyes focusing on me, his mouth pulled back in a sneer, revealing his sharp fangs, stained red.

"If you want to save your precious vampire, you must

come with me, Serenity." Balthazar's voice was full of mock sympathy.

No! No! No! I screamed in my mind, but the words couldn't reach her. She could send me her thoughts, but I couldn't do the same. I was trapped in my own head, forced to watch as she sacrificed herself for me.

"Let him go." Her voice cracked. "Don't let Dracula hurt him. I beg you. I'll do anything."

"Tell you what I'm willing to do." Balthazar circled her like a wolf stalking wounded prey. "I'll unfreeze your lover boy and allow him time to get away from Dracula. But then you have to promise me you'll come with me willingly. Otherwise—he's dead."

The lie in his words was obvious to everyone but Serenity. He hadn't specified how much time—could be seconds, could be minutes. Just long enough to make her watch as Dracula tore me apart. The perfect torture for us both.

"I want to say goodbye to him."

"By all means, please do." Balthazar's smile promised horrors to come.

"Unfreeze him."

The ice melted from my limbs, but Vlad's poison still burned in my veins. I tried to warn her, to tell her not to do this, but no words could escape my throat.

Serenity pressed her palms against my chest, and her power blazed through her skin, turning her ethereal blue. The throbbing pain vanished under her touch, her gift burning away Vlad's toxin. Even now, she was trying to protect me.

She slipped her hand around my neck and pulled me down. Though my arms remained frozen at my sides, I could feel every inch where her body pressed against mine. When she kissed me, hard and desperate, her power surged between us like lightning, like she was trying to pour every ounce of herself into me.

"Time to go." Balthazar's voice cut through the moment like a blade.

Her lips brushed my ear, her voice breaking. "I can't watch you die, Angelo. Stay alive. Come find me. You have my heart...always."

Then she was gone, leaving me stunned, her sweetness still on my lips, her power humming beneath my skin. Whatever she'd done, whatever she'd given me in that kiss—it felt ancient, felt like more than just healing.

Balthazar stretched out his hand to her. The moment Serenity's fingers touched his, they vanished like smoke in the wind.

Dracula's paralysis broke instantly. He slammed into me with centuries of hatred, dragging me from the church into the night. "I've waited a long time for this, Angelo. Don't worry. You won't die right away."

He would do to me what I'd done to countless victims over the centuries. But nothing he could inflict would compare to this—watching Serenity sacrifice herself to Balthazar while I stood helpless, knowing that the devil himself now had the only thing that had ever truly mattered to me.

Do you want to find out what happens with Serenity and Angelo?

Snippet to The Crown of Blood and Vengeance—

The church doors burst open, and we stumbled out into the night air, finally free of whatever dark magic had held us frozen. I flexed my fingers, trying to shake off the lingering numbness.

"Enzo." Keir's voice was rough. "What do we do now?"

I stared at the blood staining the marble steps—Angelo's blood. My friend. My brother. The vampire I'd sworn to protect.

"We hunt," I said, my fangs lengthening. "And we remind Balthazar why New Orleans has always feared its Enforcer."

DEAR READER

I hope you enjoyed The Curse of Blood and Silence. In the next book as you can see, the book opens with Enzo's point of view. I thought you would want to see what happened at the church after both Angelo and Serenity disappeared. I know I would.

I'm sure you're guessing that Enzo will be getting his own story. The third book, The Crown of Blood and Vengeance, in this trilogy will have more hints of Joy and Enzo's determination to find her.

I love a good romance where the heroine is missing and the hero will do anything to find her. One of my favorite movies that shows this is Mission Impossible Two. Ethan has to find Nyah before she succumbs to the deadly virus–Chimera. Once again, I play this trope out not only in the last book in The French Quarter Vampire

King, but in the next series, The French Quarter Vampire Enforcer.

Thanks for taking a chance on this series. If you want to find out more about the next book, you can join my newsletter and you'll find out how Angelo first became a vampire. You'll get a free book!

I also have a patreon where you can get more sneak peeks and goodies!

Hopefully, I'll see you around.

M Guida

ABOUT THE AUTHOR

M Guida weaves captivating tales where fantasy and romance collide in mysterious realms. From her earliest days, she was drawn to stories of magic and wonder, but it was the allure of paranormal love that truly ignited her imagination.

In her youth, she immersed herself in tales of enchantment. The discovery of romance opened a whole new world of storytelling possibilities. Now, she crafts intricate narratives that explore the supernatural, set in academies where ancient secrets and modern passions intertwine.

Her literary universe is a rich tapestry where dragons soar majestically, vampires move with timeless grace, and shapeshifters blur the lines between human and animal. Elves whisper age-old incantations in hidden groves, while otherworldly beings challenge mortals with complex choices.

When not writing her next thrilling adventure, M Guida finds inspiration in the rugged beauty of the Rocky Mountains, often accompanied by her loyal companion, Raven, on thought-provoking walks.

M Guida's stories invite readers into a world of mystery and passion, where hidden talents are uncovered and connections defy ordinary explanation. Her works explore the depths of supernatural romance, weaving tales of intrigue, desire, and unbreakable bonds.

ALSO BY M GUIDA

French Quarter Vampire King:

Chains of Blood and Darkness

Curse of Blood and Silence

Crown of Blood and Vengeance

Kiss of Blood and Sin

Goody Magic Academy:

Goody Magic Academy Year One

Goody Magic Academy Year Two

Goody Magic Academy Year Three

Red Rose Academy:

Red Rose Academy Year One

Red Rose Academy Year Two

Red Rose Academy Year Three

Red Rose Academy Year Four

Paranormal Mercenary Corps

Call Name Cupid

Operation Cupid

Mission Cupid

The Hunt Cupid

Retreat Cupid

Final Game Cupid

Beyond Mercenary

Blood Illusions

Shadows of Excess

Mirror of Vanity

Crown of Envy

Tangle of Lust and Lethargy

Wolf Princess:

Wolf Princess

Wolf Prince

Wolf Mate

Wolf Pact

Academy for Reapers:

Academy for Reapers Year One

Academy for Reapers Year Two

Academy for Reapers Year Three

Academy for Reapers Year Four

Legacy Series:

Before Legacy: The Early Years

Legacy Year One

Legacy Year Two

Legacy Year Three

Legacy Year Four

Ebony's Legacy

Ebony's Legacy Year One

Ebony's Legacy Year Two

Ebony's Legacy Year Three

Ebony's Legacy Year Four

Collections:

Legacy Academy Collection One

Legacy Academy Collection Two

Academy for Reapers Collection

Wolf Princess Collection

Before Legacy Series:

Before Legacy: Armond

Before Legacy: Gunnar

Before Legacy: Valentin

The Defenders

Wolf Defender

Vella Story:

Bite Me: Vampire's Forbidden Romance

Kiss of Blood and Sin